PENGUIN BOOKS

TOO FAR FROM ANTIBES

Bede Scott lives in Singapore, where he is an associate professor in the School of Humanities at Nanyang Technological University. He is the author of *On Lightness in World Literature* (2013) and *Affective Disorders: Emotion in Colonial and Postcolonial Literature* (2019).

Too Far From Antibes

Bede Scott

PENGUIN BOOKS
An imprint of Penguin Random House

PENGUIN BOOKS

USA | Canada | UK | Ireland | Australia
New Zealand | India | South Africa | China | Southeast Asia

Penguin Books is part of the Penguin Random House group of companies
whose addresses can be found at global.penguinrandomhouse.com

Published by Penguin Random House SEA Pte Ltd
9, Changi South Street 3, Level 08-01,
Singapore 486361

First published in Penguin Books by Penguin Random House SEA 2022
Copyright © Bede Scott 2022

ISBN 9789814954846

Typeset in Garamond by MAP Systems, Bangalore, India

www.penguin.sg

In memory of Eric Ambler (1909–1998)

You can order it in four sizes: *demi* (half a litre), *distingué* (one litre), *formidable* (three litres), and *catastrophe* (five litres).

F. Scott Fitzgerald, *Notebooks*, 1945

Contents

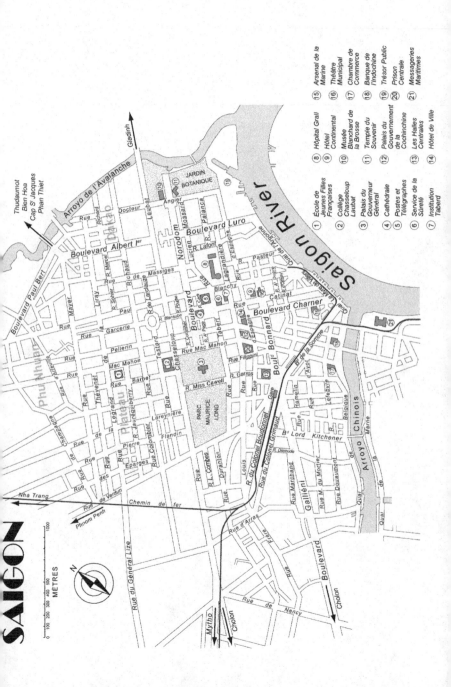

SAIGON

METRES
0 100 200 300 400 500 1000

N

Nha Trang

Phnom Penh

Mytho

Cholon

Cholon

Rue de Nancy

Boulevard

Rue du Général Lize

Chemin de fer

Rue d'Arras

Phu Nhuan

Boulevard Paul Bert

Thudaumot
Bien Hoa
Cap St Jacques
Phan Thiet

Gladinh

Arroyo de l'Avalanche

Boulevard Albert Ier

JARDIN
BOTANIQUE

Saigon River

Arroyo Chinois

Rue de Verdun

Rue des Eparges

Rue Pierre

Rue de la Champagne

Rue de l'Effort

Rue Jauréguiberry

Rue L. Cordès

Flandin

Rue Larreynière

Plateau

Legrand

Thévenet

Rue Barbet

Mac Mahon

PARC MAURICE LONG

R. Miss Cawell

Rue Mac Mahon

Rue Filippini

R. Garros

Gare

Rue Pellerin

Rue Duranton

Rue Louis

Rue du Colonel Boudonnet

Rue du Colonel Grimaud

R. Deomède

Rue Marchand

Galliéni

Rue M. du Mortier

Rue Douaumont

Quai de la Marine

Bd Lord Kitchener

Rue Hamelin

Rue de la Somme

Bd de la Somme

Boulevard Bonnard

Lefèbvre

Belgique

Boulevard Charner

Rue Catinat

Rue Pasteur

Rue d'Espagne

Rue Taberd

R. Colombert

R. Piquet

R. Chasseloup

R. de Lacorderie

R. de Massiges

Rue de Massiges

Rue Richaud

R. Sohier

Rue Paul

R. Mayer

R. Liray

Rue Garcerie

R. Blanchat

R. Testard

Boulevard Norodom

Lucien Lafont

R. Lafont

R. d'Espagne

Boulevard Luro

R. Mossard

Angier

R. Palanca

R. Richard

Rue Docteur

Laurai

Boulevard Dakao

Quai de Belgique

Quai Napoléon

Quai Francis Garnier

Quai

Rue de Belgique

Rue Blanchy

① École de Jeunes Filles Françaises
② Collège Chasseloup Laubat
③ Palais du Gouverneur Général
④ Cathédrale
⑤ Postes et Télégraphes
⑥ Service de la Sûreté
⑦ Institution Taberd
⑧ Hôpital Grall
⑨ Hôtel Continental
⑩ Musée Blanchard de la Brosse
⑪ Temple du Souvenir
⑫ Palais du Gouvernement de la Cochinchine
⑬ Les Halles Centrales
⑭ Hôtel de Ville
⑮ Arsenal de la Marine
⑯ Théâtre Municipal
⑰ Chambre de Commerce
⑱ Banque de l'Indochine
⑲ Trésor Public
⑳ Prison Centrale
㉑ Messageries Maritimes

Chapter 1

Some Preliminaries

Despite everything that subsequently happened, it's difficult to remember the first time I met Jean-Luc Guéry without smiling. I suppose he was just that kind of person: the comedic type. No matter what had transpired, no matter how dire the circumstances, one struggled to take him altogether seriously. A faint air of absurdity seemed to cling to him like the smell of the cigarettes he was always smoking and the eau de cologne he wore whenever he was suffering from one of his euphemistic 'migraines.'

On this particular day, the day he came to see me in my office at the Sûreté headquarters, it certainly didn't help that his neck was encased in a rigid cervical collar that made it impossible for him to turn his head by more than a couple of degrees in either direction. He also had a black eye, an angry welt on his left temple, and a large white plaster spanning the bridge of his nose.

'I was actually looking for Inspector Arnaud,' he said once he was seated. 'But I'm told that he's on leave.'

'Yes,' I replied, 'I'm afraid he'll be away until the end of July. And in the meantime, I'll be handling all of his cases.'

Guéry studied me with his heavy-lidded eyes for a moment or two; then he made a rather strange gesture of acquiescence and lit a cigarette.

'As you can see,' he said, 'I've been the victim of a crime. I was assaulted last night as I was walking back to my hotel. There were three of them, and they were massive too, like Henri Deglane. I didn't stand a chance.'

'You mean they looked like Henri Deglane the *wrestler*? The one who used to fight at the Élysée Montmartre?'

'Yes, that's right. Only they were fully clothed.'

This was a difficult scenario to imagine.

'Where had you been earlier in the evening?'

'In Cholon, at the Palais de Jade. Do you know the place?'

I nodded. 'And where are you staying while you're in Saigon, Monsieur Guéry?'

'The Hotel Majestic. Down by the river.'

He leaned over to use a nearby ashtray, wincing as he did so.

'Did you know the men who assaulted you?'

'No. I'd never seen them before in my life.'

'Never?'

'Well, I did notice them sitting at one of the tables in the Palais de Jade; but at the time, of course, I thought nothing of it. I was preoccupied with something else.'

I smiled. 'Of course.'

'And then later, once I left the Palais, I noticed that they were following me.'

'You say you were walking . . . '

'Yes. I'd asked the taxi driver to drop me halfway along boulevard Galliéni so that I could walk the rest of the way back to the hotel.'

'Was there any particular reason why you did this?'

'Not really.' He adjusted the leather brace he was wearing with his free hand and then reached for the ashtray once more. 'I suppose I just needed to clear my head. It had been a long day.'

'So where were you actually assaulted?' I asked.

'Near place Eugène Cuniac, in one of the alleyways running down toward the quay.'

'Your assailants forced you into this alleyway?'

'They did.'

'And then began beating you . . . like Henri Deglane.'

'Precisely.'

Guéry was sitting in an elongated rectangle of light that came from one of the two large windows in my office; and he didn't look particularly comfortable doing so. Although it was only ten-thirty in the morning, the glare was already quite intense, and it seemed to be irritating his eyes. I asked him if he would like to move his chair, but he insisted that he was fine, so we carried on as before.

'Had you done anything to provoke this assault, Monsieur Guéry? One must always be careful to observe small courtesies at a place like the Palais, you know.'

'I'd done nothing, Inspector Leclerc—nothing whatsoever. I was only there for half an hour. I didn't have the time to offend anyone.'

'Did these men say anything when they first accosted you?'

'Nothing. Not a word.'

'They simply pushed you into the alleyway.'

Guéry nodded. 'That's right.'

There was a slight tremor in the hand that was holding his cigarette, but I wasn't sure if this could be attributed to the events of the previous evening.

'Could you describe the assault in more detail?' I asked.

'It was actually very strange. When I realized what was happening, I thought I was going to die, and it made me think about all the things I haven't done in my life—and all the things I should have done.' Guéry's voice had acquired an introspective tone, and he seemed to be studying something in the far corner of the office. 'It certainly concentrates the mind, this kind of experience. It gives you a different perspective on life. I imagine it's the same when you're facing a firing squad.'

'Quite so, Monsieur Guéry, but I was really more interested in the assault itself.'

'Oh,' he said, turning in his chair, 'I see . . . Well, I tried talking to these men, but they wouldn't respond. They just started punching me, hitting me in the face, one after the other, and at a certain point I felt something in my nose give way. I'm not sure if it was cartilage or bone.'

'And then what happened?'

'The alleyway was suddenly filled with light, believe it or not, and I heard the sound of singing voices.'

'Singing voices?'

'Yes. It was all very mystical. I heard these angelic voices, and for a second I seemed to be levitating, like Padre Pio, and then I collapsed on the ground.'

'How remarkable,' I said obligingly. 'Please go on, Monsieur.'

'Then they began kicking me—you know, in the usual way.'

'Yes, I can imagine.'

'And when they were finished, one of the men told me that I should be on the first flight out of Saigon today, and that I should consider this a warning, or something along those lines.'

'Were you able to see their faces? Did they have any distinguishing features?'

'Not really. Once that strange light had gone, it was very dark in the alleyway. All I can tell you is that they were European, that they were in their mid-thirties, and that they looked like Henri Deglane.'

'That's all? European, mid-thirties, Henri Deglane?'

He shrugged painfully. 'I'm afraid that's all I can remember.'

'Very well,' I said. 'What happened then?'

'Nothing much. I must have fainted or something, and when I came to, they were gone, and there was a dog with one ear licking the blood off my face.'

I looked at him. 'The dog had one ear, you say?'

'That's right.'

'Not two?'

'No, it was definitely just the one.'

'And you're absolutely sure of this . . . '

'Yes. I can still remember it quite clearly. The left ear was missing. It gave the dog a rather asymmetrical appearance, as if it were leaning to one side.'

Guéry ran a hand through his heavily brilliantined hair and then sat there for a while in silence, contemplating the burning end of his cigarette.

I suppose he was picturing the dog—the one-eared dog that he could remember so vividly.

'Monsieur Guéry, if you don't mind my asking, what is your profession?'

'I'm a journalist,' he said. 'I work for *Le Journal d'Antibes*.'

'I'm afraid I haven't heard of it.'

Apparently, this was not the first time he had encountered such a response.

'It's a small newspaper, but it's widely read in the communes of Antibes, Valbonne, and Vallauris. Some people even prefer it to *Nice-Matin*. They say it covers local issues more thoroughly and gives the reader a better sense of place.'

'I see. And are you here in a . . . professional capacity?'

'No, not exactly.'

'So if you're not here on business, Monsieur Guéry, representing this newspaper of yours, precisely why are you here?'

'I'm here because of my brother,' he replied, as if he were stating the obvious. 'I'm here to find out who murdered Olivier Guéry.'

After pausing to light another cigarette, Guéry then proceeded to tell me the whole story, right from the beginning; and perhaps that's where I should start this narrative too—the one you're reading. Not with our first encounter in my office, or with the beating he had received in that alleyway off boulevard Galliéni, but with the discovery, a month or so earlier, of his brother's body floating in the Arroyo Chinois, just a few metres from the quai de Belgique. After all, that was what had brought him out here in the first place, all the way from Antibes, and that was why he had been beaten so severely the night before.

* * *

I can't remember now exactly who found the body, or even the specific date on which it was discovered. In those days, such cases were hardly rare. It was early 1951, and General de Lattre had just achieved a major victory in the north of the country, but in Saigon and the surrounding provinces the situation was rapidly deteriorating. There was a heavy police presence in the European quarter, and the terraces of the cafés were all covered in anti-grenade netting. Yet, despite such measures, a long list of atrocities continued to be published every morning on the back page of *Le Journal de Saigon*. Someone had rolled a grenade down the aisle of a cinema on rue d'Ormay. A local girl had detonated another one while dancing with a group of sailors in the Capriccio. An officer of the FTEO had been shot dead in broad daylight at the entrance to the Sporting Club. Etc., etc. At the time, there were also a large number of Viet Minh 'murder committees' operating undercover in the city. These operatives would emerge from nowhere, it seemed, to kill or be killed depending on the circumstances. They regularly assassinated political figures, members of the judiciary, and Vietnamese 'collaborators'; but they were also subject to reprisals from the security forces. In the latter case, we would often find their corpses abandoned on street corners with handwritten notices that read: *I am a communist murderer executed for my crimes*. And then at night, when most of the killing had been done for the day, one could sit on the roof terrace of the Majestic and, while drinking a Pernod or a cognac, gaze out over the river and watch the graceful arcs of tracer fire illuminate the night sky. The other side of the river was enemy territory, and it was only two or three hundred metres away.

So yes, when the body of Olivier Guéry was discovered floating face down in the Arroyo Chinois, one of the larger tributaries of the Saigon River, it was considered a fairly routine occurrence—and only merited a few cursory lines in the following day's *Journal*. According to the pathologist, the body had been in the river for some time, between twelve and twenty-four hours, but the murder itself had taken place elsewhere. Guéry, the elder, had been shot twice. One bullet had entered the frontal bone above his left eye and remained lodged in the opposite side of his head. The second bullet had followed another trajectory, penetrating the left temple and emerging just above the right ear, where it created an irregular hole roughly three times the size of the entry wound. The bullet that was eventually retrieved from the body came from a nine-millimetre semiautomatic pistol, most probably a Luger or a Steyr.

It was easy enough for us to identify the body as it was carrying a French ID card originally issued in Nice.

We contacted the authorities there, and they were able to verify the card's authenticity within a couple of days. It had belonged to a man by the name of Olivier Guéry, who had been living in Saigon for almost five years. He was the manager of a small company whose primary concern, we discovered, was the importation and distribution of agricultural machinery. A company representative was asked to identify Guéry's body, and then, once all the other formalities had been completed, he was laid to rest among the calcimined plane trees in the old Catholic cemetery. The funeral was sparsely attended, it has to be said. Arnaud, the investigating officer, was there, along with the assistant manager of Guéry's company (a man named Reyes) and two or three of his acquaintances. As is so often the case in the colonies, it was an entirely masculine affair, and if Guéry had a mistress—a *con gai*, as they're called around here—she had obviously decided not to perform these particular rites. A priest delivered a brief eulogy, the deceased was lowered carefully into the ground, and then everybody went home, satisfied that they had done all they could for poor old Olivier Guéry.

By this time, in fact, Arnaud had essentially given up on solving the case. Of course, he had made enquiries in all the usual places. He had interviewed Guéry's colleagues and business associates, and even discussed the case with his own colleagues in the municipal police, but this hadn't got him very far. Olivier Guéry seemed to have been an ordinary man doing an ordinary job, and there was no obvious reason why he should have ended up in the Arroyo Chinois with a bullet in his head. Arnaud had investigated the most likely scenarios as thoroughly as he could, but after reaching a dead end in every instance, after encountering a dispiriting normality in all areas of Guéry's life, he had decided to abandon the case. In my colleague's defence, I have to say that this was not atypical in those days. With so many murders to investigate, we had no time to waste on lost causes, on cases that appeared to be unsolvable. We had to prioritize, and that meant learning to distinguish between those cases that conformed to a recognizable scenario, that were amenable to a certain investigative logic, and those that made no sense whatsoever. Unfortunately, Guéry's murder belonged to the latter category, which was why his dossier was so quickly consigned to the bureaucratic purgatory of unsolved cases. We simply had more important things to do.

I suppose it was this lack of resolution that finally drove Jean-Luc Guéry to come out here and try to solve the case for himself. In some ways, this decision was admirable, but it was also hopelessly misguided and foolhardy. Saigon in those days was no place for amateurs, and it was certainly no place for someone like Guéry. He was in his late thirties when he arrived, and it was clear from the outset that he was not a particularly formidable figure. He was no General de Lattre, that is to say, nor even a Navarre or a Cogny. Leaving aside his somewhat comedic appearance (the dense, brilliantined hair, the heavy eyebrows, the stereotypical Gallic nose, the nicotine-stained fingers, etc.), he was obviously a man whose vices outweighed his virtues. For a start, he was a dedicated drinker and an enthusiastic consumer of cigarettes—usually filterless Gauloises, but any would do, even the foul-tasting *cigarettes de troupe*. He would, I'm told, have his first cigarette before he got out of bed in the morning and would usually enjoy his first apéritif not long afterward. As a young man, he had harboured literary aspirations, but these had come to nothing, and he had eventually found a job working for a local newspaper, *Le Journal d'Antibes*. Like his colleagues, Guéry covered a wide range of stories, and I believe he did so with a reasonable degree of competence, but he had never really distinguished himself in this field, and whatever money he made would usually be squandered at the roulette tables in Cannes or Nice—an addiction to gambling being another one of his many peccadilloes.

I have often wondered, in retrospect, where a man like Guéry found the courage to travel to one of the more remote colonies in order to solve the mystery of his brother's murder. He had never been particularly close to his brother, and he had never before demonstrated any kind of physical valour or aptitude for intrigue. But solve the mystery he did, and in the face of considerable personal danger too, as we have already seen. Perhaps it's just the kind of decision one makes when one wakes up in a strange hotel room on the Côte d'Azur with a crippling headache, a broken finger, no clear memory of the night before, and only three francs to one's name. Or perhaps he was simply doing it for his grieving father, whom he loved dearly and who had been devastated by the murder of his eldest (and most promising) son. Or perhaps, finally, it had something to do with his life-long enthusiasm for the work of Georges Simenon, whose novels he would often read while lying partially submerged, like some kind of gelatinous sea creature, in a tidal pool near the Plage des Ondes.

Whatever the case, whatever his underlying motive may have been (and I suspect it was probably a combination of all three), Jean-Luc Guéry arrived in Saigon in April of 1951 with the sole objective of identifying his brother's murderer— the man or woman who had shot him in the head and then dumped his body in the Arroyo Chinois. I have reconstructed everything that subsequently happened using the various sources available to me, including the case files (from which much of the above material is derived), surveillance reports, and Guéry's own testimony. In places where the factual evidence is scarce, I have allowed myself to speculate, but not excessively so, and at no point do I treat conjecture as fact. As I came to know Guéry better, he seemed to be more willing to discuss his experiences with me. Indeed, at times, his candour could be rather disconcerting, but it did prove extremely useful for the purposes of this narrative, making it possible to reconstruct even long passages of dialogue with considerable precision. As I say, there may be places where my knowledge of what transpired is only partial, but these ellipses usually coincide with Guéry's own memory lapses and have no significant bearing on the substance of the story I am about to tell. Guéry could always remember what really mattered, and the notes that he too was taking during this period proved to be surprisingly comprehensive. At times, it was difficult to make sense of these notes, and to decipher Guéry's cryptic handwriting (a disorderly scrawl full of tangled lines and strange runic flourishes). But in some ways, it's only appropriate that this should have been the case—for confusion, opacity, and sheer ignorance also have a large part to play in the following narrative.

Chapter 2

The Grey File

According to Arnaud, when Guéry came to see him on his first morning in Saigon, he was looking even more dishevelled than he usually did. For some reason, he hadn't anticipated the climate he would encounter out here in the tropics, and he was wearing a heavy flannel suit that clung uncomfortably to the perspiring angles and planes of his body. He hadn't shaved either, and there were dark circles under his eyes.

The first thing he wanted to know was why the investigation had been abandoned.

Arnaud was used to this question, and he responded as he always did: 'I'm afraid, Monsieur Guéry, that we simply don't have the time or the resources to pursue such cases indefinitely.'

'Of course,' Guéry replied. 'But I'd like to know why you decided to abandon this particular case.'

'First of all, Monsieur, I should remind you that your brother's case has not actually been abandoned. The investigation is still active; it's just been deprioritized, that's all.'

'Very well. But why, specifically, was it deprioritized?'

'We pursued every possible line of enquiry but could find no plausible explanation for what happened to your brother. He had no known enemies. He was not interested in politics. He was not involved in any illicit activities. He didn't gamble or use narcotics. And he had no *con gai*—or at least none that we could discover.'

'That's not particularly surprising.' Guéry smiled. 'Olivier never did care for such things. But he was always interested in money. That was why he was out here in the first place. And isn't money often the primary motive in cases of this kind?'

'Indeed. But everyone in Saigon is interested in money, and there was nothing we could find that distinguished your brother's commercial activities from those of anyone else.'

'Did you speak to his colleagues and business associates?'

'Naturally.'

'And did you not learn anything from these interviews?'

'I'm afraid not. In this respect too, your brother was quite unremarkable.'

Guéry fanned himself thoughtfully with his right hand. 'This company he was managing, Perec Frères, was it successful?'

'Apparently so.'

'He wasn't facing any financial difficulties?'

'No. On the contrary, he seemed to be prospering.'

Having demonstrated admirable forbearance thus far, Guéry finally allowed himself to light a cigarette. He was feeling a little tired, a little jittery, and he needed to steady his nerves.

'I wonder if you could describe for me the circumstances in which the body was found,' he said once he had settled back into his chair. 'I understand that it was in a river of some kind—the Arroyo Chinois.'

'That's right, Monsieur. It was found at approximately ten-thirty in the morning, floating alongside the quai de Belgique.'

'Who discovered the body?'

'I believe it was a teller from the Banque de l'Indochine.'

'Which is located nearby?'

'Yes. It's the big granite building on the quay itself, the one with all the pillars. The teller was walking along the quayside when she saw something strange floating between a couple of barges. At first, she thought it was a bundle of clothes, but it turned out to be . . . something else.'

Guéry found it difficult to picture his brother's body floating in a river. It was the kind of indignity that Olivier would never have suffered while he was alive, so it was hard to imagine him colliding with bridges or being jostled by rice barges once he was dead.

'Was the body in a reasonable condition when it was found?' he asked.

Arnaud shook his head slowly. 'Your brother had been in the water for quite a long time, Monsieur Guéry, and in this climate a body can reach a fairly advanced state of decomposition within a few days.'

'Poor Olivier . . . Did you find anything else on his body—aside from the identity card?'

'Nothing of any significance. But if you would like to wait for a moment, I may be able to give you a more precise answer.'

Arnaud rose and left the office. Once he was alone, Guéry looked around for a piece of paper on which to write some notes. It very rarely occurred to him to prepare for such an eventuality, so his notes were usually scrawled on anything that came to hand—a discarded envelope, say, or the torn-off corner of a railway timetable. In this case, rather than pilfering something from Arnaud's office, he used a tariff card that he had picked up in the foyer of the Majestic, and here's what he wrote:

> *Enemies: none.*
> *Political activities: none.*
> *Illicit activities: none.*
> *Vices: none.*
> *Mistresses: none.*
> *Financial difficulties: none.*
> *Body found c. 10h30.*
> *Arroyo Chinois.*
> *Teller (Banque de l'Indochine).*
> *Quai de Belgique.*

As Arnaud still hadn't returned by the time he had finished making these notes, Guéry compiled a list of everything he needed to do that day (including his laundry). And then, after a brief pause, he jotted down the following musical notation:

It mystified me when I later saw this incongruous piece of music among Guéry's notes. As soon as I had the chance, I asked him about it, and he told me that it was something he had heard that morning as he was buying a packet of cigarettes. It was a song one of the street vendors had been singing, and he simply couldn't get it out of his head. (Looking at his notes and the information he considered worthy of recording, it was sometimes difficult to believe that Guéry was a practising journalist who had once interviewed the ambassador of the Dominican Republic.)

After another couple of minutes, Arnaud returned carrying a grey file.

'This is all the information I have on your brother's case,' he said, turning to the first page. 'Apparently, a wallet containing fifty-five piastres was found on the body. And the identity card too, of course—issued in Nice.'

'Was there anything else?'

The inspector ran his finger slowly down the page. 'Nothing of note. A cigarette lighter, some keys, a lottery ticket, a pair of sunglasses, a bottle of vitamin capsules.'

'What brand was the cigarette lighter?'

'It says IMCO here. One IMCO cigarette lighter, silver.'

'And what kind of sunglasses were they?'

'There's no record of the brand, Monsieur Guéry, but I believe the frames were made of celluloid. They probably came from Italy—such things usually do. Otherwise, the keys belonged to your brother's apartment and his office. The lottery ticket was illegible. And the vitamin capsules were of the B-12 variety, which is apparently good for nerve injuries, cirrhosis of the liver, and fatigue.'

This was all news to Guéry.

'Does the file contain the autopsy report too?' he asked.

'I'm afraid not. It seems to be missing. But there should be a copy at the coroner's office on rue Pasteur.'

'Would I be allowed to see it?'

'Yes, I believe so—if you follow the necessary procedures.'

Balancing the tariff card on his knee, Guéry added a few more lines to his notes.

'Could you tell me, Inspector Arnaud, who identified the body?'

'Once the authenticity of the ID card had been confirmed, one of your brother's colleagues agreed to do so.'

'This was at the morgue . . . '

'That's right.'

'Would you be able to give me his name, please?'

'Certainly.' Arnaud had to turn two or three pages before he found what he was looking for. 'His name was Jacques Fourier.'

'And do you have an address for this Monsieur Fourier?'

'The only address I have listed here belongs to Perec Frères: 39 rue d'Espagne.'

Guéry wrote this down on his tariff card too, along with the name of the man who had identified his brother's body.

'Thank you, Inspector,' he said finally. 'You've been very obliging.'

'You're welcome, Monsieur Guéry . . . But before you go, I feel I ought to make sure of something.'

Guéry paused.

'The detailed nature of your enquiries would seem to suggest that you are interested in pursuing this case further. Is that so?'

'I suppose it is, yes. I would like to find out what happened to my brother.'

'I understand this impulse, Monsieur Guéry, and sympathize, but I would strongly urge you to reconsider. Saigon is not a very congenial place for amateur detectives. It's a city where people are dying like your brother every day—sometimes two or three times a day. And it would be most unfortunate if you were to meet a similar fate.'

Arnaud was an older man with grey hair and tired, ironic eyes; and when he delivered these last two lines, I imagine they must have made quite an impression on Guéry. After all, this was not the kind of thing one typically heard in the cafés and casinos of the Côte d'Azur.

'Moreover,' he continued, 'I fear that you may be wasting your time. Saigon is also a very complicated place, and I find it difficult to believe that you, having arrived here only yesterday, will succeed where we, the police, have failed. If I may put it bluntly, Monsieur Guéry, and I feel an obligation to do so, you would be far better off returning to France with the information you already have and accepting that some things simply defy understanding.'

Guéry lit another cigarette.

'Inspector Arnaud, everything you're saying is quite true, I'm sure. But Olivier was my only brother, and I have a duty to investigate the circumstances surrounding his murder, regardless of the outcome.'

'Yes, Monsieur, but it's precisely the outcome that concerns me—and it should concern you too. As I say, Saigon can be an unforgiving place for dilettantes.'

A look of injured pride passed momentarily over Guéry's face.

'That may be so,' he replied, 'but I don't really feel that I have a choice. And what would it matter, anyway, if I were to fail? The world is full of failure, Inspector. We can't all succeed, and we can't all be heroes.'

Arnaud found this attitude rather mystifying, and in his place, I suppose I would have too. He didn't understand that Guéry had become, over the years, something of an authority on failure. As a young man, he had wanted nothing more than to play football for FC Antibes, but of course this had come to nothing. He had soon discovered that he lacked the physique, the mentality, and the aptitude for such things. He was, he eventually decided, destined to become an intellectual instead. So he turned his attention to literature and spent many an hour labouring over his old Imperial typewriter. But there too he had failed. The narratives he imagined, the intricate masterpieces he constructed in his head, simply refused to make their way into the world; and those that did emerge from his typewriter, derivative and laboured as they were, ultimately pleased no one. The editors of the popular literary magazines of the day (*La Nouvelle Revue Française*, *Les Temps Modernes*, etc.) were all equally unimpressed by his stories. And the long experimental novel he wrote, closely modelled on Gide's *Counterfeiters*, was rejected by almost every publisher in France. In the end, utterly discouraged, he had given up on this particular ambition too and accepted that his destiny lay elsewhere. After failing to complete a degree at the University of Nice, he finally found a job working for *Le Journal d'Antibes*, and that was how he had made his living ever since: following the vicissitudes of local politics, interviewing the odd visiting dignitary, and reporting on the latest burglaries and traffic fatalities.

'And what of the danger you may face, Monsieur Guéry, does that not concern you at all?'

At this point in time, Guéry still seemed to have a rather unrealistic sense of his own invincibility. He somehow imagined that his brother's murder was a unique and unrepeatable occurrence—that it was the only time in the history of Saigon that anyone had ever been shot in the head and dumped in the Arroyo Chinois.

'Inspector Arnaud,' he said, 'I appreciate your concern, but there's really no need to fear for my safety. I'm sure I'll be perfectly fine.'

Arnaud looked at him for a second before replying. 'Very well. If you're determined to proceed, there's nothing I can do to stop you. But may I suggest that you apply for accreditation as soon as possible. That will at least give you some official status here in Saigon, and it may also make it easier for you to conduct your . . . enquiries.'

Guéry promised to visit the Information Service that very morning.

'And one more thing before you leave, Monsieur. I've just remembered something else they found on your brother's body. Something rather odd.'

Arnaud reached over to a wire tray labelled *Miscellaneous* and, after searching through its contents for a moment or two, produced a small, rectangular piece of paper.

He handed it to Guéry.

Although the paper had partially disintegrated, it was obviously the title page of a book, and the printing on it was still legible. It said:

TU PARLES D'UNE INGÉNUE

UN ROMAN

par

JEAN BRUCE

The name of the publisher was written at the bottom of the page (Fleuve Noir), and just above this was a circular library seal that read: CENTRE SAINT-LAZARE—ROME.

Guéry turned the page over. Apart from the usual copyright information, which gave the date of publication as 1949, there was nothing on the other side.

He looked up at the inspector. 'So this was found on my brother's body?'

'Yes.'

'Are you familiar with this . . . ' He turned the page over once more: '*Tu Parles d'une Ingénue?*'

'I can't say that I've read it, no. But I believe it's the first in the OSS 117 series. Some kind of spy thing apparently.'

'I see. And have you any idea why my brother might have been carrying it when he died?'

Arnaud smiled. 'I'm afraid not, Monsieur. But if I were you, I wouldn't attach too much significance to it.'

'No? And why not?'

'Because this is not a novel. You are not OSS 117. And in real life such "clues" are usually rather disappointing. More often than not, they turn out to mean nothing at all.'

Chapter 3

Bergerac

Later that evening, so I'm told, Guéry made his first appearance on the terrace of the Hotel Continental. One of my men was there too, and the following day he reported what he had seen. From his description (heavy eyebrows, Gallic nose, etc.), I immediately recognized Jean-Luc Guéry.

Apparently, Guéry arrived around five-thirty. The terrace was crowded, as it always is at that hour of the day. Although there were two free tables by the wall, Guéry wandered around for some time before locating them. He was shortsighted, I later learned, and found it difficult to see beyond the range of a few metres. The fact that he didn't wear glasses always struck me as a curious vanity for a man who neglected his physical appearance in so many other ways, but there you go—people can be strange sometimes. Once he had found a table, Guéry ordered a Pernod and lit one of his ubiquitous cigarettes.

Around this time, as night begins to fall, the square in front of the Continental is particularly active, and while he was waiting for his drink to arrive, Guéry should have been able to see the beautiful Vietnamese women drifting by in their tailored *ao dai*; the legionnaires and the soldiers of the Expeditionary Corps congregating wherever they found the space to do so; the innumerable bicycles, the Merciers and the Aviacs, following their erratic trajectories between the cars and the lorries; and the young boys—the ones who so often carried grenades too in those days—selling cigarettes and shining shoes outside the Municipal Theatre. But of course, being shortsighted, he couldn't see any of this; and he probably wouldn't have appreciated it anyway, as he never did have much of a taste for the picturesque.

At some point, Guéry noticed two men sitting at a nearby table whom he vaguely recognized. He had seen their faces somewhere before. They seemed to be discussing a topic of great importance, and every so often they would accentuate what they were saying with an emphatically masculine gesture— jabbing the air with their cigarettes, for instance, or slicing the palm of one hand with the edge of the other, as if they were cutting into something hard. After several minutes, Guéry finally remembered who they were. One of the men was Lucien Bodard, the celebrated correspondent for *France-Soir*; the other was Jean Lartéguy of *Paris-Presse*.

No one likes to see another person being embarrassed in public, so I won't dwell for too long on the following scene. My colleague later told me that Guéry rose from his chair and walked tentatively over to Bodard and Lartéguy's table. On arriving at his destination, he introduced himself, rather formally, as Monsieur Jean-Luc Guéry and explained that he was on assignment here in Saigon, representing *Le Journal d'Antibes*. Neither Bodard nor Lartéguy had heard of this newspaper, but Guéry was able to provide them with a brief summary of the *Journal*'s history—from its establishment in 1908, through the difficult war years, and up until the present day. Although the two men listened politely, they may well have wondered why a local newspaper in the city of Antibes, which had a population of about thirty thousand people, should find it necessary to employ a foreign correspondent at all. In any case, the pleasantries that followed were stilted, to say the least, and punctuated by increasingly lengthy silences—until Guéry finally brought things to a close. He apologized for interrupting, stammered something about Haiphong and the frontline, and then retreated as quickly as he could to the safety of his own table.

As I say, this was all very embarrassing for Guéry. He deeply admired these two men, who were famous throughout France for their courage under fire (Lartéguy had been awarded the Légion d'Honneur not long before) and for their journalistic integrity. But the encounter I have just described only reminded Guéry of his own place in the universe; and this was probably what he was contemplating as he sat there, on the inner edge of the terrace, drinking his Pernod, smoking his cigarettes, and observing all the usual toing and froing one associates with such places.

After a while, Guéry grew tired of doing this, and he was just about to leave when a man emerged from the hotel doorway and walked directly over to his table.

'May I?' he said, gesturing toward an empty chair.

'Of course,' Guéry replied. 'Please do.'

The man was in his early fifties, with a receding hairline and ears that jutted at a perpendicular angle from his head. His face was pale, strangely so for the tropics, and yet his forehead was scored with deep horizontal lines, and when he smiled his eyes disappeared into a profusion of intersecting wrinkles. He was conspicuously overweight too, and the jacket of his linen suit only just covered a large, spherical belly—what was called, in those days, an *oeuf colonial*. He was carrying a cane, which he leaned carefully against the table before he sat down, and on two of his fingers he wore heavy silver rings.

Guéry offered the man a cigarette.

'Thank you, Monsieur, that's very kind of you . . . My name is Bergerac.'

'Guéry.'

'A pleasure.'

He called the waiter over and ordered a vermouth.

'I don't believe I've seen you here before, Monsieur Guéry.'

'No. I've only just arrived in Indochina.'

'Really? Where are you staying?'

'At the Majestic.'

Bergerac nodded approvingly. 'And what do you think of Saigon so far? Not too disorientating, I hope.'

'Not at all. It's very agreeable.'

'Good, good. It often confuses people at first, but in fact it's a very easy city to understand. There are no mysteries here, no ambiguities. It's all perfectly straightforward.'

Guéry raised his eyebrows. 'That's interesting. I had been told the opposite.'

'The city has many different layers, Monsieur Guéry, and this may be rather bewildering for the novice. But there's one thing that unifies us all: the people at these tables, the prostitutes in the hotel bar, those legionnaires over there—even the lepers who live among the gravestones in the cemetery.'

'And what might that be?' Guéry asked.

'Money, my friend, plain and simple. The almighty seventeen-franc piastre. That's the only thing that carries any value around here.'

As he was saying this, Bergerac's vermouth arrived, giving Guéry the opportunity to order another Pernod. If it had been a socially acceptable practice, he would have ordered two at the same time, perhaps even three. It had been a long day, and he was far from home.

'So what brings you to Saigon, in any case?'

'I'm here on assignment,' Guéry said cautiously. 'I'm a correspondent for *Le Journal d'Antibes*.'

'Forgive my ignorance, but I'm not familiar with that particular newspaper.'

'No? Well, apparently you're not the only one.'

By now this was becoming a rather sensitive subject for Guéry. Acting on Arnaud's advice, he had gone to the Information Service earlier that day to apply for accreditation. The service was housed in a large bureaucratic building on rue Lagrandière, and it had taken him almost half an hour to find the appropriate office. After waiting for another twenty minutes or so, he had been interviewed by a junior officer called Auteuil, who hadn't heard of *Le Journal d'Antibes* either. Indeed, he had made it quite clear that he was only accepting Guéry's application out of common courtesy (and a certain amount of pity). The latter was told that his accreditation would have to be approved at a higher level before the *carte de presse* could be issued, and that this process could well take three or four days— if, of course, it was approved at all. During this time, the officer had suggested in a tone usually reserved for the wives of minor functionaries, he might like to enjoy the facilities at the Sporting Club or spend a couple of days at Cap Saint-Jacques. In the end, Guéry had left the office in a fury, and had only recovered his equanimity with the aid of a large 'apéritif' and four or five rapidly consumed cigarettes.

'And what do you do for a living, Monsieur Bergerac?'

This question brought a strange smile to the man's face. 'I suppose you could say I provide one of the more essential military services.'

'Is that so?'

'Indeed. Without my assistance, the war would have been lost long ago.'

'So what is it, precisely, that you do?' Guéry asked.

'I provide personnel and logistical support for the BMCs.'

'And what are they?'

Bergerac laughed. 'You *haven't* been here long, have you, Monsieur Guéry . . . I'm referring to the *bordels militaires de campagne*.'

Guéry had, in fact, heard of this particular service. It was one the colonial forces in Morocco had been enjoying for many years.

'So what are your actual responsibilities, Monsieur Bergerac, if you don't mind my asking?'

'I supply the women for the BMCs. They're all volunteers, naturally—many of them from the Ouled Nail desert tribe.'

'In Algeria?'

'That's right.'

'But why do you use these women in particular? Why go to the trouble of bringing them all the way out here?'

'It's something the women of the Ouled Nail have always done. They work to put together their dowries, and then they go home and get married. In their culture, I believe it's considered perfectly acceptable to do so. There's no shame attached to it at all.'

Guéry nodded slowly. 'But you must employ other women too, women of other nationalities.'

'Of course, Monsieur Guéry.' His smile returned. 'One must cater to all tastes, but there's something special about the women of the Ouled Nail, something unique.'

'I see. And what kind of logistical support do you provide for these women?'

'When the BMCs are sent out into the field, they're required to service various sectors, and I'm responsible for preparing their itineraries—making sure that they're evenly distributed throughout the different combat zones.'

'That's a big responsibility.'

'Indeed, Monsieur. Nothing is more important, during a war, than the morale of the troops.'

Although the sun had disappeared behind the Municipal Theatre, it was still hot on the terrace, and Bergerac was beginning to sweat quite heavily. As he did so, the reason for his strangely pallid appearance became clear to Guéry. He seemed to be wearing some kind of mineral powder on his face, and where the perspiration had gathered in the lines of his forehead and the wrinkles around his eyes, this powder was gradually liquefying.

'So tell me,' he said, apparently oblivious to his dissolving maquillage, 'what is the nature of your assignment here in Saigon? Have you been asked to write about anything in particular?'

Guéry hesitated for a moment before replying. He knew that he should probably give an evasive answer, but it was difficult to feel threatened by a man who looked like an overheated Louis XIV.

'Actually, Monsieur, the truth is that I'm here to investigate the death of my brother.'

Bergerac lifted one hand to the side of his face in a rather theatrical gesture of surprise. 'How *terrible*,' he said. 'What was your brother's name?'

'Olivier Guéry. Did you know him by any chance?'

'I'm afraid not.'

'He was working for a company called Perec Frères.'

'And what do they do?'

'I'm not sure of the specifics, but I believe they import agricultural machinery.'

Bergerac seemed to be on the verge of smiling. 'I suspect your brother and I may have moved in different circles, Monsieur Guéry.'

'Of course.'

By this time, Guéry's second Pernod had arrived, and Bergerac watched in silence as he diluted it with iced water from a jug.

Then he said, 'If it's not too intrusive, may I ask how your brother died?'

'He was murdered, actually. They found his body in the Arroyo Chinois.'

Again Bergerac responded with a slightly theatrical gesture—of pity this time, rather than surprise. 'What an absolute tragedy. Please accept my condolences . . . But are you really sure that this is something you want to investigate, Monsieur Guéry? Aren't cases of this kind better left to the police?'

'The police seem to have reached a dead end, so I'm going to see what I can do.'

'Forgive me for saying so, Monsieur, but surely there's very little chance of you succeeding where the police have failed.'

'That's what the officer I saw this morning said. And I imagine you're both probably right. But it's still something that I feel I have to do. My brother and I were never particularly close, but family is family, after all.'

'Indeed.'

Another silence followed, during which Guéry finished his second Pernod and contemplated ordering a third. Although he was growing a little tired of this Monsieur Bergerac, with his ridiculous *oeuf colonial* and his powdered face, he no longer had any real desire to leave. It was comfortable sitting out there on the terrace, watching the blurred figures moving around in the square, and he was beginning to feel the sense of peace and well-being that often descended on him at this time of day, as the hour of the *apéro* was drawing to a close.

He lit another cigarette and called the waiter over.

Once they had ordered, Bergerac said, 'Anyone here, anyone on this terrace, could have been responsible for your brother's murder, you know. One shouldn't be deceived by appearances, Monsieur Guéry.'

This directly contradicted his earlier claim that there were no mysteries or ambiguities in Saigon, but Guéry refrained from saying so.

'Take Monsieur Vitelli, for instance, the hotel proprietor.' He gestured toward a man with an affable face and sharp, agile eyes, who was standing as unobtrusively as possible in the doorway. 'He doesn't look particularly forbidding, does he, Monsieur? But believe me, he can be very dangerous indeed.' At this point, Bergerac lowered his voice and leaned forward conspiratorially. 'He's a respectable businessman who has lived here for many years, but there's another, more sinister side to him too.'

Guéry waited.

'He's allegedly involved in the smuggling of gold, currency, and narcotics. In fact, some say he's the leader of the Corsican underworld here in Saigon—*un vrai monsieur*. But you wouldn't want to say that too loudly, and you certainly wouldn't want to accuse him of anything in public.'

'No?'

'Not if you value your life. Only last year, a young journalist by the name of Hugo Lefèvre came out here to investigate the illegal trafficking of piastres. He publicly accused Vitelli of being involved in the piastre trade, and within a month or so he was dead. He was returning to Paris on a DC-4 when it crashed into the Persian Gulf, just off the coast of Bahrain, and he was killed instantly. It was all very sad.'

Guéry whistled softly. 'Did they ever find out what caused the accident?'

'Not conclusively, no. But everyone agreed that Vitelli must have had something to do with it. He's a man with considerable influence, you know, and these Corsicans are very sensitive when it comes to matters of honour.'

'Indeed they are,' Guéry replied. 'But I doubt my brother was involved in anything along those lines. He was far too conventional and law-abiding.'

'So was Hugo Lefèvre. He was just doing his job, but he went too far. He wrote things he shouldn't have written, said things he shouldn't have said—and ultimately paid the price for it.'

Guéry looked over at the man standing in the doorway again. It was hard to believe that such an innocuous figure could have been responsible for a crime of any kind, let alone someone's murder. Surely it was just another one of those rumours that circulated so freely, so irresponsibly, out here in the colonies.

'Or it's also possible that your brother's murder had something to do with politics.'

'That too is rather unlikely,' Guéry said. 'He had no interest in politics. None whatsoever. He was only interested in selling agricultural machinery.'

Bergerac smiled. 'In a place like Saigon I'm afraid you're always involved in politics, whether you like it or not. Just being here is a political act, or at least that's the way the Vietnamese see it.' He paused. 'You've heard of these "murder committees," I suppose.'

'Only in passing.'

'Well, they're very active. Almost every day someone is assassinated. Usually, it's a public figure or a member of the military, but ordinary people like your brother are often killed too. People who were simply in the wrong place at the wrong time.'

Guéry gave the crowded square an apprehensive glance.

'In fact, as a journalist, you need to be particularly careful. Just the other day they assassinated the editor of *L'Union Française*. He was being driven to his house on boulevard Luro, when a jeep with the yellow plates of the Consular Corps appeared out of nowhere. The person sitting in the passenger seat of the jeep threw a grenade into his car and—*bang*.' Bergerac made a detonating gesture with his hand. 'No more editor.'

This topic of conversation wasn't doing much for Guéry's sense of peace and well-being; and not for the first time in his life, he began to regret staying for a third Pernod.

'May I offer you some advice, Monsieur Guéry?'

'Of course.'

'Forget about investigating your brother's murder. Go home and leave it to the police.'

'But the police aren't doing anything. They've abandoned the case.'

'Then you should do the same. If they have failed, then you will too; and you may get yourself killed along the way.'

Bergerac's manner had suddenly changed. He had lost some of his earlier congeniality, and there was a hard, unyielding edge to his voice.

'There are too many dangerous people in this city, Monsieur Guéry, and any one of them could have been responsible for the death of your brother . . . If I were you, I would go back to Antibes, back to the beautiful Côte d'Azur, and forget all about this dirty, dangerous place.'

This was, of course, wise counsel. Monsieur Bergerac may have been a rather strange man, one of those oddities that the tropics tend to produce, but he was talking a lot of sense—and I have often wondered since why Guéry didn't take his advice. Arnaud had suggested he leave, as had Bergerac, but he simply refused to do the sensible thing. It's not that he was a particularly courageous person; indeed, quite the opposite. He was prey to all manner of phobias and neuroses: a fear of enclosed spaces, a fear of open spaces, a fear of flying, certainly a fear of landing, a fear of deep water, and a fear of venereal disease, to name only the most debilitating. Despite his avid consumption of cigarettes, he was also tormented by the thought of losing his tongue to cancer—or simply being killed outright by the dreaded disease. So why, we may ask ourselves, would a man like Guéry choose to pursue such a dangerous course of action, and all for the sake of a brother he had never particularly liked in the first place? Why didn't he take the advice he was given and simply leave Saigon? I suggested earlier that it may have had something to do with his father or his admiration for the fictional Inspector Maigret, but I'm only speculating. In fact, it could have been anything. All I know for sure is that Guéry repeatedly ignored the advice he was given by people like Arnaud and Bergerac, people who knew the place far better than he did, and continued to pursue this most improbable of enquiries. He somehow found the courage to do so, and that's what really fascinates me about this story: not the mystery of his brother's murder, which in some ways was actually quite banal, but the mystery of where Jean-Luc Guéry—with his brilliantined hair and Gallic nose, and his long history of literary failure, and his addiction to alcohol and gambling, and his nicotine-stained fingers and inappropriate clothes—where he found the courage to do something so unbelievably stupid.

That evening, on the terrace of the Continental, he simply explained to Bergerac that he had come a long way and felt a certain responsibility to find out what had happened to his brother. 'I don't imagine I'll solve the case,' he conceded. 'But I do feel obliged to try, and you never know, I may even discover something. After all, I have learned a thing or two about homicide cases over the years. I'm familiar with all the procedures. I've read Vidocq, and I do have a good memory for faces.'

Bergerac chose to disregard this last utterance. 'Be that as it may,' he said, 'I fear you are still playing with fire, Monsieur. This is not Antibes or Cannes or Nice. They do things differently here—even the Unione Corse.' He raised his eyes once more to the figure standing in the doorway. 'And it would be a great shame if you were to be found floating in the Arroyo Chinois like your brother.'

As I say, if Guéry had only heeded this warning, things might have turned out very differently indeed. But he didn't listen; or if he did, he didn't take the warning as seriously as he should have. I suppose Bergerac's timing could have been better too. It was still the hour of the *apéro*, you see, and at that time of day, poor old Jean-Luc Guéry always regarded the world as a place of peace and tranquillity and eternal brotherhood; and in a world of this kind, a world without pain or suffering, without venereal disease or cancer of the tongue, nothing could ever go wrong.

Chapter 4

Perec Frères

The following day, despite the fact that he was enduring one of his notoriously severe 'migraines,' Guéry decided to visit the Perec Frères offices on rue d'Espagne. He had not yet been placed under surveillance, so I only found out about this much later when he came to see me at the Sûreté. It was, he said, the obvious place to begin his investigation as this was where Olivier had spent the last five years of his working life.

Perhaps naively, Guéry was expecting the company to be located in a grand neoclassical building, something befitting an enterprise as distinguished as Perec Frères (which had been established in the 1920s by two brothers from the Languedoc), but when he finally found the place, it turned out to be rather unprepossessing. The foyer was spacious, with an elaborate tessellated floor, but everything felt just a little bit grimy, as if none of the surfaces had been cleaned in a very long time. To the left of the doorway, barely visible in the gloom, there was a printed directory in a glass case. According to this directory,

Perec Frères was located on the fifth floor, surrounded by public notaries, secretarial services, and insurance agencies.

Guéry climbed the stairs as slowly as possible, then made his way along a narrow, dimly lit corridor until he came to a bronze plaque that read as follows:

Perec Frères
Importateurs de Machines Agricoles de Qualité
Ventes et Demandes de Renseignements

He rang the bell and waited. Eventually, the door was opened by a middle-aged Vietnamese woman with marcelled hair and pencil lines for eyebrows. Guéry identified himself and explained that he was looking for a Monsieur Reyes. After presenting the woman with his card and subjecting himself to a moment or two of close scrutiny, he was ushered inside.

'Please wait here,' the woman said, before disappearing through another doorway into an adjoining office.

Guéry lit a cigarette and remained standing. The room was sparsely furnished and smelled strongly of some unidentifiable leafy fragrance. On the wall to the right of the door there was a poster advertising the company's wares: *Vendeuvre Diesel France—Moteurs Diesel, 6 à 90 CV, 1 à 6 Cylindres, Groupes Électrogènes, Tracteurs 17-35-55 CV, Presses, Semoirs, Batteuses,* etc. As he was reading this poster, Guéry wondered, and not for the first time either, how his brother could have dedicated his life to something so utterly banal. Surely there were more interesting ways to make money, if that was what you wanted to do. And how did a man importing and selling agricultural machinery end up with a bullet in his head anyway? Even if it wasn't necessarily tragic, in the classical sense, it certainly seemed rather incongruous.

After several minutes, the woman with the marcelled hair returned.

'Monsieur Reyes will see you now,' she said.

Guéry followed her into the adjoining office, where he was greeted by a man in his late forties with bifocal glasses, a bald head, and the pronounced bone structure of a third-century ascetic.

'Monsieur Guéry,' he said once they were both seated, 'please accept my sincere condolences. Olivier was a dear friend of mine—and a valued colleague.'

'Thank you. As you can imagine, it's been a difficult time for our family, but we're very grateful for all the support the company has provided.'

Reyes waved a deprecatory hand. 'Not at all. It was the least we could do. I'm only sorry that you weren't able to be here for the funeral. The ceremony was really quite moving.'

'I understand that the priest read from Ecclesiastes.'

'Indeed. It was a beautiful passage. Very appropriate.' He paused for a second as if recalling the scene. 'But tell me, Monsieur Guéry, what brings you to Saigon?'

'I'm actually here to find out what happened to Olivier. I'd like to know why he was murdered.'

'This is something we would all like to know,' Reyes said, nodding his head gravely, 'but unfortunately the police were unable to solve the case.'

'Yes, I've been to see the investigating officer, Inspector Arnaud. He told me that they had reached a dead end. But even so, I thought I might be able to discover something that the police have overlooked.'

'Given the circumstances, Monsieur Guéry, I fear this may be a little optimistic. Since the beginning of the war, there have been many such cases in Saigon, and very few of them have been solved.'

'So I've heard. But I was wondering if you could tell me a bit about my brother's case in particular.'

'Certainly.'

Guéry lit another cigarette and looked around for something on which to write his notes.

'A piece of paper, Monsieur?'

'Thank you; that's very kind.' He folded the sheet of paper he was offered in half and balanced it on his knee. 'Could you begin, perhaps, by telling me about the discovery of the body?'

'Of course. It was found some time around ten or eleven in the morning, as far as I can remember, by an employee of the Banque de l'Indochine. She saw it floating in the river, just over there.' Reyes gestured vaguely toward the Arroyo Chinois. 'The police were immediately called, and the body was taken to the morgue, where I believe an autopsy was performed.'

'Inspector Arnaud told me that one of my brother's colleagues was asked to identify his body, a man by the name of Jacques Fourier.'

'That's right. Monsieur Fourier had worked closely with your brother for several years.'

'Would it be possible for me to speak to him?'

Reyes lifted his shoulders in a regretful shrug. 'I'm afraid Monsieur Fourier resigned shortly after your brother passed away, and I haven't seen him since.'

'Do you happen to have his address?' Guéry asked. 'Perhaps I could contact him that way.'

'Yes, it should be somewhere around here. I'll give it to you before you leave.'

There was a strange watercolour hanging on the wall of Reyes' office. It was clearly a landscape, but it was so generic, so bland, that it could have been a depiction of almost any location in the world. Earlier, it had reminded Guéry of the *calanques* between Marseille and Cassis, but now, when he glanced over at the painting, it looked more like Rio de Janeiro.

'I'm also curious about Olivier's business dealings,' he said. 'Do you think they might have had something to do with his murder?'

Reyes smiled. 'I don't believe so, Monsieur Guéry. The work we do here could hardly be described as dangerous.'

'And what is it that you do here, precisely?'

'It's very simple. We import agricultural machinery from the factory in Vendeuvre—rotary hoes, hydraulic presses, that kind of thing—and then we sell this equipment locally.'

'Have you found this to be a profitable enterprise?'

'Moderately so. Your brother arrived in Saigon at the end of 1946, just as the war was beginning; and since then we've had some difficult times, but we've never once fallen into the red.'

As he spoke, Reyes was toying with a silver cigarette lighter, opening and closing its circular lid. The lighter had the word IMCO written on the side, and it occurred to Guéry, in passing, that the same kind of lighter had been found on his brother's body. But of course this was of no significance whatsoever; it was just a rather irritating sound.

'What type of manager was Olivier?' he asked.

'A very good one,' Reyes replied. 'Dedicated and industrious. He put a great deal of effort into making sure that everything ran smoothly and that the customers were always satisfied.'

'Did he ever encounter difficulties of any kind?'

'Nothing that would have led there, Monsieur Guéry.' Again he gestured toward the river. 'As I say, there's nothing we do in this place that could be considered even remotely dangerous.'

'I was speaking to someone yesterday who mentioned the name Vitelli—Pierre Vitelli. Did my brother ever have any business dealings with him?'

Reyes laughed. 'No, none at all. In fact, I would be surprised if they were even acquainted with one another. I don't imagine that Monsieur Vitelli has much need for rotary hoes or hydraulic presses.'

Guéry paused for a moment to write the following notes on his piece of paper:

Fourier resigned February.
Moderately profitable.
Customers satisfied.
Difficulties: none.
Danger: none.
Vitelli's need for agricultural machinery: none.

'By the way,' Reyes said, 'if it's of any interest to you, the office we're now sitting in used to belong to your brother. This was where he spent his days.'

For the first time, Guéry sat back in his chair and surveyed the place. It was a relatively large office, with four balustraded windows overlooking rue d'Espagne. Unlike the room he had just left, it was conspicuously cluttered and untidy. There were papers, files, trade catalogues, invoices, overflowing correspondence trays, and even small pieces of machinery covering every available surface. A grey filing cabinet stood in one corner, and on the wall facing him there was a framed map of Saigon, the aforementioned watercolour, and a commercial calendar advertising Vendeuvre agricultural machinery. It was all fairly unremarkable, Guéry later told me—the typical office of a busy managing director. Only one detail seemed a little odd, and it was something he would remember later too. The commercial calendar on the wall was open to the month of July 1949, making it almost two years old.

'And now this is your office, Monsieur Reyes?'

'It is.'

'I presume you were promoted when Olivier died.'

'Yes,' Reyes said in a neutral tone of voice, 'I was.'

'Tell me, Monsieur, if you don't mind, do you have any theories as to why my brother was murdered? Apparently, he lived a very ordinary life here, managing an ordinary company, and yet for some reason he was killed in this quite horrific way. To me, it just doesn't make any sense.'

'I'm afraid I really can't help you, Monsieur Guéry. I find it rather mystifying too. As you say, your brother was a very ordinary man. Certainly not the kind of person who would have had anything to do with Monsieur Vitelli or his associates. And yet . . . ' He hesitated. 'Well, no—there's really nothing more to say.'

'Please, Monsieur Reyes. Even the smallest detail may be useful.'

The managing director studied him closely through the upper half of his bifocal glasses. He seemed to be considering something, turning it over in his head; and then, apparently, he made his decision.

'Well, Monsieur Guéry, there was one aspect of your brother's life that may have brought him into contact with certain disreputable types, let's say. It's still nothing out of the ordinary; in fact, it's rather typical for men living out here in the colonies. It can be a solitary life, as you can imagine, and one does sometimes feel the need for more refined company . . . '

'Go on, Monsieur.'

'Some time ago, I discovered that your brother had been spending his evenings at a nightclub called the Palais de Jade, and I believe he had developed a rather strong attachment to one of the dance hostesses there. A girl by the name of Weiling.'

Guéry frowned. 'Forgive my ignorance, Monsieur Reyes, but what exactly is a dance hostess?'

'They're young Vietnamese or Chinese women who will dance with you for a small fee. I'm told that some of them can be quite charming. But the reality of it isn't so glamorous. The girls are often very poorly paid. They live in squalid dormitories. And they're sometimes obliged to entertain their customers after hours too, charging as little as forty or fifty piastres for the privilege.'

This struck Guéry as a remarkably detailed answer, particularly coming from someone who looked like one of the early Desert Fathers.

'Where is the Palais de Jade?' he asked.

'It's down the far end of boulevard Galliéni, in a district called Cholon.'

'The Chinese quarter?'

Reyes nodded.

'And you think this dance hostess, this Weiling, may have had something to do with Olivier's murder?'

'I really couldn't say. But Cholon itself can be a dangerous place, and apparently your brother had also taken to gambling at some of the casinos there. The Grand Monde in particular, along with two or three others.'

The suggestion that his brother had been frequenting casinos surprised Guéry far more than the revelation that he had found himself a *con gai*. Olivier Guéry had always enjoyed a fairly easy and unproblematic romantic life. That was all part of his normality, his 'well-adjustedness,' and also one of the main things that had distinguished him from Guéry, whose encounters with women were almost always farcical exercises in humiliation and failure. So yes, he could see his brother romancing a local girl, in that carefree and conventional way of his, but he found it hard to imagine him sweating over a baccarat table or putting his last two hundred francs on red-27. His brother had always been a deeply pragmatic man. Everything he did was designed to serve a larger purpose, to move him ever closer to some ultimate objective, usually financial. So it was almost inconceivable to Guéry that he could have given in to the lure of the casino, to the *diablerie* and dreaming and self-deception that necessarily accompany the act of gambling.

'It surprises me to hear you say this, Monsieur Reyes. I must admit I find it difficult to recognize the man you're describing as my brother.' He paused. 'But tell me, why is this Cholon such a dangerous place?'

'The French administration has no authority there. It's run by the Binh Xuyen, and they can be very dangerous indeed.'

'Who are they?' Guéry asked.

'A private army, I suppose you might say. They started off as river pirates operating on the southern fringes of Saigon in the 1920s. But eventually they moved in to Saigon itself, where they formed an alliance with the French authorities and pledged their loyalty to the emperor. In exchange for their assistance with the counterinsurgency, they were allowed to establish themselves in Cholon—and they now have complete control over the gambling, prostitution, and narcotics in that part of the city.'

'I see.'

Guéry wrote the words *gambling, prostitution*, and *narcotics* on his piece of paper.

'So when you travel down boulevard Galliéni and enter Cholon,' Reyes continued, 'you're really entering foreign territory. The Binh Xuyen have laid claim to the entire place. Until last year, the Grand Monde was run by a Macanese gambling syndicate, but the Binh Xuyen finally managed to drive them out too. And now they really do own everything.'

'Wasn't the Grand Monde where you said Olivier had been gambling?'

Reyes nodded. 'I believe he was seen there more than once.'

'So do you think the Binh Xuyen may have been involved in his murder?'

'Not necessarily, although it's always possible. Once you start frequenting such places, once you start gambling in their casinos and consorting with their dance hostesses, you do expose yourself to another way of life. And you can easily run into trouble.'

'What kind of trouble?' Guéry asked.

'In your brother's case, of course, it may have had something to do with the girl. These attachments often lead to difficulties of one kind or another. But I've also been told that he may have borrowed money to cover his gambling losses.'

'Really? It's difficult to imagine Olivier losing.'

'Perhaps so, Monsieur. But at a place like the Grand Monde, it's equally difficult to imagine anyone winning—even a man as gifted as your brother.'

Guéry took a moment to add to his notes.

'Monsieur Guéry,' Reyes said once he had finished writing, 'may I offer you a piece of advice?'

'Please do.'

'I think it would be rather unwise for you to pursue this investigation of yours any further. Particularly if you're intending to do so at the other end of boulevard Galliéni. Your brother, Olivier, had been living here for almost five years when he was murdered. He knew the place as well as anyone, and yet he still ended up in the Arroyo Chinois. If I were you, Monsieur, I would go home and try to forget about everything that has happened here. If you don't, quite frankly, I fear for your safety.'

Guéry smiled. It was the third time in as many days that he had been offered such advice. 'I appreciate your concern, Monsieur Reyes. But I still feel that I need to clarify the circumstances surrounding my brother's murder; and once I've done so, I can assure you that I'll be going straight home.'

'Very well,' Reyes said with an air of polite finality. 'Then I wish you the best of luck with your enquiries. And if you do happen to find Monsieur Fourier, I would be grateful if you could please let us know. We still have his last pay cheque.'

'Of course, Monsieur. I'll notify you immediately.'

After giving him Fourier's address, Reyes escorted Guéry through the adjoining office and out into the corridor, where they exchanged the usual civilities.

As he turned to go, however, something occurred to Guéry. 'Is it true that the company maintains a warehouse here in Saigon?' he asked.

'Yes, naturally.'

'In that case, I wonder if I might be able to take a look at it one day.'

The managing director seemed surprised by this. 'But why? It's really not very interesting.'

'Even so, if you don't mind, I would very much like to see it before I leave. I'm just curious, that's all. And I would like to get some sense of Olivier's daily routine while he was here. The places he visited, the things he did.'

'I see.' Reyes shrugged. 'Well, if it means so much to you, Monsieur Guéry, I'm sure that something could be arranged. I'll discuss it with my colleagues and drop you a line at the Majestic in a couple of days.'

'Thank you,' Guéry said. 'Is the warehouse very far away?'

'No, it's within walking distance—probably about fifteen minutes from here. It's down by the river, opposite the Ogliastro building.'

'I'm sorry, Monsieur, but I still don't really know my way around the city . . . '

'Of course. If you turn right when you leave the Majestic, and then turn right again immediately after boulevard de la Somme, you'll find it just beyond the Banque de l'Indochine.'

Guéry raised his eyebrows. 'The Banque de l'Indochine? So it's on the quay that runs alongside the Arroyo Chinois?'

'Yes.'

'Where Olivier's body was found?'

Reyes glanced to his left, along the corridor, as if there might be someone else there. 'Yes,' he said after a momentary pause, 'where your brother's body was found.'

Chapter 5

Tu Parles d'une Ingénue

I must admit that I have only read one or two of Guéry's journalistic pieces, and those were the articles he would later send me from France, along with a large folder containing his notes on the case. Like most of the people he encountered during his time here, I had never heard of *Le Journal d'Antibes*, and to this day I still haven't seen a copy of that particular newspaper. I am, however, familiar with the kind of material such a newspaper would typically contain: the mundane controversies, the petty crimes, the provincial intrigues, etc., etc. This was Guéry's world, the one he had mastered, the one he found most comforting. So it must have been rather traumatic for him to have been plunged, without warning, into another kind of world altogether—a world of dance hostesses and gambling syndicates and murder committees.

Although he claimed to have 'learned a thing or two about homicide cases over the years,' this wasn't quite true. Everything he knew about such cases had been gleaned from the *romans policiers* he read so avidly. And over the following days, it was this knowledge (rather than any familiarity with actual cases) that would determine almost everything he did. It was as if he were acting out his very own detective novel—the only difference being that the consequences for the protagonist, on this occasion, were entirely real. If he were to be shot in the head, for instance, and dumped in the Arroyo Chinois, that would be the end of the story; there would be no 'close shaves' or miraculous escapes, and certainly no epilogues.

Anyway, the point I'm trying to make here is that Guéry's decision to visit the coroner's office on rue Pasteur, the day after his meeting with Reyes, was determined not by the investigative logic of the case itself but by the generic features of the classic detective novel. In other words, he only went there because that was what someone like Maigret would have done in his place. Within the first couple of chapters, a fictional detective would always make his way to the morgue, where more often than not he would discover some vital piece of evidence that would eventually lead to the resolution of the case (or at least provide a way forward). Guéry may not have had any first-hand knowledge of police procedures, but he did recognize the value of the morgue scene. This was the point at which the narrative of the crime and the narrative of the investigation intersected— in the form of a cold, mute body lying on an autopsy table or a steel refrigerator-tray. This was where one story typically came to an end and the other began. Only, in Guéry's case, of course, things weren't quite that simple.

As his brother had been buried a month or so earlier, there was nothing much to see at the coroner's office. There was no body to be dramatically unveiled, and therefore no opportunity to commune with the dead or discover vital forensic evidence. The only thing he could do was talk to the pathologist who had conducted the original autopsy. This was a man by the name of

Cabral, it turned out, who had a large, airy office on the third floor. He was in the middle of typing something when Guéry entered, and seemed rather startled by the intrusion, but once he understood what his visitor was looking for, he was able to find the relevant file with surprising ease.

'Let me see,' he said, running his finger down the first page of the report. 'Caucasian, male, early forties, 183 centimetres, 79 kilograms . . . No distinguishing features . . . Gunshot injuries to the head . . . Suspected homicide . . . It's all quite typical, really.' He paused. 'Is there anything in particular you would like to know, Monsieur?'

Guéry thought for a moment. 'Perhaps you could describe my brother's injuries in more detail,' he said finally.

'Of course.' Cabral consulted the report once more. 'He had been shot twice in the head. One bullet had entered his skull just above the left eye, and the other had entered through his left temple. I'll spare you the technicalities.'

'So does that mean that the shots were fired in quick succession?' Guéry asked.

'Most probably, yes.'

'But only one bullet was found in his head, I believe.'

'That's right. The first bullet was found lodged in the right parietal lobe. That's here.' Cabral tapped the back of his own head with a pencil. 'The other one emerged from a point two or three centimetres above his right ear.'

'And based on the bullet you found, were you able to identify the type of gun that was used?'

'Yes. It was a nine-millimetre semiautomatic pistol— probably a Luger or a Steyr.'

'Are these pistols widely available here?'

'I'm afraid so. The Luger is particularly common. It's standard-issue for both the police and the army, and I believe the legionnaires use them too.'

'Were you able to determine exactly when my brother died?'

Cabral shook his head. 'Not precisely. We were able to estimate that he had been in the river for somewhere between twelve and twenty-four hours, and that he was dead when he entered the water. But it's far more difficult to tell you exactly when he was killed. Water complicates these matters, you see. All I can say with any degree of certainty is that he died no more than five days before his body was found.'

There was a brief silence as Guéry jotted these figures down on the back of an advertising flyer he had been given earlier that morning. (I have it before me as I write, incidentally. On one side of the flyer there is a perfectly ordinary advertisement for Vittel-Délices; but if you turn it over, you find something that looks like one of Poe's cryptographic challenges or a fragment of Linear B.)

'What else can you tell me about the manner in which my brother was killed?' Guéry asked once he had completed his notes.

'He was shot from a distance of a metre or so. In each case, the bullet followed a largely horizontal trajectory. And that's about it, really.' Cabral looked up from the file. 'I'm afraid there isn't much more to say, Monsieur.'

Guéry nodded slowly. 'Was the body photographed at any point during the autopsy?'

'No. It's not customary to keep a photographic record in such routine cases.'

'I see. And was it difficult to identify the body, given the fact that it had been in the water for so long?'

'It wasn't easy. Some bloating and maceration of the skin had occurred; and there was also considerable soft-tissue damage. But there's no doubt that the identification was a positive one.'

'So you're confident that it was my brother . . . '

'Absolutely. The ID card that was found on the body obviously belonged to the deceased, and one of your brother's colleagues later confirmed his identity.'

'A Monsieur Fourier.'

Cabral glanced down at the file. 'Yes, that's right. Monsieur Jacques Fourier.'

At this point, Guéry later said, he was becoming rather frustrated. He had been told very little that he didn't already know, and there was something about Cabral's insistence on the routine nature of the case that he was beginning to find irritating.

'Do you yourself have any theories as to why my brother might have been killed?' he asked.

The pathologist gave him a fatigued smile. 'I'm sorry, Monsieur Guéry, but that's not my field. My job is to tell you as much as possible about the manner in which he was killed, based on the physical evidence alone. Everything else I leave to the police.'

'Of course. But you seem to be suggesting that what happened to Olivier is an everyday occurrence around here. Is that really the case?'

'Unfortunately so. You just need to look around to see what kind of place Saigon has become—the corpses left on the street corners every other morning, the anti-grenade netting over the café terraces, the armed sentries posted outside all the government buildings. Only yesterday a young girl detonated a grenade in the foyer of the Olympic. We had five dead bodies arrive here within half an hour, and we spent most of the night trying to put the right pieces into the right bags.'

'So was there nothing at all remarkable about my brother's case?'

Cabral turned the pages of the report for some time before responding. 'Well,' he said at last, 'there was one thing that might interest you—although it's hardly unusual here either.'

'Yes?'

'When we did the toxicology report, we discovered that your brother had traces of opiates in his blood. Quite a large quantity, actually, given the circumstances.'

'Really?' Guéry was stunned. 'But the police told me that there was no evidence of drug use.'

Cabral shrugged. 'They must have missed this detail—or decided that it didn't matter.'

'But opiates? I can hardly believe it.'

'The figures are right here, Monsieur.'

'I'm sure they're accurate. It's just that my brother wasn't the kind of person who would have used narcotics of any kind.'

'Well, I'm afraid he did. The evidence is indisputable. As I say, though, it's hardly rare that this should be the case. Once they've been here for a while, many people acquire local . . . proclivities.'

'But hasn't the opium trade been outlawed?' Guéry asked.

'It has, yes, since 1946.'

'So . . . '

'So it's going to take quite a few years to close every *fumerie* in Saigon. And in the meantime, well, nothing much has changed.'

Guéry sighed quietly. 'But even so . . . my brother, of all people . . . it just doesn't make sense . . . '

This seemed to be the kind of thing that Cabral had heard before. He gave another one of his world-weary smiles, and then uttered some banality about everyone leading double lives, to a certain degree, and the importance of forgiving the dead for what they may (or may not) have done while they were still alive.

At the time, Guéry found it all rather persuasive, but once he had left the coroner's office and made his way to a nearby bar, where he ordered two 33 beers and a large cognac, he wasn't quite so sure.

The Olivier he was beginning to discover here in Saigon was scarcely recognizable. First, there was the suggestion that he had been frequenting casinos with a dance hostess from the Palais de Jade, and now this. It was all too bewildering. On the one hand, his brother seemed to have developed some rather uncharacteristic 'proclivities' since arriving in the city; yet on the other hand, he was still the same old Olivier, a dedicated and industrious managing director who simply wanted to do the best he could for the company he was representing. Cabral was right, of course: we all lead double lives to some degree. It was just that the contrast here was so pronounced and the 'other life,' the other Olivier, so difficult to imagine. The *con gai* he could understand, and perhaps even the odd sociable flutter at the casino; but if you added something like opium to the picture, it became completely inconceivable. After all, this was the same Olivier who had only ever been interested in entry strategies and percentages and strategic alliances, and considered everything else a complete waste of time. This was the same Olivier who, at their father's behest, had once interrupted Guéry in the middle of a particularly long and debilitating binge in Cannes. It was the off-season, when Guéry could more easily afford to pay for a hotel room, but even so he was staying at one of the dingier places by the railway station, just off rue des Serbes. And he could still vividly remember the disdain in his brother's eyes when he saw the place, and the word he had used to describe Guéry, as if it were no ordinary noun but some terrible curse imposed on him by a higher being. '*Degenerate*,' he had said. 'You are nothing but a *degenerate*.' And now here he was, gambling and ingesting opiates and God knows what else. It was all rather disconcerting—not least because Guéry could see, for the first time in his life, something of himself in his brother, something undisciplined and self-destructive and, yes, degenerate.

It was almost enough to make him feel sorry for the poor dead fool.

* * *

Guéry stayed at the bar for another hour or so. Then around midday, feeling suitably fortified and with nothing better to do, he decided that it was time to find Jacques Fourier, the man who had identified his brother's body.

The address Reyes had given him belonged to a dilapidated art deco building on place du Joffre. There was a caged elevator in the foyer, but as Guéry had a strong aversion to such machines, he elected to climb the stairs instead. Fourier's apartment turned out to be on the top floor; and by the time he got there, he was sweating profusely and beginning to feel some rather disturbing gastric twinges.

He rang the doorbell several times.

Somewhere in the building he could hear a radio playing flamenco music, but behind this particular door there was complete silence.

After a while, he tried the bell again.

Still nothing.

'Good day, Monsieur. Can I help you?'

Guéry turned around. An old man was standing two or three paces away, regarding him inquisitively. He was about seventy or so, with a thin grey face and slightly misaligned eyes.

'I'm the concierge here,' the man said. 'I heard you ringing.'

'I'm actually looking for a Monsieur Jacques Fourier. I believe he lives in this apartment.'

'Indeed he does, Monsieur, but you won't find him there.'

'He's gone out?'

'He's been gone for a long time.'

'You mean he's moved somewhere else?'

'No, Monsieur. His belongings are still inside. Nothing has been touched. It's just that Monsieur Fourier himself has gone.'

This sounded ominous, like something you might read about in *Détective* magazine.

'Did he tell you where he was going?' Guéry asked.

'I'm afraid not. He just disappeared. One day in late February, I believe it was.'

'Without any warning?'

'That's right.' The man hesitated. 'May I ask if you are another one of Monsieur Fourier's business associates?'

'No,' Guéry was surprised to hear himself say, 'I'm actually his brother. I've just arrived here from . . . the Antilles. Yes, the French Antilles, that's where I live.'

'Is that so? Well, Monsieur Fourier, I'm pleased to make your acquaintance. My name is Cotillard.'

'The pleasure is all mine, Monsieur Cotillard. But you asked if I was another one of Jacques' business associates—does that mean someone from Perec Frères has already been here?'

'Yes. When Monsieur Fourier first disappeared, back in February, a man by the name of Reyes came to find out what had happened.'

'I know Reyes.'

'Very good. And then a week or so later, another two men came. I can't remember their names. They said they were from the SDECE.'

'The intelligence agency?'

Cotillard nodded.

'And did they give you any indication of what might have happened to . . . er, Jacques?'

'None. They spent an hour or so looking through his apartment, and then they left without saying anything.'

'They didn't tell you what they were looking for?'

'No, Monsieur, I'm afraid not.' He gave a rather philosophical shrug. 'The men of the SDECE are not typically known for their candour—or their volubility.'

'No,' Guéry agreed, 'I don't suppose they are.' He turned slightly and gestured toward the enamel nameplate on Fourier's door. 'If Jacques left in February, may I ask why you haven't yet found another tenant to take his place?'

'The apartment belongs to your brother, Monsieur. It's not a rental property.'

'But you do have a key?'

'Yes, for cleaning purposes. Would you like me to show you around?'

'If it's not too much trouble . . . '

'Not at all, Monsieur. I have it right here.'

He produced a large set of keys and, after trying two or three, eventually located the right one.

The apartment was just as Fourier would have left it. In fact, it looked as if he might have stepped out only a few minutes earlier to buy a packet of cigarettes. Cotillard led him into the living room, where there was an old typewriter standing on a mahogany writing table. On either side of the typewriter there were various loose papers (invoices, brochures, letters, etc.), as well as a ceramic jug, some used glasses, and a half-empty jar of olives. Several liquor bottles had been casually deposited on the sideboard, and on another table, by the door, there was an overflowing ashtray balanced on a pile of magazines. The only things that suggested the place may have been unoccupied for any length of time were the lizards scurrying across the parquet floor and the patches of mould growing on the ceiling.

Cotillard was horrified by the latter. 'I'll have to get my wife to do something about this,' he said. 'It's one of the curses of the tropics, you know.'

Guéry glanced surreptitiously at some of the papers on the table, but there was nothing of any significance there—only what the SDECE agents had left behind when they searched the place.

He followed Cotillard through the rest of the apartment, stopping from time to time to study an imitation Sèvres vase or an engraved cigarette case or an old 78.

'Tell me, Monsieur Cotillard,' he said at one point, 'do you have any idea why the intelligence service was trying to find Jacques?'

'No, Monsieur, I'm afraid I don't. Your brother tended to keep to himself when he was living here. He was always very civil, of course, but we didn't really learn much about his private life or his business activities.'

'You do know that he worked for a company called Perec Frères . . . '

'This we only discovered when Monsieur Reyes came looking for him in February.'

'I see. Did you ever happen to meet a man by the name of Guéry—Olivier Guéry?'

Cotillard smiled. 'Unfortunately not, Monsieur. As I say, we had very little to do with your brother and no knowledge at all of his private life.'

It gave Guéry a rather uncanny feeling, he later told me, to be inspecting the apartment of a complete stranger—and particularly as there was still so much evidence of his intimate domestic life on display. An unmade bed shrouded in grey mosquito netting. A bag of soiled clothes hanging from a door handle. A collection of medicine bottles standing on top of the refrigerator. It made him feel uncomfortable to be sifting through the minutiae of another man's life in this way, and he wasn't even sure how productive it was to do so. All he had learned so far was that Fourier smoked cheap Bastos cigarettes, that he liked the music of Charles Trenet, and that he suffered from atopic dermatitis and hives.

Only later would Guéry realize that he had in fact learned something of value by noticing, by remembering, what was *not* there. Despite the fact that the apartment still looked inhabited, there were no personal photos to be found anywhere, and all the official documentation and money had disappeared too. This suggested that Fourier had most probably left the place of his own free will, taking only what really mattered to him, and that he had done so quite deliberately, knowing that he was unlikely to return. Although his motives for leaving were still a mystery, then, it was clear that he was gone for good.

In one corner of the living room there was a small bookcase, and once the tour was finished, Guéry crouched down to read some of the titles. Fourier, it seemed, was a man with literary tendencies. There was some Céline, some Balzac, and even some Alfred Jarry. He was pleased to see his preferred genre represented there too—the latest Simenon, two or three Séries Noires, and a battered copy of *The Lerouge Affair*. On a lower shelf there were also several atlases, some dictionaries, and a three-volume history of the Napoleonic Wars.

Guéry was just about to stand up again when he noticed a small paperback book that had been pushed a few centimetres further in than the others. It was the 1949 Fleuve Noir edition of *Tu Parles d'une Ingénue*.

He took the book out and studied the cover for a minute or two:

Then he turned to the title page.

It was missing.

Guéry settled back on his haunches and flicked through the remaining pages. Eventually, he found the confirmation he was looking for: the circular seal of the Centre Saint-Lazare in Rome. The loose page that was discovered on his brother's body had been torn from this very copy of *Tu Parles d'une Ingénue*.

'Monsieur Cotillard,' Guéry said, getting to his feet, 'would you mind if I borrowed something? It's a book I gave Jacques a couple of years ago—some light reading for the plane.'

After glancing at the cover, Cotillard smiled in an understanding way. 'Of course, Monsieur. I like reading about spies too.'

It was at this moment, quite without warning, that Guéry's stomach made the most alarming noise. (The phrase 'distant thunder' comes to mind, although the sound did have a muffled, subterranean quality too, suggesting, perhaps, some kind of large-scale seismic disturbance.)

'I beg your pardon, Monsieur,' he said, attempting to smile graciously. But even as he smiled, he heard another ominous rumbling and tasted, not for the first time that day, an acrid intermingling of beer and cognac on his tongue.

Cotillard looked at him with concern. 'Would you like a glass of water, Monsieur?'

'No, thank you. I'm fine. It's just the humidity in this place— and the tropical climate more generally. It's taking me some time to acclimatize.'

Cotillard nodded sympathetically. 'Yes, it can be rather difficult for the first few days. But you'll get used to it eventually. Everyone does.'

There was a brief silence, and then they heard what sounded like a coal mine collapsing in on itself two or three hundred metres beneath the ground.

'Actually, Monsieur, perhaps it would be best if I used the . . . facilities. I'm suddenly feeling rather ill.'

'Of course,' Cotillard said. 'Please do.'

Guéry only just reached the toilet in time. Crouching over the bowl, he watched as everything he had eaten that morning, along with surprisingly large quantities of beer and cognac, reentered the world. It made a colourful *millefleurs* pattern on the side of the toilet that reminded him of the Tapestry of the Apocalypse in Angers. But this first outpouring was

soon followed by another, and then another, and then several
more—none of which bore the slightest resemblance to any
masterpieces of the late Middle Ages.

'Monsieur Fourier.' Cotillard's voice came through the door.
'Monsieur Fourier, are you all right?'

Guéry answered in the affirmative, although the gurgling
sound he produced in order to do so suggested that this was not
entirely true.

'Would you like me to call a doctor, Monsieur?'

He managed a more convincing response this time, and
Cotillard seemed satisfied.

'Very well. But please let me know if you need any assistance.'

'I will,' Guéry replied, as persuasively as he could, before
returning once more to the business at hand.

As I said at the very beginning of this narrative, it was
sometimes difficult to take Guéry seriously. Even in the
most critical of circumstances, he would often find a way to
undermine his own dignity, to reduce whatever was happening
to the level of farce. Quite frankly, I would have preferred it
if this wasn't the case. But that was simply the kind of person
he was. At a time when an ordinary detective would have been
speculating as to the significance of the missing page from
Tu Parles d'une Ingénue, he was on his knees, staring into a toilet
bowl full of regurgitated beer and cognac.

It was all rather unfortunate; but that was Guéry for you,
I suppose. He never did have a very good sense of timing.

* * *

Two days later, still feeling a bit rough around the edges, Guéry
paid a visit to the Perec Frères warehouse on the quai de Belgique.
He would much rather have spent the day convalescing in bed,

but Reyes had made it quite clear in his message that this would be Guéry's one and only chance to see the warehouse. So when the designated hour arrived, he made his way, rather gingerly, along the quayside until he came to a large concrete building with a corrugated-iron roof and two unadorned flagpoles. Above the central doorway, one of three, a row of raised concrete letters spelled out the company's name: PEREC FRÈRES.

As it happened, Guéry had arrived a few minutes early, so he sat for a while on a wall overlooking the Arroyo Chinois, smoking a cigarette and observing the activity on the river. This, of course, was where Olivier's body had been found, floating face down, just a couple of metres from the quay itself. But his body could have been dumped almost anywhere along the river and simply drifted to where it was eventually discovered. The Arroyo Chinois is a busy, working river, lined with sampans, barges, and floating wooden structures that often house entire families. This floating city is known as Roseauville, the City of Reeds, and it stretches from the Saigon River all the way to Cholon, where many of the illicit opium refineries are located. So it was really impossible to say precisely where Olivier's body had been disposed of; and the fact that it was found floating relatively close to the warehouse may have been nothing more than a coincidence.

After finishing his cigarette, Guéry made his way across the quay to the Perec Frères building. All three of the large doors at the front of the warehouse were closed, so he walked around to the side, where there was a narrow alleyway full of metal debris and old tractor engines. Halfway down this alley, he found a small door with a sign on it that said BUREAU. He rang the bell and waited, but he didn't have to wait for very long. Almost immediately, the door was opened by a rotund Vietnamese man in his late fifties.

'Monsieur Guéry,' he said with a smile. 'Please come in. I've been expecting you.'

Once he was inside, Guéry found himself standing in a square, windowless office. The linoleum flooring was a dirty grey colour, and the walls were covered in Alberto Vargas pictures, most of which had been torn out of calendars and magazines.

'Monsieur Reyes told me that you would be coming, and he's asked me to show you around.'

'That's very kind of you,' Guéry said. 'I presume you're Monsieur Chiang.'

'Yes, indeed. And as you can see, I'm the only one here today.' He made an expansive gesture to indicate the emptiness of the office. 'I'm afraid that business has been rather slow over the last few days.'

'How long have you worked here, Monsieur Chiang?'

'Quite a long time. Almost twenty years.'

'So you obviously knew my brother, Olivier Guéry.'

'Yes, I did. He was a good man, and I was very sorry when he died.'

Guéry had heard this before, but the warehouse manager seemed sincere.

'And you must also know a man by the name of Jacques Fourier.'

'I do,' he said. 'But Fourier no longer works here, and perhaps that's not such a bad thing.'

'Really?'

'Yes.' Chiang's features darkened momentarily. 'Unlike your brother, he was a rather difficult man to have as a colleague.'

'I see. And do you, Monsieur Chiang, have a theory as to why my brother was murdered?'

'I'm afraid it's a complete mystery to me, Monsieur Guéry. I find it hard to believe that a man as good-natured as your brother could have had any enemies.'

After a brief pause, during which he idly contemplated one of the Vargas pictures, Guéry said, 'Perhaps you could tell me a bit about the company itself. I understand that it was established in the 1920s.'

'Yes,' Chiang replied, 'that's right. It was founded in 1923 by a couple of brothers from the Languedoc. They came out here after the war, having been told that they could make a fortune trading in rubber and rice. But when this fortune failed to materialize, they decided to import agricultural machinery instead. So they established Perec Frères, and as the plantations expanded during the twenties and thirties, they managed to make quite a bit of money after all. Not a fortune exactly, but enough to retire at a reasonably young age.'

'Are they still alive, these two brothers?'

'I believe so. About ten years ago, they sold the company to Vendeuvre and moved back to France. I'm told they now live in a village near Béziers, where they've bought themselves a vineyard.'

'So Olivier was managing the company on behalf of Vendeuvre?'

'Yes, and he was very good at his job too. Over the last couple of years, the company has become increasingly profitable.'

Guéry looked around the office with half-closed eyes while nodding his head slowly, as if to suggest that he was deeply impressed by what he had just heard.

'And now, Monsieur Guéry, would you like to see the warehouse itself?'

Chiang led him through another doorway and into an enclosure that was at least five hundred square metres in size. It was illuminated by two skylights and a row of dirty windows that spanned the rear wall. On three sides, he could see the steel substructure of the building itself, and on the fourth side, the interior of the large wooden doors that faced the Arroyo Chinois. The building was uninsulated, and the heat emanating from the gabled roof was intense.

'So, Monsieur Guéry,' his guide said, 'this is it, the Perec Frères warehouse.'

At the rear of the building there was a collection of about twenty or thirty wooden crates. These crates were of varying sizes and had all been stamped with the name of the company and the words HAUT, BAS, and FRAGILE. It was, of course, precisely what one would expect to find in a warehouse; and Guéry suddenly felt a little foolish to have insisted on seeing a place that was so obviously unremarkable.

'How fascinating,' he said. 'So this is where you actually store the agricultural machinery.'

'Yes,' Chiang confirmed. 'This is where it goes when it first arrives in the country.'

'And what a convenient place to have a warehouse too, so close to the river and everything.'

Chiang agreed that the location was a good one.

'So when you receive an order for a particular piece of machinery—a tractor engine, let's say, or a rotary hoe—this is where it can be found.' He gestured toward the wooden crates. 'Right here. In these very crates.'

'Yes, Monsieur Guéry. That's usually the case.'

Guéry surveyed the warehouse admiringly. Then he walked over and touched one of the dirty steel girders with an air of expertise. 'You know,' he said, having finally made his evaluation, 'this really is a very good warehouse.'

'I'm pleased you like it, Monsieur Guéry. It certainly serves its purpose.'

At that moment, to Guéry's relief, a telephone rang in the adjoining office.

'Excuse me,' Chiang said, disappearing through the doorway. 'I should really answer this.'

While he was waiting, Guéry wandered toward the rear of the building. He sat down on a rectangular crate and lit a cigarette. The dust he unsettled when he touched the crate was illuminated by the slanting light from the windows at the rear of the building. It reminded Guéry, rather incongruously, of the cathedral in Antibes, with its altarpiece depicting Our Lady of the Rosary. And then he thought about how far he had come just to sit in a warehouse and smoke a cigarette. It was a fairly demoralizing thing to contemplate.

After a couple of minutes, Guéry stood up again, and as he did so, he felt the crate suddenly shift beneath him. It was a large crate, perhaps the size of a dinner table, and he was surprised that it should move so easily. He pushed it with the side of his shoe, and it turned out to be much lighter than it looked. Guéry threw his cigarette away and tried to open the lid. It was fastened, but not too securely; and by agitating it, by moving it from side to side, he was able to lift the timber by two or three centimetres. He bent over and peered inside. The crate was empty.

Needless to say, there was nothing particularly remarkable about this either. But out of curiosity, he then lifted the lid of another crate, a smaller one this time, and found that it too contained nothing.

Guéry would later tell me that he looked inside at least half a dozen crates in the warehouse that day, and every single one of them was empty.

When Chiang finally returned, however, Guéry chose not to say anything about the empty crates. He simply uttered a few more complimentary phrases and then explained, regretfully, that he had a pressing engagement somewhere else. But it was a discovery that bothered him for the rest of the day. Perec Frères was obviously a respectable company. It had been operating in Saigon for almost thirty years, and during this time, it had gained a reputation for providing merchandise of the highest quality. But how could it be expected to do so when its warehouse was full of empty crates? And why hadn't Chiang acknowledged this fact during his visit, when they had discussed every other aspect of the business in such excruciating detail? It was all very strange, and the thought of that warehouse down by the river, where his brother's body had been found floating just metres from the quayside, the thought of that gloomy warehouse full of Alberto Vargas pictures and empty crates, like something out of a de Chirico painting, with its asymmetrical shapes and elongated shadows, the very thought of it, of all that emptiness, those blank inventories, that pile of inexplicable zeroes labelled HAUT, BAS, and FRAGILE, yes, the very thought of it was enough to give him the heebie-jeebies.

Chapter 6

Weiling

The Palais de Jade was located in a modern two-storey building at the southern end of boulevard Galliéni. On the ground floor there was a restaurant specializing in Chinese cuisine, and on the first floor there was a nightclub, a relatively expensive one, where a band from the Philippines played every evening between eight and two. In those days, it was one of the more popular places in Cholon, despite the anti-grenade netting on the terrace and the armed guard at the door.

When Guéry arrived it was still early. The band had only just started playing, and aside from a few isolated couples, the dance floor was deserted. He found a table by the wall and ordered a cognac and a bottle of Vichy water. It was unusual for him to order the latter, but only two days had passed since the episode at Fourier's apartment, and he was still feeling rather fragile.

After swallowing half an Entero-Vioform tablet, he lit a cigarette and looked around. The nightclub was a large place, only a little smaller than the warehouse he had visited the day before. There were about fifteen or twenty tables, and every so often a thin white pillar rose to the ceiling, where it sprouted a decorative fringe of stucco palm leaves. A varnished balustrade separated the tables from the dance floor, beyond which there was a narrow stage for the band. The wall behind the stage had been decorated with dancing figures, geometric shapes, and oversized musical notes. There was also a small bar in one corner, and to the left of this, he could see a group of young women sitting at several adjacent tables. These, he assumed, must be the dance hostesses.

'Good evening, Monsieur. Are you expecting anyone else?'

Guéry looked up to find a young Vietnamese man standing at his table. His hair had been carefully combed to one side, and Guéry could smell the brilliantine he had used to keep it in place.

'No, I'm here alone.'

'In that case, if you're ready, would you care to dance with one of our hostesses?'

'I would certainly be interested,' Guéry said, 'but I'm not sure of the formalities.'

The man smiled. 'It's really very simple, Monsieur. You decide which girl you like, and then you pay to dance with her.' He gestured toward the waiting hostesses. 'The only difficulty lies in deciding which one you prefer. As you can see, they're all equally charming.'

'Indeed they are,' Guéry conceded. And it was true; they were.

'Some of our patrons prefer the local hostesses. Others like the ones from Hong Kong or Shanghai. But they're all the same price.'

'I see. And once I've chosen a girl, what do I do then?'

'Then, Monsieur, you buy one of these.' He held up a small book of tickets. 'The standard price is one hundred piastres for an hour. Or, if you prefer, you can pay by the dance.'

Guéry asked if it was possible to request a particular hostess.

'As long as she's available, yes, of course.'

'In that case,' he said, 'I'd like to dance with a girl called Weiling.'

The man glanced over at the hostesses. 'She's a popular girl, but you've come at a good time. I believe she's free.'

'Would you mind telling me which one is Weiling?'

'Certainly, Monsieur. She's the one in the red *cheongsam*, sitting at the table by the bar. The one with the flower in her hair.'

After paying his one hundred piastres, Guéry made his way over to the girl he had been told was Weiling. She looked to be in her early twenties, and her pale face was dominated by two large, mascaraed eyes. He introduced himself rather stiffly, as if he were inviting her to perform a waltz or a quadrille, and she followed him out onto the dance floor. The band was playing a song he vaguely recognized—something that had been fashionable several years before in the nightclubs of Cannes and Nice. As you can imagine, Guéry was not a particularly accomplished dancer, but he managed to survive by imitating the other men on the dance floor and by trying to imagine what the ambassador of the Dominican Republic would have done in his place.

Like Cotillard a couple of days earlier, Weiling seemed to be regarding him with genuine sympathy.

'Have you been in Saigon long, Monsieur?' she asked.

'No,' Guéry replied. 'I only arrived on Tuesday.'

'And what do you think of it so far?'

'It's a very nice place, although I'm not sure about the climate. I prefer the Côte d'Azur.'

She smiled. 'I imagine we would all prefer the Côte d'Azur. But one makes do.'

After dancing in silence for a few more minutes, Guéry said, 'I believe you may have known my brother, Olivier Guéry.'

He had been hoping for some kind of telling response, but there was none. She simply smiled again and said, 'Yes, I do know Monsieur Guéry.'

He noticed her use of the present tense.

'I'm not sure if you've heard, Mademoiselle, but my brother is dead. He died about a month ago.'

This time there *was* a response, a sudden intensity in her eyes, but it passed quickly, and once it was gone, he wasn't even sure if it had been there in the first place.

'I'm very sorry to hear that,' she said. 'Monsieur Guéry was a nice man—always very polite. May I ask how he died?'

'He was shot. Twice.'

'I see.'

'They found his body in the Arroyo Chinois.'

'That's terrible, Monsieur. Please accept my condolences.'

A tone of professional cordiality had entered her voice, as if she were commenting on the death of someone she barely knew. It was a very convincing performance.

'One of my brother's colleagues, a Monsieur Reyes, suggested I come to see you.'

'Really?'

'Yes. He said that you knew my brother rather well.'

There was no response.

'In fact, he said that you and he were very close indeed.'

She studied him carefully for a moment before replying. 'Monsieur, I'm sorry to hear about the death of your brother. He was very kind to me, and yes, we were . . . close. But that was a long time ago now, and if you don't mind, I'd rather talk about something else.'

'I understand,' he said. 'It's just that I'm trying to find out what happened to Olivier, and I thought you might be able to help.'

She shrugged apologetically. 'I'm afraid there's nothing I could tell you that would be of any use. I simply didn't know your brother that well. We enjoyed ourselves. We had a good time. And then one day he disappeared, and I never heard from him again.'

'That may be so, Mademoiselle, but it's important that I find out everything I can about Olivier's life here in Saigon, and you're the only one I've met who knew him personally.'

At that moment, the band finished the song they had been playing and, after a brief pause, launched into another one. This time it was easy to recognize: 'Les Feuilles Mortes.'

'A beautiful song,' Guéry said as they moved across the dance floor.

Weiling nodded her head and smiled. 'Where do you live in France, Monsieur?'

'Antibes.'

'And what is your profession?'

'I'm a journalist.'

'How interesting,' she said a little too quickly.

'Yes, I write for *Le Journal d'Antibes*.'

'What kind of things do you write about?'

'Local politics. Football matches. Court cases.' He thought for a second. 'I once interviewed someone who had worked on a screenplay with F. Scott Fitzgerald. This was during the late thirties, when he was contracted to Metro-Goldwyn-Mayer . . . '

Weiling seemed genuinely impressed by this reference to Hollywood. 'Have you ever interviewed any movie stars?' she asked.

'No, but I did meet Gisèle Pascal a few years ago, in a café in Cannes.'

'Really? What was she like?'

'Well, I didn't actually *meet* her, I suppose. She was busy at the time, and I didn't want to get in the way. She was there with some of the other actresses from *La Vie de Bohème*. I did catch her eye as I was leaving, though, and she gave me a very nice smile.'

Weiling nodded solemnly, and they danced for a while longer in silence.

Then, to his surprise, she said, 'Tell me, Monsieur, what is it that you would like to know about your brother?'

I'm not sure if it was his story about Gisèle Pascal or the quality of his dancing or simply the vague feeling of pity he so often inspired in women—even those half his age. But whatever it was, she had obviously changed her mind about poor old Guéry and decided to help him with his enquiries.

'Perhaps,' he said, 'you could start from the beginning. How did you first meet Olivier? Was it here?'

'Yes. He came one night with some of his colleagues. We danced together, but only for half an hour or so. Then he came back the following night, and we danced again. Before long, he was coming all the time, every other night, just to see me. He would give the *taipan* a thousand piastres, and we would dance together until two in the morning . . . '

Weiling's voice trailed off into silence, and after a while it became clear that she had finished speaking.

'When did Olivier first come here?' Guéry asked.

'Some time early last year, I suppose it was.'

'And when did you begin to see him elsewhere too, away from the Palais?'

'Around June or July.'

'Then one day, without warning, he just disappeared?'

'That's right. I assumed that he had gone back to France or that he had simply grown tired of me.'

'This would have been in February, I imagine.'

Weiling thought for a moment, looking over his shoulder as she did so. 'Yes,' she said finally. 'Some time in late January or early February.'

'That makes sense. Olivier was killed on the eleventh of February. At least that was when they discovered his body. He may have died several days earlier.' Guéry paused briefly as they passed another couple on the dance floor. 'And you didn't try to find out where he had gone, or why?'

She smiled. 'That's not how things are done around here, Monsieur. I did go to his apartment after a week or so, to see if he was there, but it was empty. They were redecorating.'

Guéry was beginning to regret the fact that the band was playing 'Les Feuilles Mortes.' It was altogether too appropriate, what with the dead leaves and the cold wind and everything.

'Did Olivier ever talk to you about the kind of work he was doing at Perec Frères?' he asked.

'No. I knew that it had something to do with importing agricultural machinery, but that was all.'

'So I don't suppose you ever met a colleague of his by the name of Fourier . . . '

'Not that I can remember. After the first night, Olivier mostly came here alone.'

'I see. And when you went out together, just the two of you, where would you go?'

'Depending on the time, we might go to a restaurant or a bar—or sometimes to another nightclub. He liked the Paradis and the Tour d'Ivoire. On the weekend, during the day, he would take me to the Sporting Club or to one of the cafés by the river.'

'Did you ever go to the Grand Monde together?'

'No.' She smiled again. 'That wasn't really Olivier's kind of place.'

'I was told by Monsieur Reyes that he had taken to gambling there.'

Weiling looked surprised. 'He must have been mistaken,' she said. 'Olivier hated gambling. I remember him telling me once that it was a waste of money and that only stupid people gambled.'

'Really? But Reyes was quite definite about it when I spoke to him a few days ago. He said that Olivier had been seen gambling at a number of different casinos. And he suggested that he may have been in debt too—that he may have borrowed money from someone to cover his losses.'

'I'm afraid that's simply untrue, Monsieur. For as long as I knew Olivier, he never once gambled. He would always avoid the roulette tables wherever we were. He didn't even like watching other people gamble. He said it was like watching someone burn money.'

Guéry considered this as they carried on dancing. The line about burning money certainly sounded like the kind of thing that Olivier would say. In fact, he had probably said it to Guéry himself more than once. But if Weiling was right, and Olivier hadn't been gambling in any of the casinos, then Reyes must have been lying to him, and it was difficult to understand why he would have done so. Why slander the dead in this way? What possible motivation could he have had for lying, when it would have been so much easier simply to say nothing? Guéry had only been making general enquiries, after all, nothing too specific, nothing too threatening or accusatory. So why go to the trouble of providing him with a false lead—if, indeed, that was what Reyes had done?

After one last chorus, the band finally came to the end of 'Les Feuilles Mortes' and began to play something with a faster tempo. It was another song that Guéry vaguely remembered from several years before—from the summer of 1949, to be precise—and it carried with it some rather unpleasant memories. Listening to it now, he was reminded of the time he had lost two thousand francs in one evening and been obliged to walk all the way from Cannes to Antibes (a distance of roughly eleven kilometres) because he had somehow managed to forget the name of his hotel and would have been unable to pay the bill anyway, even if he had found the place, due to the unfortunate peripeties he had suffered at the baccarat table. (In case you're wondering, the band had been playing this particular song as he left the casino, and the damn thing had stayed in his head all night long—taunting him with its moronic gaiety.)

Guéry looked at Weiling as they circled the dance floor together. She was precisely the kind of woman one would expect to encounter under such circumstances: coiffured hair, languid eyes, vertiginous curves, etc., etc. It was as if she had emerged, fully formed, from the pages of a novel like *Tu Parles d'une Ingénue*. And this contributed to the sense of unreality that Guéry had been feeling ever since he arrived in Saigon—a sense of artifice and insubstantiality, as if everyone he had encountered thus far were simply playing a part in a larger narrative whose overall shape he could never quite discern. The real difficulty, of course, lay in determining exactly which role each of the characters was playing. Had Weiling been assigned the role of the *femme fatale* or the loyal, grieving lover? Was Reyes a genuinely concerned colleague or something more sinister? And what about Arnaud and Cabral and Bergerac, and even the mysterious Monsieur Fourier—which roles were they supposed to be playing?

'I went to the coroner's office a couple of days ago,' Guéry said eventually, 'and the man I spoke to there told me something rather strange.'

Weiling waited.

'He told me that they had found traces of opiates in Olivier's blood. Quite a lot apparently . . . Did you ever see him using narcotics? Did he ever take you to a *fumerie*?'

'No,' she said, shaking her head slowly. 'In fact, he didn't really approve of that kind of thing either.'

'Are you sure?'

'Quite sure, Monsieur. I'm afraid I simply don't recognize the man you're describing. As far as I know, Olivier never gambled and he never used drugs. I'm sorry, but that's just the way he was, at least when he and I were together.'

'Yes,' Guéry said, 'I remember him the same way. Of course, it's always possible that Reyes lied, but then how does one account for the presence of opiates in his blood? According to the pathologist, there was no doubt about the identity of the body—or the drug use.'

Weiling said nothing.

'Do you think Olivier might have been leading some kind of double life?'

She smiled. 'Don't we all lead double lives, Monsieur, in one way or another?'

Guéry had a feeling that he had heard this before. And then he remembered: it was something the pathologist, Cabral, had said to him—and this repetition, this echo, only added to his sense of unreality. These characters were now quoting each other, it seemed, as if they were all trying to persuade him of the same thing, as if they were all conspiring to perpetrate the same elaborate fraud.

Nevertheless, he persisted: 'Did Olivier undergo any kind of change before he disappeared, before he was killed?'

She frowned slightly. 'I don't understand.'

'Did his personality change in any way? Did he start behaving strangely or doing things that were out of character?'

'No, not that I could tell. But as I say, Monsieur, I never did get to know your brother very well.'

Guéry nodded. 'Nor did I,' he said. 'We were two very different people. Wholly incompatible. Or so I always believed.'

Over her shoulder, Guéry could see that the place was becoming more crowded. The tables beyond the balustrade were all occupied, and there were several people standing at the bar waiting to be served. Many of the hostesses had been 'hired' and were now plying their trade on the dance floor.

'Is there anything else you could tell me that might help in some way?' Guéry asked.

There was a pause. Then she said, 'No. I'm sorry. Nothing comes to mind.'

'And do you have any idea at all why Olivier might have been murdered?'

'If I did, Monsieur, I would tell you. Please believe me. But like you, I find it quite mystifying. Your brother was an ordinary man, no different from anyone else here.' She tilted her head in the general direction of the surrounding tables. 'I can think of no reason why anybody would want to kill him. As I say, he was . . . '

All of a sudden he felt her body become tense.

'What is it?' he asked.

She was staring at something over his shoulder. He turned but could see nothing out of the ordinary: just tables full of people doing what they usually do in such places.

He turned back again. 'Is there something the matter?'

'No, Monsieur. But please, I think you should leave. I've told you everything I know about your brother. And now it's time for you to go.'

She detached herself and turned away.

'Mademoiselle,' he said, touching her gently on the shoulder. 'Please tell me what's wrong.'

She paused. 'Monsieur Guéry, you need to leave. For your own safety, and for mine too. And please take my advice: forget about your brother, forget about his murder, go home to Antibes. This place is far too dangerous for a man like you.'

Guéry, it seemed, had been assigned his own role in the narrative.

'I'm sorry,' she said, giving him no chance to reply, 'but our dance is over. Good evening, Monsieur.'

Then she turned and walked away without a backward glance.

* * *

I suppose it was typical of Guéry that he didn't immediately recognize the danger he was facing. Anyone else would have seen the fear in Weiling's eyes and very quickly understood the gravity of the situation. But not our old friend Jean-Luc Guéry. Perhaps it had something to do with the sense of 'unreality' he claimed to be feeling at the time or his tendency to see things from a purely literary perspective. Whatever the case, when he left the Palais that evening he certainly wasn't as careful as he should have been. He hailed a taxi and told the driver to take him to the Majestic, but then halfway along boulevard Galliéni, rather unwisely, he decided to get out and walk the rest of the way back to his hotel. ('I just needed to clear my head,' he would later tell me. 'It had been a long day.') This was obviously a mistake, the kind of thing that only an amateur like Guéry would have done, and it very nearly cost him his life.

In those days, there wasn't much in the way of foot traffic on boulevard Galliéni, so it didn't take Guéry long to notice the three men who were following him at a distance of about fifty metres. They were walking in complete silence and maintaining a steady pace, as if they had something important to do.

At first, he thought nothing of it, but when he paused to light a cigarette, he could see out of the corner of his eye that they had also stopped walking. Although one of the men was kneeling down to tie his shoelace, it was obvious that they had only come to a halt because Guéry had done so.

He began moving again, and the men did too. After a couple of minutes, he crossed the road to see if they would do the same thing. They did. And when he crossed over once more, just to be sure, they immediately followed him back to the other side.

It was at this point, Guéry later told me, that he finally became scared. His heart began palpitating in a rather alarming way, and he suddenly remembered all the times he had been told that Saigon was a dangerous place and that if he wasn't careful he would end up in the Arroyo Chinois like his brother. Up until now, despite these warnings, his investigation had been conducted in a fairly detached and abstract manner. He never did get to see his brother's body, with its macerated skin, opaque eyes, and suppurating bullet holes. When he talked to Arnaud, the investigating officer, or Cabral, the pathologist, it was as if he were discussing the plot of a classic Série Noire. And when he spoke to the dance hostess at the Palais de Jade, this Weiling, it was as if he had actually *entered* one (what with all the languid eyes and vertiginous curves). So yes, it must have come as quite a shock for him to find himself suddenly walking along a deserted street at eleven in the evening, with three strangers—three very *real* strangers—following close behind.

In those days, as I say, the northern end of boulevard Galliéni was not particularly lively, but as he walked, Guéry could see the lights of place Eugène Cuniac not too far ahead. And he knew that if he reached this square he would be safe. There were people there, and most probably policemen to be found in the railway station or at the entrance to the

CFI building. He quickened his pace. If he turned his head to one side and lowered it slightly, he could see the dark outlines of his three pursuers, and it was clear that they were also walking more quickly. In fact, every time he glanced over his shoulder, they seemed a good deal closer than they had been before. He considered breaking into a run, but the square was still three or four hundred metres away, and he knew that they would be able to catch him long before he made it to safety. He thought about hailing another taxi too, but the road was deserted.

According to the report I have before me, Guéry was only a hundred metres or so from the intersection when it happened. He suddenly felt a hand on his shoulder, and he was pushed roughly from behind into one of the alleyways that lead from boulevard Galliéni down to the Arroyo Chinois.

At this precise moment in time, Guéry later said, he was convinced that he was about to be killed, and he felt an almost overwhelming urge to cry. There was so much that he hadn't done. He had wasted his life on fripperies and minor indulgences. He had filled his days with Pernod and cognac and foul-tasting cigarettes and ridiculous games of chance. He had let himself go at such a young age too, so that looking in the mirror every day was like surveying the site of some natural disaster. He had achieved nothing in his thirty-eight years of life. His destiny was still unfulfilled. He would leave nothing behind, at least nothing of any permanence or durability. No children, no grieving wife, no eternal masterpiece—not even a second-rate work of genre fiction that might one day be discovered in a bookstall and taken home and read, thus guaranteeing its poor dead author a degree of immortality. No, he had done nothing with his life, and he would now die as he had lived, in a state of shame and disgrace and abject failure. On his knees in an alleyway, crying like a baby. He wouldn't even merit a proper obituary in *Le Journal d'Antibes*—

just a few lines if he was lucky, lines that only the elderly or the unemployed would bother to read. The local police would be obliged to investigate his murder, of course, but their investigation would only last a day or two. Arnaud would very quickly decide that the case was unsolvable and move on to something else, something of greater significance. And that's where it would end, that's what he would become—an abandoned case, a forgotten file, a vague recollection in the head of a man he scarcely knew. A man with grey hair and tired, ironic eyes.

You can see, I hope, why Guéry felt like crying. I imagine that I would too under similar circumstances.

I would later ask Guéry to describe the three men who had assaulted him, but he was unable to do so. It was dark in the alleyway, and as we know, he was also rather shortsighted. All he could tell me was that they were European, that they were in their mid-thirties, and that they looked like Henri Deglane, a professional wrestler from Limoges who was famous for his Olympian physique.

Once his eyes had adjusted to the darkness, Guéry gave his assailants an ingratiating smile and said, 'Messieurs, I'm afraid there must have been some kind of mistake.'

He was about to say something else too, something equally placatory, when the taller of the three men stepped forward and punched him hard in the face.

Guéry hadn't been hit like this in a long time, not since he was a schoolboy, and it took him completely by surprise.

'Please, Monsieur . . . '

Before he could finish his sentence, however, the same man punched him a second time on the bridge of his nose, and he felt something—either cartilage or bone—immediately give way.

'My nose,' he said rather unnecessarily. 'You've broken my nose.'

There was no reply.

Guéry swallowed a mouthful of his own blood and touched his nose gingerly.

Then, without warning, one of the other men hit him in the same place. The pain was intense, like nothing he had experienced before, and he felt a sudden surge of anger.

'Leave me alone!' he shouted. 'I've done nothing to you!'

In the silence that followed this outburst, Guéry's rage quickly dissipated, and he decided to approach the matter from a different angle.

'Listen,' he said in a more reasonable tone of voice. 'This must surely be a case of mistaken identity, so if you'll just let me go, we can forget all about it.'

He then delivered what he considered to be his most agreeable smile (actually a queasy, blood-filled grimace), but again there was no response—or at least no articulate response. The last of the three men simply lunged forward and struck him with immense force on the left-hand side of his face. A bright light immediately filled the alleyway. It was like some kind of religious experience. At first, he was blinded by this sudden luminescence, then he heard the sound of singing from above, then he felt a strange floating sensation, as if he had risen two or three centimetres into the air, then his knees gave way and he collapsed.

Once he was lying on the ground, the men formed a semicircle and began kicking him viciously in any unprotected place they could find. They seemed to favour the ribcage and the kidneys, although from time to time one of their shoes would graze his face or some other, more tender part of his anatomy. He defended himself as well as he could, but after a while he became resigned to the inevitability of the beating and to his complete helplessness in the face of such violence.

When it was finally over, he was left lying there on the ground, clutching his torso and groaning.

'Consider this a friendly warning,' one of the men said. 'You need to leave Saigon immediately. If you're not on the first plane out of here tomorrow morning, you're going to die like your brother.'

'That's right,' another voice added. 'Go home and mind your own business. This is no place for someone like you . . . Do you understand?'

Guéry nodded his head as vigorously as possible. 'Yes,' he said. 'Tomorrow morning, the first plane. I've got it.'

'Good.'

Guéry closed his eyes, and when he opened them again, the men were gone.

He was alone in the alleyway.

He turned onto his back and looked up at the night sky. It gave him a strange feeling of peace to do so, and for a moment he thought he was lying in a tidal pool near the Plage des Ondes. It was nice and warm there, and he could hear the sound of children playing by the water's edge. They were laughing and shouting and splashing each other, just as he and Olivier had done many years before.

Guéry closed his eyes again, and he must have fallen asleep or lost consciousness, because this time when he opened them it was morning, and the sky was a vivid blue and his nose was throbbing and felt twice as large as it usually did, which was fairly large after all, and there was a mangy-looking dog with one ear licking the dried blood off his face.

Chapter 7

The Cervical Collar

As I said at the very beginning, I would never have met Jean-Luc Guéry if Arnaud hadn't been obliged to take leave, for personal reasons, some time in early April. While he was gone, I was given the responsibility of handling his cases, and that meant that when Guéry turned up at the Sûreté headquarters on the morning after his beating, he was shown directly into my office.

It was clear that he had seen better days. He had a black eye, a blood-engorged wound on his left temple, and a large white plaster spanning the bridge of his nose. As mentioned earlier, he was also wearing one of those ridiculous cervical collars that prevent you from turning your head without also turning the entire upper half of your body. That morning, moreover, his eyes were particularly red and inflamed, his hair particularly undisciplined and greasy, and his nose particularly Gallic.

He settled painfully into a chair, lit a demoralized cigarette, and told me everything that had happened the night before.

When I asked him what he was doing in Saigon in the first place, he said, 'I'm here because of my brother. I'm here to find out who murdered Olivier Guéry.'

And he then proceeded to tell me everything else that had happened to him over the last couple of days.

'As soon as I got here,' he said, 'I went to see your colleague, Inspector Arnaud, and he described the case to me in some detail.'

I nodded.

'He told me that Olivier's body was discovered one morning floating in the Arroyo Chinois. It was found by a teller from the Banque de l'Indochine. Olivier had been shot twice in the head. Once here.' He indicated a spot just above his left eye. 'And once here.' He pointed to the raised ridge of purple skin on his left temple. 'When they pulled the body from the water, they found that it was carrying an identity card issued in Nice. And within a few days, the authorities in Nice were able to confirm that the card was genuine—it belonged to my brother.'

'Did they discover anything else of interest on the body?'

At this point, Guéry produced what looked to be a hotel tariff card and, turning it over, read out the following inventory. 'They found,' he said, 'a cigarette lighter, some keys, a lottery ticket, a pair of sunglasses, and a bottle of vitamin capsules.'

'So nothing of any significance.'

He gave me a rather enigmatic smile. 'They also found a page torn from a book called *Tu Parles d'une Ingénue*, written by Jean Bruce. It was the title page of the 1949 edition, and apparently the book had been borrowed from a library in Rome, the Centre Saint-Lazare.'

'I'm afraid I've never read it.'

'I've only just started it myself,' he said. 'It's set in Paris in 1948. The hero, an agent of the OSS, is trying to recover a stolen file that relates in some way to international arms trafficking.'

'And why do you think this novel might be important?'

'Well, for one thing, the narrative itself may tell us something about my brother's murder.'

This time it was my turn to smile. 'I don't imagine that's very likely, Monsieur. In my experience, murder cases are usually far more prosaic. We don't tend to find clues of this kind on dead bodies . . . It was probably just a book that your brother was reading, and he accidentally tore out the title page. If I were you, I wouldn't waste too much time scrutinizing it for clues. I would be very surprised if it turned out to carry any deeper significance.'

Guéry seemed a little disappointed by this response. 'That may be so,' he said, 'but I did discover something else about the novel, something very interesting indeed . . . '

'Yes?'

'The title page that my brother was carrying at the time of his murder came from a book I later found in the apartment of a man named Jacques Fourier, who was one of his colleagues at Perec Frères.'

'Perec Frères?'

'The company Olivier used to manage. They import and sell agricultural machinery. I was particularly interested in talking to Fourier as he was the one who had identified Olivier's body. But when I went to Perec Frères a couple of days ago, I was told that he hadn't been seen since February, having disappeared around the time of my brother's murder.'

'Was Inspector Arnaud aware of this?'

'I don't think so.'

'And you say that the page in question came from Fourier's copy of the novel.'

'That's right.'

'May I ask, Monsieur, how you gained entry to his apartment?'

'The concierge was very obliging.'

'He let a complete stranger into an apartment belonging to someone else?'

Guéry trained his eyes on an electric fan that was swivelling to and fro in the corner. The fan typically makes a loud whirring sound as it moves, and visitors to my office can sometimes find this distracting.

After observing two full cycles in silence, Guéry said, 'To be honest, Inspector, I may have allowed the concierge to believe that I was in some way related to Monsieur Fourier.'

'You *allowed* him to believe this.'

'Yes.'

There was a pause.

'Very well,' I said after another two cycles had elapsed. 'Please continue.'

'So while I was there, I discovered the very same copy of *Tu Parles d'une Ingénue* in Fourier's bookcase.'

'And what do you think the significance of this might be?'

'It proves that Fourier was somehow involved in my brother's murder.'

'Does it, though, Monsieur Guéry? Or does it simply mean that your brother borrowed this particular copy of the novel from his colleague, read it, and then returned it without the title page—having accidently torn it out and forgotten to replace it?'

Guéry was forced to concede that such a contingency was not impossibly remote.

'I'm sorry to say this, Monsieur, but life very rarely resembles the plot of a detective novel or a thriller. As in science, the least complicated theory is usually the right one. *Pluralitas non est ponenda sine necessitate* . . . Plurality should not be posited without necessity.'

'Again that may be so, Inspector, but you must admit that Fourier's sudden disappearance around the time of the murder is suspicious.'

'Or perhaps it's simply a coincidence. He may have had some other reason for leaving, one that had nothing to do with your brother's murder.'

'Such as?'

I laughed. 'I don't know, Monsieur. Perhaps he was suffering from a crisis of some kind, like Gauguin, and wanted to start over again in the Marquesas. Perhaps he was tired of selling agricultural machinery and wanted to dedicate his life to painting instead.'

'And you really think he would have done so without informing his employers?'

'It's always possible.'

'Perhaps. But the concierge also told me something else while I was there. He said that Fourier's apartment had been searched by two men from the SDECE.'

This, admittedly, I did find interesting. 'He told you that?'

'Yes. Apparently, they searched the place in February—a week or so after Fourier's disappearance.'

'Did they say what they were looking for?'

'No, they didn't tell him anything.'

'That's a pity.'

There was a brief silence, then Guéry said, 'What is the SDECE anyway? What do they do?'

'They're an intelligence agency like any other, I suppose. And of course they're particularly active these days. In addition to providing all the usual services, they also have a military base at Cap Saint-Jacques, where they train our supplementary forces.'

'Supplementary forces?'

'That's right. Over the last year or so, the SDECE has been recruiting volunteers from the hill tribes to safeguard certain territories. Mostly T'ai and Meo, I believe.'

'And they're trained at Cap Saint-Jacques?'

'Yes. They're trained, given supplies, and then sent back out there to fight for us.'

'I imagine they're paid to do so,' Guéry said.

'Of course.' I smiled. 'Such loyalty always comes at a price.'

'So why do you think the SDECE might have been interested in Fourier?'

'I've got no idea, Monsieur Guéry. They could have searched his apartment for any number of reasons, and once again it may have had nothing to do with your brother's murder.'

Guéry regarded me sceptically. 'Forgive me, Inspector Leclerc, but I find it hard to believe that these are all simply coincidences. Particularly given some of the other strange things I've heard over the last couple of days.'

'About your brother?'

He nodded.

'And what is it exactly that you've heard?'

'When I went to see Monsieur Reyes, the managing director of Perec Frères, he told me that Olivier had taken to gambling at some of the local casinos. And he also suggested that he may have borrowed money to cover his losses.'

'I'm afraid this is not so unusual, Monsieur Guéry.'

'Perhaps not. But it is unusual for Olivier. He despised gambling.'

'People change, Monsieur. Particularly out here in the colonies. I believe it has something to do with the tropical climate; it can be very debilitating.'

Guéry chose to ignore this. 'The pathologist also told me that traces of opiates had been found in my brother's blood. And yet Olivier would never have used narcotics. He didn't even care for alcohol.'

'Again, Monsieur, people change.'

'But he *didn't* change, that's precisely the point I'm trying to make. Before he died, Olivier was seeing one of the hostesses at the Palais de Jade, and when I spoke to her last night, she said the same thing. She said that Olivier had no interest whatsoever in gambling or drugs—or any other vices for that matter.'

'Then how do you explain the presence of opiates in his blood?'

'I don't know,' Guéry said, putting his cigarette out in the ashtray. 'That's a mystery. But as far as the gambling is concerned, it's quite obvious that Reyes lied to me.'

'Reyes, the managing director of Perec Frères . . . '

'Yes. My brother's successor.'

'Have you any idea why he might have done so?' I asked.

'I'm not sure. Perhaps he knew more than he was letting on. Perhaps he had something to do with Olivier's murder and was trying to protect himself by providing me with a false lead.'

'But he also gave you Fourier's address, I presume.'

'He did.'

'And if I understand you correctly, you believe that Fourier was somehow involved too, which would make them accomplices.'

Guéry said nothing.

'I think you'll agree, Monsieur, that this is all rather confusing. Everything you've told me so far involves a great deal of conjecture. We have a few coincidences and some circumstantial evidence, but nothing more. Are there any certainties at all here? Have you discovered anything that could be regarded as incontrovertible?'

Guéry lit another cigarette and considered this question for some time before replying. 'I know that Reyes lied,' he said eventually. 'I know that whoever arranged for me to be assaulted last night also killed my brother. And I know that there's something very peculiar going on at Perec Frères these days.'

'Really? And what might that be?'

'First of all, when I was talking to Reyes in his office, I noticed a calendar hanging on the wall. It was a commercial calendar advertising Vendeuvre agricultural machinery, and I could see that it was almost two years old. For some reason, it had been hanging there, unused, since 1949 . . . '

'Go on, Monsieur.'

'And then a few days later, I paid a visit to their warehouse on the quai de Belgique. I was shown around by a man named Monsieur Chiang, who was very hospitable. But at one point he was called away to answer the phone, leaving me by myself in the warehouse. While I was waiting, I happened to notice that one of the wooden crates was much lighter than it looked, so I decided to open a couple to see what was inside. Just out of curiosity, you understand.'

I sighed audibly. 'And what did you find inside these crates, Monsieur Guéry?'

'Nothing.'

'Nothing at all?'

'That's right. They were empty.' He leaned forward rather painfully, it seemed, and lifted his damaged eyes to mine. 'So tell me, Inspector, what kind of managing director doesn't use a calendar for two years? And what kind of company takes the trouble to maintain a warehouse full of empty crates?'

Suddenly, a lot of what he had been saying thus far made perfect sense.

'If the company's warehouse is empty, Monsieur, then I imagine they're most probably involved in the illegal piastre trade. And that would also explain why the managing director lied to you.'

Guéry looked confused. 'I'm sorry,' he said, 'but I'm not entirely sure what this trade involves.'

'It's all quite simple, really. In 1945, acting on the advice of the Banque de l'Indochine, the government decided to set the official rate of exchange for the piastre in France at seventeen francs, which was twice its actual value at the time. So piastres worth eight and a half francs in Saigon could be exchanged for seventeen francs in Paris.'

'And this is still the case today?'

'Indeed. The real value of the piastre has depreciated several times since then, but the franc has remained fairly stable, making the trade even more profitable these days.'

'But why would the government have done this in the first place?' Guéry asked. 'Why create this artificial rate of exchange?'

'To encourage people to settle here,' I said, 'to do business here, and to fight here. In short, Monsieur, to make the colony more profitable for all concerned.'

'So the soldiers are also allowed to remit their salaries at this inflated rate of exchange?'

'A percentage of their salaries, yes.'

'And how is this trade regulated? It must be controlled in some way.'

'In theory, the remittances are controlled by the Banque de l'Indochine. One must apply at the foreign exchange office on rue Guynemer for permission to remit piastres to France, and have a good reason for doing so. But in practice, of course, it's very difficult to assess the validity of such requests, and the system itself is not without its loopholes.'

'How so?'

'There are many ways to arrange for the remittance of piastres, Monsieur Guéry. You can pay someone else to do it on your behalf, someone who has the right to apply for a transfer. You can bribe one of the officials at the exchange office. Or you can import useless or obsolete merchandise from

France—paying for it all with BIC piastres. This last practice is particularly common. In one case, for example, a Paris publishing house created a subsidiary in Saigon, to whom it sold all of its remaindered titles. Once the books arrived here, they were immediately pulped, but the publisher was able to double its money by exchanging the piastres it had received in "payment" at the official rate of exchange in Paris.'

'I see.'

'And in some cases, of course, the companies don't even bother importing anything. The bills of lading they present at the exchange office are completely false. They're importing nothing but thin air, and making a fortune in the process.'

'Hence the empty crates in the Perec Frères warehouse.'

'Yes, hence the empty crates.'

Guéry frowned slightly and ran a hand through his greasy hair. 'But Perec Frères was first established in 1923,' he said, 'and they're a very reputable company.'

'Perhaps they were, Monsieur—originally. Bogus companies are usually created in order to remit piastres; but sometimes you'll find companies that were once perfectly legitimate also being used for this purpose. In the case of Perec Frères, someone probably realized that remitting piastres was far more profitable than actually importing agricultural machinery.'

After thinking for a moment, Guéry said, 'Is it possible that the company may have been taken over forcibly and obliged to participate in the piastre trade?'

'Possible,' I replied, 'but unlikely.'

He persisted. 'So it's also possible that Olivier may have been killed by someone who wanted to appropriate the company and use it to remit piastres instead?'

'Perhaps. But your brother was only killed in February, Monsieur, and didn't you say that the calendar on the wall was two years old?'

Guéry nodded unhappily.

'In any case, I think it's far more likely that he was complicit in the trafficking—and then had some kind of falling out with one of his colleagues or with his employers, whoever they were.'

'So it's really just a question of finding out whose money was being used to run Perec Frères; and once we've done that, we should know the identity of Olivier's killers.'

He said this as if it were the simplest thing in the world, and for a moment I envied him his innocence.

'Not necessarily, Monsieur.'

'But you do think this is the most likely scenario.'

'I suppose so,' I conceded reluctantly, 'if what you say is true and your brother had no other vices. But unfortunately that doesn't get us very far.'

'Why not?'

'I'm afraid almost everyone in Saigon is involved in the piastre trade, so you're going to have a hard time finding out precisely who your brother's employers were.'

'Almost everyone, you say?'

'That's right. The emperor and his associates, the Banque de l'Indochine itself, various syndicates and companies—anyone with a bit of money, really. Even the local representatives of certain political parties in France.'

'Is that so?'

I nodded. 'A couple of years ago, the RPF sent a former inspector of finances out here to arrange for the remittance of piastres to Paris. I'm told their profit was somewhere in the region of seventeen million francs, and that it helped to finance their election campaign in 1948.'

Guéry raised his eyebrows.

'But what they're doing at Perec Frères is of a different nature altogether,' I went on, 'so in this particular case, you're probably looking for someone less . . . official. Someone who doesn't have the authority or the influence to do it any other way.'

'And who might that be?' Guéry asked.

'Again, Monsieur, I'm afraid there are numerous possibilities. Your brother may have been working for the Binh Xuyen, or for a Chinese or Macanese syndicate. He may even have been collaborating with the Viet Minh, who are also said to be dealing in piastres these days.'

'What about this Monsieur Vitelli, the proprietor of the Continental? I was talking to someone just recently who suggested that he might be involved too.'

I smiled. 'Monsieur Vitelli is involved in a lot of things.'

'Including the piastre trade?'

'I can't really comment on that directly . . . but I wouldn't contradict you either.'

'I see.' He meditated for a moment or two. 'So where does that leave us, then?'

'Basically, Monsieur, we can assume that your brother was probably involved in the piastre trade; and we can assume that this involvement probably led, in some way, to his demise.'

'But we still don't know who killed him or why they did so.'

'Indeed. He could have been killed by almost anyone, and for almost any reason. This is Saigon, remember. Nothing is ever simple here.'

Poor old Guéry seemed rather dispirited by this observation. He lit another cigarette and lapsed into silence. Looking at him sitting there in his heavy flannel suit, with his black eye and broken nose, I suddenly felt a strong surge of pity for the man. He was so obviously ill-equipped to be investigating a murder case; and yet there he was, doing it all the same, risking his life in order to bring his brother's killer to justice. If it hadn't been so foolhardy and naive, it might have been admirable—even heroic.

'Monsieur Guéry,' I said finally, 'may I offer you a piece of advice?'

'Let me guess,' he replied. 'You're going to advise me to forget about my brother's murder. You're going to tell me that Saigon is a dangerous city and certainly no place for someone like me. You're going to tell me that I should go home to Antibes and leave the investigation to the police.'

I admitted that this was more or less precisely what I had been going to say.

'In that case, Inspector, let me save you the trouble. Almost everyone I've met in Saigon has advised me to go home, even the men who did this.' He lifted a hand to his face. 'But I'm not going to leave. Not yet anyway. I need to see this through to the end.'

'I admire your determination, Monsieur Guéry, but the assault you suffered last night makes it perfectly clear that your life is in danger, and if you stay in Saigon much longer you'll . . . '

'End up in the Arroyo Chinois like my brother?'

'Yes. Quite.'

Guéry brushed some stray dog hair off his trousers. 'That may be so,' he said solemnly, 'but I'm not leaving until I've done everything I can to find the man who killed Olivier.'

I almost smiled because it sounded so much like something a character from a Série Noire might say. But I could see that he was being quite sincere, so I simply inclined my head in a gesture of resignation.

'Very well,' I replied. 'But please allow me to give you one more piece of advice before you go. This is a city of subterfuge and lies, Monsieur Guéry, and if you are to survive, you need to understand that no one can be trusted. Not even those who claim to be on your side.'

In retrospect, I have to say that this was actually rather sound advice, and Guéry would have done well to heed it.

But of course it was not in his nature to do so. In addition
to being a neurotic, an alcoholic, a gambler, a hypochondriac,
a failed writer, and a general reprobate with melancholic
tendencies, he was also incredibly obstinate and had a strong
aversion to what most people would call 'common sense.' If
he had listened to my advice that day, a great deal of trouble
might have been avoided. But on the other hand, if he had
done as I suggested, the case would most probably never have
been solved. So, on reflection, I suppose there is something to
be said after all for obstinacy and stupidity and the ill-informed
meddling of dilettantes.

As soon as he left my office, I immediately arranged for
Guéry to be placed under surveillance. Although I didn't
really think his investigation would lead anywhere, I did feel
an obligation to try to protect him from his enemies (whoever
they may have been). So I made sure that at least one of my
officers would be observing him at all times, and much of what
follows is based directly on their reports. To be honest, these
daily summaries can be a little disturbing in places:

> At 10.23 in the morning, the subject entered the
> Capriccio, where he consumed three Armagnacs in quick
> succession before continuing on his way . . . The subject
> arrived at the Cloche d'Or around 9.40 and spent the rest
> of the evening at the roulette tables, where he appeared
> to sustain considerable losses . . . After emerging from
> his hotel room at 11.36 the following morning, the
> subject proceeded directly to the Pharmacie Centrale,
> where he purchased twenty aspirin capsules, a bottle of
> quinine bisulphate, and an unidentified eau de cologne
> . . . Etc., etc.

But it is precisely this voyeuristic quality that makes the reports so informative, allowing us to trace the unfolding investigation in some detail. I only regret the fact that when Guéry finally did need our assistance, we were unable to provide any. At the very moment when he was facing the greatest danger to his life, with a nine-millimetre Luger jammed into his ribcage, my men could do absolutely nothing about it—having been left stranded, like amateurs themselves, on the quai Le Myre de Villers.

As it turned out, of course, Guéry acquitted himself rather well; but who would have been able to predict such a thing?

When he left my office that day, with his ridiculous cervical collar pressing against the underside of his unshaven jaw, and his black eye and his broken nose and his nicotine-stained fingers and everything else I've described above, I really did fear for his life.

He looked tired, confused, and ill at ease, like a man who hadn't seen the Côte d'Azur in a very long time.

Chapter 8

Solvitur Ambulando

The following morning, after a coffee at the Continental, Guéry returned to the Information Service on rue Lagrandière to collect his *carte de presse*. He had been told that it would be ready within three or four days, and he was eager to be accredited as soon as possible.

Once again, he was obliged to wait for around twenty minutes or so before being shown in to see Monsieur Auteuil, the junior officer who had assisted him the last time he was there.

Auteuil was a young man with perfectly symmetrical features and an air of supreme confidence. When Guéry entered his office, he was reading an illustrated magazine of some kind and smoking a cigarette.

'Yes?' he said, looking up from the magazine. 'How can I help you?'

'My name is Jean-Luc Guéry. I came here several days ago to apply for a *carte de presse*, and I was hoping to collect it today.'

'I see.' He studied Guéry's battered face for a moment in silence, then gestured toward an empty chair. 'And what's the name of your newspaper, Monsieur?'

'*Le Journal d'Antibes.*'

'That's right,' he said. 'I remember you now, Monsieur Guéry. *Le Journal d'Antibes.*' He said this slowly, as if he were savouring the punchline to a joke. 'Yes, I remember you very well indeed.'

'So . . . my card. Is it ready yet?'

'Just one moment, please.'

Auteuil turned in his chair and opened the middle drawer of a filing cabinet that was standing against the wall to his left.

'Guéry, Guéry, Guéry . . . '

After locating the relevant file and glancing at the first page, he turned around to face his visitor once more.

'I'm afraid, Monsieur, that your accreditation has not yet been authorized.'

'But you told me that it would be ready within three or four days.'

Auteuil shrugged his shoulders. 'That's usually the case. But sometimes it takes a little longer . . . Why don't you come back again in another couple of days? We should have heard something by then—either way.'

'Either way?'

'Yes. By then we'll know if your application has been accepted or rejected.'

'And on what basis might it be rejected?'

Auteuil gave him a rather patronizing smile. 'Please don't worry, Monsieur. I'm sure your newspaper . . . what was it called again?'

'*Le Journal d'Antibes.*'

'Yes, quite. I'm sure it's perfectly reputable. But of course these things need to be investigated thoroughly before accreditation can be granted.'

'So it may take another couple of days?'

'No more than two or three, I assure you.'

Guéry thanked him and stood up to leave.

'By the way, Monsieur Guéry, did you manage to get out to Cap Saint-Jacques?'

The details of their earlier encounter were obviously coming back to him now.

'No, I'm afraid I haven't had the time. I'm not really here to go sightseeing.'

'That's unfortunate,' Auteuil said. 'It's a wonderful place. Only a couple of hours by car, or you can take the ferry if you prefer. I believe the first one leaves around nine-thirty every morning.'

Guéry nodded obligingly.

'The swimming is very good out there, you know, and the cool sea breezes are a welcome relief after Saigon. You'll think you're back in Antibes. If I were you, I would go for the weekend. Leave first thing Saturday morning and come back in the afternoon on Sunday. But if you're travelling by car, you should allow plenty of time for the return journey. One can't be too careful these days.'

Guéry could see that he wasn't being taken seriously. 'Thank you for your advice,' he said. 'I'll be sure to make my way there as soon as possible.'

'Not at all, Monsieur,' Auteuil replied, smiling once more. 'Enjoy yourself, and I'll see you again in due course.'

According to the officer who was following him at the time, Guéry walked around the city for several hours after leaving the Information Service. He didn't seem to have a specific destination in mind. One assumes that he was thinking—considering everything he had learned thus far and trying to decide how best to proceed with his enquiries. Some time later, Guéry told me that everyone should have a motto, and that he had taken his from Diogenes: *Solvitur ambulando*. It is solved by walking. So I imagine that was what he was doing on the morning in question—trying to work through the complexities of the case in his head while walking aimlessly around the city. First, he strolled up and down boulevard Charner several times. Then he walked along the quay to the Messageries Maritimes building at the entrance to the Arroyo Chinois. He sat there for some time, I believe, smoking cigarettes and watching the traffic on the river. Then he made his way to Les Halles Centrales, the large covered market on place Eugène Cuniac, where one can buy all manner of strange Asiatic commodities. But Guéry, of course, had no interest in such things. He simply walked in one end of the building and out the other, as if the place were nothing more than a convenient thoroughfare connecting the square to the Sporting Club. He did pause for an 'apéritif' at the latter, however. In fact, I'm told that he enjoyed two or three, sitting out on the concrete terrace by the pool. Then he started walking again, and he didn't stop until he reached the Catholic cemetery at the far end of rue de Massiges.

The cemetery is a large one, and it took Guéry some time to find his brother's grave. My colleague followed him at a discreet distance as he made his way along the intersecting, tree-lined avenues—pausing every so often to read an inscription on one of the gravestones or to smoke a cigarette in the shade.

Eventually, he found what he was looking for. It was in the northeastern corner of the cemetery, not far from the outer wall, in a slight declivity between two calcimined plane trees.

I believe Guéry stood there for almost half an hour, contemplating the small white gravestone that marked his brother's final resting place. It felt strange, he later said, to be confronted by such tangible evidence of Olivier's demise. Up until this point, it had all seemed so unreal. Guéry hadn't seen the body, with its opaque eyes and suppurating bullet holes; and he hadn't been to the funeral either, or had anything to do with settling his brother's estate. So this was the first time that he had been obliged to confront the unassailable reality of the situation. And there it was, right in front of him, indisputably etched in stone: *Olivier Guéry, 1909–1951, Priez pour lui.*

Needless to say, Guéry felt sorry for his brother, who hadn't really deserved to die in such a gruesome manner and with such indignity, being shot in the head like a common criminal and dumped in the Arroyo Chinois. And he also felt a twinge of regret that they hadn't seen more of each other in recent years. They had never really got along, of course, being completely incompatible in so many different ways; but it would have been nice, Guéry thought, to have seen a bit more of his brother before he died. It would have given him a chance, at least, to create some more agreeable memories while he still could. But for one reason or another it hadn't happened, and now there was nothing to replace or even mitigate that image of Olivier standing in the doorway of his hotel room in Cannes, disdainfully scrutinizing the interior as if he had never seen overflowing ashtrays or empty bottles or dirty clothes before in his life, and then uttering, if you remember, the terrible malediction that his younger sibling would carry with him for the rest of his days: '*Degenerate*,' he had said. 'You are nothing but a *degenerate*.'

To Guéry's surprise, however, these feelings of pity and regret weren't particularly strong. In fact, if he were being honest, he would have to admit to feeling almost nothing at all.

And this, he realized, was because he was standing at the graveside of someone he barely knew. Precisely who was this Olivier Guéry (1909–1951) anyway? What was his brother actually like? Was he a secret gambler and user of narcotics, who had been killed as a consequence of these vices? Or was he simply an innocent bystander who happened to be in the wrong place at the wrong time? Or, as I had suggested the day before, was he a legitimate businessman, an importer of agricultural machinery, who had somehow become involved in the trafficking of piastres and paid for it with his life? And if this was the case, was Olivier killed for threatening to reveal what was happening at Perec Frères or merely because he had been involved in some kind of sordid dispute with one of his colleagues?

There were at least four or five different possibilities to consider, each of which presupposed the existence of a different Olivier. And it was clear to Guéry that he wouldn't be able to leave Saigon until he had discovered which of these four or five Oliviers was the real one, until he had found out exactly whose death he was supposed to be mourning and whose salvation he was being asked to pray for.

The first of these possibilities—that Olivier had been gambling and using narcotics—was, from Guéry's perspective, the least likely. He simply couldn't picture his brother doing either of these things. The possibility that he was an innocent bystander who somehow got caught in the crossfire was also looking increasingly implausible. There was clearly something going on at Perec Frères, and the investigation had already accumulated far too many peculiarities to be so simply and easily resolved. What had happened to the mysterious Jacques Fourier, for instance, and why were the SDECE also trying to find him? Why had Reyes lied? What was the significance of the title page torn from *Tu Parles d'une Ingénue*? What had frightened Weiling in the Palais de Jade two nights previously, and who had ordered the severe beating that Guéry had suffered shortly thereafter? No, it was obviously more than just a matter of being in the wrong place at the wrong time. And that brought him to the final scenario, the most likely of the three: the possibility that Olivier had been involved in the trafficking of piastres.

Such a scenario would certainly explain why Reyes had lied to him the other day, and it would also explain the empty crates in the Perec Frères warehouse. Moreover, it was something he could quite easily imagine Olivier doing. As far as his brother was concerned, money had always carried a kind of transcendental value. In other words, for Olivier, what made money was good, and what didn't make money was, by definition, bad. It was as simple as that. Almost every profitable enterprise you can imagine fell under the first category, while under the second category, he included such contemptible activities as writing, gambling, drinking, and smoking. (And of course this was particularly the case if you happened to be writing an unpublishable novel modelled on Gide's *Counterfeiters* or gambling away your last five hundred francs at the Municipal Casino in Cannes.) So yes, it was quite conceivable that Olivier could have been involved in the trafficking of piastres. After working for several years in Saigon, importing and distributing agricultural machinery, he may well have decided that this particular field was not sufficiently lucrative; and if someone had then proposed to him that he move into the piastre trade, the decision would have been a fairly easy one to make. All he had to do was liaise with an accomplice in France, create false bills of lading, apply for the necessary currency transfers, and maintain an empty warehouse on the quai de Belgique. As an enterprise, it also had the advantage of being situated not too far beyond the parameters of legality. In fact, in one way or another, almost everybody seemed to be doing it these days—the soldiers of the Expeditionary Corps, the officials of the Banque de l'Indochine, even the representatives of the Gaullist RPF party. So why shouldn't Perec Frères also benefit from these advantageous economic circumstances? After all, such a profitable business could only be a 'good' thing.

But if Olivier really had been involved in the trafficking of piastres, then there were two further possibilities to consider. Either he had threatened to reveal what was going on at Perec Frères and was killed before he could do so. Or he had simply had a falling out with one of his colleagues—an argument over percentages, let's say, or some other financial matter—and was killed as a consequence of this dispute. In either case, though, it did seem rather strange that he should have ended up where he did, floating in the river with a bullet in his head. The trafficking of piastres was certainly illegal, but it wasn't the worst thing one could do out here in the colonies either. And no one at the foreign exchange office on rue Guynemer seemed particularly interested in detecting or even discouraging such fraudulent practices. So why kill someone in order to conceal what was happening at Perec Frères? Was it really necessary to do so, given the fact that it was such a common practice and so rarely investigated by the authorities? Or similarly, if the second scenario were the correct one, would a disagreement over percentages really have led to murder, given the fact that piastre trafficking was essentially the same as any other business these days? He supposed it was all a question of who your employers were. If you were working for the RPF or the Banque de l'Indochine, then such an outcome was obviously improbable. But perhaps it was the kind of thing that might conceivably transpire if your employers happened to be a private army of erstwhile river pirates or a syndicate of Corsican gangsters.

Whatever the case, it was clear to Guéry that he had more investigating to do. If Olivier really had been involved in the trafficking of piastres, and had been killed as a consequence, then he had to find out as soon as possible whose money was being channelled through Perec Frères. Once he had done so, it would be much easier to put all the pieces together and try to identify whoever was responsible for his brother's murder.

* * *

It was early afternoon by the time Guéry left the cemetery, and the temperature was steadily rising. Although he had taken off his heavy flannel jacket and rolled up his shirtsleeves, it was obvious that he was struggling with the humidity. He was perspiring heavily, and every so often he would tug at his cervical collar and grimace, as if it were a pillory or some kind of medieval torture device. According to the surveillance report that was subsequently filed, Guéry took the quickest possible route back to the Majestic, but even so, he was visibly distressed and disorientated by the time he got there. He sat for a moment in the foyer, gathering his resources, before making his way up to his room on the third floor, where I imagine he spent the rest of the day recovering from the ordeal he had just endured.

Around nine-thirty that evening, having bathed and added a further layer of brilliantine to his hair, Guéry left the hotel and hailed a taxi. My colleague immediately caught another one and instructed the driver to follow Guéry's at a reasonable distance. As soon as they reached place Eugène Cuniac, it became clear where Guéry was going. The taxi turned left onto boulevard Galliéni, and within fifteen minutes it had arrived in Cholon, where our 'subject' was deposited outside the Grand Monde. He had never actually been there before, but given Guéry's proclivities, it was inevitable that he would eventually find his way to the city's largest and most profitable casino.

In those days, the entrance to the casino was always guarded by several heavily armed Binh Xuyen foot soldiers, and they would have searched Guéry thoroughly before allowing him to pass through the gates. Once he had done so, he would have found himself in a large courtyard illuminated by low-hanging strings of multicoloured electric lights. Within this courtyard there were roughly twenty or thirty corrugated-iron structures, each of which contained half a dozen gaming tables. This was where the ordinary people of Saigon gambled, squandering their meagre earnings on traditional games of chance like *bau cua* and *tai xiu*. At every table there was a croupier who would roll the dice and then announce the winning numbers in a loud, incantatory voice. Before initiating a new round, the croupiers would have to gather in the losing stakes, and this was something they did with considerable expertise, as if they had been performing the same fluid motion all their lives. The atmosphere in the courtyard was festive, and it was hard to hear anything over the noise of the crowd; but the casino itself was a different kind of place altogether. It was located on the southern side of the quadrangle, in a building with high, coffered ceilings, and it was obviously the preserve of the élite. Money was not used to gamble here. Instead, one was obliged to purchase tokens ranging in value from a hundred piastres to a thousand. In the main room there were at least a dozen roulette tables, attended by uniformed croupiers, and it was at one of these tables—the one in the far corner, between the palm tree and the statue of the flamingo—that Guéry elected to spend the rest of his evening.

The report I have before me as I write is unnecessarily detailed, so allow me to provide just a brief summary of what followed.

Apparently, there was a Vietnamese man standing to Guéry's left at the roulette table. He was in his early sixties and had yellow, jaundiced eyes. His name was Nguyen Van Loc, and he had been known to the intelligence services in Saigon for some time.

After half an hour or so, Nguyen turned to Guéry and said, 'You've brought good fortune to the table, Monsieur.'

Guéry smiled. 'For others, perhaps.'

'I haven't noticed you here before.'

'No,' Guéry replied. 'I only arrived in Saigon a couple of days ago.'

'And you've already run into some trouble, I see.' Nguyen gestured vaguely toward Guéry's bruised face.

'Yes. I've been unfortunate elsewhere too.'

There was silence for a moment as they placed their bets. Guéry put two hundred piastres on 33 and another two hundred on odd, just to be safe. The croupier set the wheel in motion.

'So what brings you to Saigon, Monsieur?' Nguyen asked, without lifting his eyes from the spinning wheel.

'I'm trying to find out what happened to my brother.'

'He's gone missing?'

'Not quite. He was actually killed. Murdered. They found his body in the Arroyo Chinois.'

Nguyen gave him a sympathetic glance. 'How very sad,' he said. 'Please accept my condolences.'

There was something about the wheel that made the ball spin for longer than usual—almost indefinitely, it seemed—but it finally came to rest on 28, and Guéry watched as the croupier collected his four hundred piastres.

'I'm told my brother came here quite regularly,' he said, putting another two hundred on odd. 'Perhaps you knew him. His name was Olivier Guéry.'

Nguyen shook his head slowly. 'No, I'm afraid not, Monsieur. I don't recall meeting anyone by that name.'

'Would you mind if I showed you a photo of my brother?'

'Please do.'

Guéry took an old photo of Olivier out of his wallet and gave it to Nguyen, who studied it for some time before responding.

'I'm sorry,' he said. 'I don't recognize this man at all.'

'You've never seen him at the casino before . . . '

'No.'

'But you come here regularly yourself?'

'I do. At least three or four times a week.' He paused to light a cigarette. 'And every time I come, I gamble with my life.'

Guéry was so surprised by this dramatic revelation that he smiled inadvertently. 'But why should that be the case, Monsieur?'

'When I was a young man, I worked for the French intelligence service. I believed it was my patriotic duty to do so.'

'I see.'

'And I've been told that my name is now on the list that circulates among the Viet Minh murder committees here in Saigon. So it's only a matter of time before they kill me.'

'But how can you be so sure?'

'Sooner or later, Monsieur, they always get you. Last year, they assassinated Marcel Bazin, the deputy chief of the Sûreté. They shot him four times as he was about to get into his car. This was in the centre of the city, in broad daylight, and his killers still managed to escape.'

The roulette wheel came to a halt once more. This time the ball landed on 30, and Guéry lost another two hundred piastres.

'Corner,' Nguyen declared, placing a hundred piastres of his own between the squares marked 10, 11, 13, and 14. Then, turning to Guéry, he said, 'The funny thing is that Bazin knew they were coming for him. He knew his killers had arrived in the city. Every day on the Viet Minh radio station, they would say, "Bazin, you are going to die. Bazin, you are going to die." And of course that's precisely what happened. He died.'

'But is the casino not a safe place to be?' Guéry asked. 'It's heavily guarded, after all.'

'On the contrary, Monsieur. Nothing could be easier than to infiltrate this place and kill someone. It's impossible to tell where anyone's loyalties lie—or who they're really working for.' He leaned forward and lowered his voice. 'None of these Binh Xuyen mercenaries can be trusted. If you paid them enough, they would kill anyone.'

'So why come here at all, then, if it's so dangerous? Surely there are other, safer places you could go.'

Guéry was expecting Nguyen to say, in response, that it was an act of defiance on his part or an affirmation of life or something along those lines; but the answer, when it came, wasn't quite so heroic.

'I'm addicted to gambling, Monsieur. It's as simple as that. I can't stop myself from coming—even if I'm risking my life by doing so.'

When Guéry later spoke to me about this encounter, it was clear that he had been deeply impressed by Nguyen's dedication to the vice they both shared. Here was a man whose desire to gamble was stronger than his desire to live, and this was something that Guéry could quite easily understand. It goes without saying that his brother would have found it disgusting and mystifying in equal measure, but for Guéry it really was something to admire—and not a bad way to go either, when all was said and done, to die as you had lived, surrendering yourself to the vagaries of fate and the inevitability of the 'house edge' (i.e., the average amount of money a player will lose during a given period of time at the roulette table). It was, in short, a better way to die than any other Guéry could imagine, and certainly better than whatever might have happened to Olivier in his final hours.

This conversation between Guéry and Monsieur Nguyen went on a good deal longer, but there's no need to record it in full here. Nothing else of any significance transpired that evening either. In fact, in almost every particular, what followed was entirely predictable. Guéry stayed at the casino until two in the morning. The losses he sustained at the roulette table during this time were substantial—far exceeding, as it turned out, the house edge. According to the surveillance report, he also consumed a large quantity of Otard cognac and may not have been in full control of his faculties by the time he left the place. All in all, then, it was just another typical night for Jean-Luc Guéry. At one point, he was joined by a young woman who made her living at the casino; but after talking to Guéry for several minutes, she must have realized that she was wasting her time. In many ways, Guéry was a poor degraded soul who was often consumed by an overwhelming *nostalgie de la boue*, but this yearning for the mud did not include the solicitation of prostitutes. That part of his life—like the investigation he was currently conducting—was far too complicated to be so easily resolved. Having recognized this fact almost immediately, the young woman left him in peace with his roulette and his cognac, and moved on to more promising pastures.

Over the course of the evening, as mentioned above, Guéry lost a great deal of money at the roulette table; but there's really nothing to be gained by offering a detailed enumeration of these losses. Suffice it to say, when he got back to the Majestic later that night and opened his wallet, he found himself to be in possession of two twenty-piastre notes and thirty-five centimes in loose change. Everything else had been squandered at the casino. Over the years, Guéry had adopted a number of different strategies in order to avoid such losses. As a young man, he had developed a complicated liturgy of rituals that were supposed to ensure good fortune at the roulette table (spitting into his own urine, arranging his tokens in multiples of three, carrying an ivory cigarette holder that had once belonged to his grandfather, etc.). But when all of this came to nothing, he decided to approach the matter from a more scientific perspective, becoming what the croupiers, with some irony, refer to as a *licencé en roulette* (a graduate, that is to say, of gambling studies). He read everything there was to read on the subject—including volumes such as *Insurance Against All Losses at Monte Carlo* and *Mathematical Observances Relating to the Game of Roulette*—before finally settling on a classic strategy known as the martingale.

According to this particular theory, if a gambler such as Guéry doubles his bet after every loss, he will eventually win and, in so doing, recover all of his previous losses, along with a profit equal to his original stake. So, for example, if Guéry were to bet one hundred francs on red-36 and lose, he would increase his wager to two hundred francs for the following round (again placing it on red-36). If he were to lose once more, he would simply double his money, and continue doing so until the ball finally landed in the desired place. Needless to say, this was an infallible strategy—as long as the gambler in question had an infinite supply of money and time. In Guéry's case, however, he would inevitably squander everything he had (and sometimes more) within a couple of hours, at which point he would be obliged to leave the table in a state of utter dismay and abject disgrace. At times, having lost his entire salary and all of his savings, in the darkness of some godforsaken hotel room, I suspect that he may even have considered taking his own life. But he obviously resisted the temptation to do so, and continued to experiment with various different strategies, all of which were based, to a greater or lesser degree, on a statistical misconception known as the Monte Carlo fallacy—and all of which, to a greater or lesser degree, resulted in the kind of losses he had just suffered at the Grand Monde.

On this particular evening, Guéry later told me, he found it difficult to get to sleep; and so he lay awake for several hours, staring at the ceiling through half-closed eyes. Everything that had happened over the last few days, everything he had seen or heard, came back to him in a disjointed collision of disparate images and memories. His brother floating in the oily water of the Arroyo Chinois. A bullet lodged in his right parietal lobe. Traces of opiates in his blood. Fifty-five piastres. A nine-millimetre Luger . . . *Je voudrais tant que tu te souviennes* . . . The empty crates in the Perec Frères warehouse. HAUT, BAS, and FRAGILE. An Alberto Vargas picture. A commercial calendar from 1949. Rotary hoes and hydraulic presses. An imitation Sèvres vase and an old 78 . . . *Des jours heureux où nous étions amis* . . . No one can be trusted. Not even those who claim to be on your side. The girl on the cover of *Tu Parles d'une Ingénue*. Languid eyes and vertiginous curves. He felt something give way, either cartilage or bone. A bag of soiled clothes hanging from a door handle . . . *En ce temps-là la vie était plus belle* . . . Where was the elusive Jacques Fourier? The Tapestry of the Apocalypse in Angers. A cigarette lighter, a pair of sunglasses, some keys. A half-empty jar of olives. An identity card issued in Nice . . . *Et le soleil plus brûlant qu'aujourd'hui* . . . The mineral powder on his face was gradually liquefying. No one can be trusted. Spies. Detectives. Mercenaries. Not even those who claim to be on your side. Two twenty-piastre notes and thirty-five centimes in change. A dog with one ear licking the dried

blood off his face . . . *Les feuilles mortes se ramassent à la pelle* . . .
He needed to buy some more 4711 and a bottle of chloral
hydrate. *Olivier Guéry, 1909–1951, Priez pour lui.* Calcimined
plane trees. They shot him four times as he was about to get into
his car. Two hundred piastres on 33 and another two hundred
on odd . . . *Les souvenirs et les regrets aussi* . . . Piastres. So many
piastres. A strange leafy fragrance. The sound of a coal mine
collapsing. He should really send his father a postcard . . .

Just as Guéry was losing consciousness, a detail
occurred to him—something he had overlooked, something of
great significance.

But when he awoke the following morning, it was gone, and
the only thing he could think about was finding some aspirin
capsules to alleviate the searing pain in his temples, behind his
eyes, and on the bridge of his broken nose.

Chapter 9

Grilled Oysters

Only an amateur would have done what Guéry did later that same day—only an amateur with a terrible 'migraine' and a peculiar indifference to his own safety.

He was sitting at the bar of the Continental, nursing a medicinal cognac, when he noticed an unassuming male figure standing in the doorway that led to the terrace. The man looked to be in his late fifties, and he was occupying a position that allowed him to see both the interior of the bar and the terrace outside, depending on which way he turned his head. He was wearing an immaculate tussore suit, and his hair had been slicked back in a style that was known locally as *le tango*. It was, of course, the proprietor himself, Pierre Vitelli.

Vitelli, if you remember, was a perfectly respectable businessman who had come to Saigon at the end of the First World War and quickly established himself within the city's more elevated social circles. He was an unofficial financial advisor to the emperor and on familiar terms with the high command of the Expeditionary Corps. But there was another side to him too. In addition to his proprietorial duties, he was said to be heavily involved in the smuggling of contraband between Saigon and metropolitan France. Although this was common knowledge at the time, it wasn't an accusation one would have made lightly; for Vitelli was also rumoured to be the head of the local Unione Corse and a close associate of the Guerini brothers, who were practically running Marseille in those days. Indeed, only the year before, as Bergerac had mentioned, a journalist by the name of Hugo Lefèvre had died in mysterious circumstances after publicly accusing Vitelli of being involved in the piastre trade.

Given all of the above, then, one might have expected Guéry to proceed carefully (or not to proceed at all); but as we know, it was not in his nature to do things that were obviously sensible or life-preserving. If it had been, he certainly wouldn't have summoned the bartender and asked to speak to Monsieur Vitelli, who duly appeared at his side several minutes later.

'Good afternoon,' the proprietor said with an affable smile. 'How may I be of assistance?'

Guéry returned the smile as well as he could. 'I'm very sorry to bother you,' he said, 'but I was wondering if I could ask you a couple of questions about my brother, Olivier Guéry.'

As he was saying this, Guéry searched Vitelli's face for a sign of recognition, but there was no change to the congenial disposition of his features.

'I'm afraid I don't know anyone by that name,' he said. 'Does your brother live here in Saigon?'

'Not anymore. He's actually dead. He was killed in February.'

'I'm sorry to hear that, Monsieur. It's an all-too-common occurrence these days.'

'So I'm told.'

There was a pause while Vitelli lit a cigarette. It was an imported brand that Guéry had never seen before, and the burning tobacco smelled like pineapples.

'Well, Monsieur, as I didn't have the pleasure of making his acquaintance . . . '

'Actually,' Guéry interjected, 'I wonder if I could have a minute of your time anyway. I've been told that you know a great deal about what goes on in this city.'

Vitelli studied him closely for a moment or two, paying particular attention to the soiled bandage spanning the bridge of his nose. 'Very well, Monsieur,' he said finally. 'What is it that you would like to know?'

'My brother worked for a company called Perec Frères. Have you heard of it by any chance? Their offices are on rue d'Espagne—number 39, I believe.'

Again there was no visible reaction to this question. Vitelli's features remained serene and undisturbed, as if he had spent a lifetime fielding enquiries of this kind.

'I'm afraid I can't help you there either, Monsieur Guéry. I've never heard of a company called Perec Frères. What do they do?'

'They import agricultural machinery.'

'That doesn't sound like a particularly dangerous occupation,' Vitelli said. 'May I ask how your brother died?'

'He was shot in the head. They found his body floating in the Arroyo Chinois.'

Vitelli raised his eyebrows as if to indicate surprise. 'How tragic . . . And what is *your* business, Monsieur Guéry, if you don't mind my asking?'

'I'm a journalist.'

'Is that so? Well, you've come to the right place. The Continental has always been very popular with your colleagues.'

'Yes, I ran into Lucien Bodard and Jean Lartéguy on the terrace just the other day.'

Vitelli nodded. 'They're fine men,' he said, 'and fine journalists too.' Then, with a perfectly straight face, he added, 'So what publication do you write for, Monsieur Guéry? *Le Monde*, *Le Figaro*, or one of the other dailies?'

It was a question that Guéry was beginning to dread. 'I write for *Le Journal d'Antibes*,' he replied.

There was another momentary pause.

'I'm afraid I'm not familiar with that particular newspaper. Are you serving as their correspondent here in Saigon?'

'Not officially,' Guéry said. 'Not yet, at any rate. I've applied for accreditation, but apparently there's been some kind of delay. And in the meantime, I've been told that I might like to visit Cap Saint-Jacques.'

'Well, Monsieur, it's certainly nice out there at this time of year. It's not too crowded, and the sea breezes are really quite invigorating. It's like Ajaccio in spring.'

'So they say. But if I could return to the matter at hand . . . '

Vitelli bowed slightly. 'Of course.'

'Several days ago, I discovered that there was something rather strange going on at Perec Frères. And when I spoke to one of the police officers at the Sûreté about it, he suggested that they might be involved in the trafficking of piastres.'

'It wouldn't be unusual if that were the case, Monsieur. But I don't see why you should be discussing this matter with me.'

'I was told that you know Saigon better than anyone else, so I thought you might be able to . . . help me with my enquiries.'

Vitelli produced another one of his proprietorial smiles. 'I'm afraid there's not much I can tell you, Monsieur. But I would be interested to hear what you've discovered yourself thus far.'

'Well,' Guéry said, after hesitating just briefly, 'I know that the Perec Frères warehouse is full of empty crates. I know that one of my brother's colleagues, a Monsieur Jacques Fourier, went missing immediately after he was murdered. I know that the SDECE are looking for him too. And I know that the current managing director of Perec Frères hasn't been particularly forthcoming with me.'

'I see. And this?' Vitelli gestured toward Guéry's face with his cigarette. 'Does this also have something to do with your enquiries?'

'It does. I was told that it was a warning and that I should leave Saigon immediately.'

'And where was this warning delivered, Monsieur Guéry?'

'In one of the alleyways off boulevard Galliéni. Three nights ago.'

Vitelli nodded his head reflectively. 'If I may say so, Monsieur, you are lucky to be alive. Warnings are a rare commodity in Saigon these days. So would it not be wise to do as you are told?'

'And leave Saigon?'

'Indeed.'

'Yes,' Guéry said, 'I imagine that would be the wise thing to do. But I can't leave until I've found out who killed my brother. And in order to do so, I need to find out what's going on at Perec Frères.'

'I'd like to help you, Monsieur Guéry, but I'm afraid I know nothing of this world. Only what I hear out on the terrace during *l'apéro*, and that's just gossip and hearsay.'

'So there's nothing you can tell me about the illegal trade in piastres?'

As soon as he had said it, Guéry realized that this question was far too direct and unambiguous. Dangerously so. And yet

Vitelli seemed unperturbed by it. He merely smiled and said, 'No, nothing at all. I'm sorry, Monsieur.'

And at that moment, Guéry suddenly understood what was happening. Vitelli was simply amused by everything he had to say. He was humouring him because it was his proprietorial duty to do so, but he hadn't felt even mildly threatened or discomforted by a single one of Guéry's questions. All Vitelli could see, sitting beside him at the bar, was a strange man in his late thirties, with greasy, dishevelled hair, a stereotypical Gallic nose, bruised and bloodshot eyes, nicotine-stained fingers, a slight tremor in the hand that held his cigarette, and a ridiculous cervical collar that made him look like some kind of primitive Bronze Age figurine. In short, it was obviously quite impossible for a man like Vitelli to take a man like Guéry at all seriously. And I believe it was this fact that most probably saved his life that day.

'Good luck with your enquiries, Monsieur Guéry, and if you do make it out to Cap Saint-Jacques, may I recommend the grilled oysters at the Negresco. They're absolutely splendid.'

'Thank you, Monsieur. I appreciate the time you've given me. And I'll be sure to try the oysters should the opportunity arise.'

'Grilled not fried.'

'Of course, Monsieur. Grilled oysters from the Negresco.'

'With or without garlic, depending on your taste.'

'Which would you recommend?' Guéry asked.

'I prefer them without garlic.'

'Then without garlic it shall be.'

'But still grilled.'

'Naturally—grilled and without garlic.'

'And they do go very well with a bottle of Sancerre,' Vitelli added.

'Then I shall buy a bottle of Sancerre too.'

'Very good, Monsieur. I trust you'll enjoy it . . . And I sincerely hope you manage to find out what happened to your brother.'

Once Vitelli had gone, Guéry quickly finished his cognac and walked to the door. It had been yet another dispiriting encounter, and he no longer had the energy to be out in public. It was time to return to the Majestic, where he could lie in bed and read, if he felt like it, or go through his notes to see if he had missed anything of significance.

As he was leaving the hotel, however, someone called out to him from the terrace. It was Bergerac.

Guéry walked over to his table.

'Monsieur Guéry, what a pleasant surprise. Will you join me for a drink?'

'Yes, of course.'

Guéry settled into a chair and resigned himself to another cognac.

'But my dear friend,' Bergerac said, 'you look terrible. What happened?'

'I ran into some trouble a couple of nights ago. Three men assaulted me in an alleyway.'

'That's appalling. Did they have any particular reason for doing so?'

'They were trying to deter me from investigating my brother's murder.'

'Oh,' Bergerac said gravely, 'I see.'

'Perhaps I should have listened to your advice.'

'Yes, perhaps you *should* have.'

Bergerac's appearance had not changed since their last encounter. He was still perspiring heavily, still nursing an oversized *oeuf colonial*, and when he smiled his eyes still disappeared into a profusion of intersecting wrinkles. It was also clear, as it had been a week or so earlier, that a thin layer of mineral powder had been applied to the deeply lined contours of his face. As you can imagine, the overall effect, once all of these features had been combined, was rather disconcerting.

'So what brings you to the Continental today?' he asked.

'Nothing in particular,' Guéry replied, 'although I did take the opportunity, while I was here, to speak to Monsieur Vitelli.'

Bergerac looked surprised. 'Really?' he said. 'And what did you speak to him about?'

'I asked him if he knew my brother.'

'Did he?'

'No.' Guéry paused to light a cigarette. 'I also asked him if he knew anything about the trafficking of piastres.'

Bergerac lifted a beringed hand to his face in horror. 'But, Monsieur, why would you have done such a thing?' He lowered his voice. 'Did I not tell you that Monsieur Vitelli is a very dangerous man?'

Guéry acknowledged that he had in fact done so.

'And did I not tell you about Hugo Lefèvre and the DC-4 that crashed into the Persian Gulf only last year?'

'Yes,' Guéry admitted, 'you did.'

'So why would you go ahead and talk to the man about the piastre trade? Are you tired of living?'

'Actually, I have to say he was very amiable. Very obliging. It's hard to believe that all the things they say about him are true.'

'Well, they are, Monsieur. And his amiability is what makes him so dangerous. It's impossible to predict what he's going to do because he always does it with a smile on his face.'

Bergerac was obviously quite dismayed by what he had heard. He produced a piece of tissue paper from his pocket and pressed it to his forehead in several different places. Then he folded it into a tight little square and left it on the table.

'What you've done,' he murmured, 'is very unwise. Very unwise indeed.'

'To be honest, I don't think he felt particularly threatened by anything I had to say.'

'Perhaps not, but it was still an exceedingly dangerous thing to do.' Bergerac gave him a speculative glance, then said, 'May I ask why you should be interested in this topic in the first place?'

In reply, Guéry launched into a detailed account of everything that had happened over the last few days. Among other things, he mentioned the empty crates at the Perec Frères warehouse, the missing Jacques Fourier, his visit to the Palais de Jade, and my suggestion, two days earlier, that his brother may have been involved in the trafficking of piastres.

'How fascinating,' Bergerac said once he had finished. 'This Jacques Fourier, you say you visited his apartment. Did you find anything of interest there?'

'Only the book with the missing title page: *Tu Parles d'une Ingénue.*'

'And the concierge wasn't able to tell you anything?'

'No.' Guéry hesitated. 'Actually, yes. He did say that the SDECE had searched Fourier's apartment around the time of his disappearance.'

Bergerac let out a low whistle. 'Fancy that. The SDECE. This is like something out of a spy novel or one of those Disque Rouge adventures.'

'Yes, I keep thinking that myself.'

'So did they manage to find anything there?'

'I'm not sure. And the concierge hadn't been told either. He said that the men of the SDECE are not typically known for their candour.'

'No. Quite.'

For a moment, they both contemplated the square without saying anything. It was crowded now, as it always was at this time of day, but Guéry couldn't see very much of what was happening beyond the periphery of the terrace. He could only imagine what the blurred shapes and colours that filled the square might actually be—a boy selling cigarettes, say, or a group of carousing legionnaires.

After a while, Bergerac broke the silence.

'Have you finished reading *Tu Parles d'une Ingénue* yet?' he asked.

'Not yet, no.'

'And I don't suppose you have any idea what the significance of the title page might be.'

Guéry shrugged his shoulders. 'It could mean anything, or it could mean nothing at all. I simply don't know.'

'What about the novel itself? Is there any connection there?'

'Not that I can tell. Not unless Olivier was involved in international arms trafficking, which doesn't appear to have been the case.'

Bergerac smiled. 'No, Monsieur, I imagine that would be highly improbable.' He gazed out over the square for a minute or two, then turned to face Guéry once more. 'Perhaps it's simply a coincidence that he happened to be carrying that page at the time of his death. It wasn't all he was carrying, I suppose.'

'No. He also had a pair of sunglasses, some keys, a cigarette lighter, that kind of thing.'

'And what about the dance hostess at the Palais de Jade? Did she have anything useful to say?'

'She confirmed that Olivier wasn't gambling or using narcotics.'

'Why would you suspect that he was using drugs?' Bergerac asked.

'The pathologist found traces of opiates in his blood.'

'Opiates, you say?'

'That's right. Quite a large quantity too.'

'And does that surprise you, Monsieur Guéry?'

'Yes, quite frankly, it does. It wasn't the kind of thing that Olivier would have done. Not the Olivier I knew anyway.'

This time it was Bergerac who shrugged. 'People change, Monsieur. Particularly out here.'

Once again, Guéry had a strong feeling of déjà vu. Different people kept telling him the same thing, as if they were all part of the same elaborate conspiracy. In this particular case, he was remembering what I had said only two days before about people changing—and especially out here in the tropics.

'Does it have something to do with the climate, Monsieur Bergerac?'

'I'm sorry?'

'Do people change out here because of the climate? Is it particularly debilitating?'

Bergerac smiled uncertainly. 'I'm not sure, Monsieur. But the place does sometimes have a strange effect on people's personalities.'

'That may be so,' Guéry said, 'but I still find it difficult to imagine Olivier using drugs. And Weiling, the hostess at the Palais, said that he had never once used them in her presence.'

'I see. And did she have anything else to say?'

'Not really, no. At a certain point, she saw something that scared her, and she refused to go on talking.'

'What did she see?'

'I'm not sure. We were dancing, and she must have noticed something over my shoulder—most probably the three men who later assaulted me in the alleyway.'

Bergerac regarded him with a certain sympathy. 'What a terrible ordeal it must have been for you,' he said. 'Is it still painful?'

'Only here.' Guéry indicated his nose. 'And here.' He touched his left temple gingerly.

'Have you any idea who these three men were?'

'No, none at all.'

'Did they say anything to you?'

'They said that I should consider the beating a warning and that I should leave Saigon immediately. Otherwise I would end up like Olivier.'

'Dead . . .'

Guéry nodded.

'So I imagine these men must have been working for whoever killed your brother.'

'Probably—but that doesn't get me very far.'

Bergerac closed his eyes for a moment, as if he were considering a matter of some profundity, then he opened them again and said, 'If I understand you correctly, Monsieur, you believe that your brother was involved in the trafficking of piastres, and that he was killed either by one of his accomplices or by his employers.'

Guéry confirmed that this was indeed the case.

'But the trafficking of piastres is so common these days. I don't understand why it would lead to murder. Who would kill someone over a couple of empty crates and some phony bills of lading?'

'That's something I don't understand either.'

'So you still have no idea whose money is being remitted through Perec Frères . . .'

'I'm afraid not. According to Inspector Leclerc, it could belong to anyone—the Binh Xuyen, the Corsicans, even the Viet Minh.'

Bergerac laughed quietly. 'Yes, that's often the problem in Saigon. There are so many people involved in so many different . . . activities. It does make it all rather confusing.'

'I remember you telling me the last time we met that there were actually no mysteries here, no ambiguities.'

'Did I? Did I really?' Bergerac was obviously amused by this recollection. 'And why did I say such a thing, pray tell?'

'You said that everyone in Saigon is interested in the same thing.'

'Money.'

Guéry nodded.

'Well, it's true, Monsieur. We all have different allegiances and objectives, but underlying everything you'll find the same basic motive—the desire for money. As Bodard said in one of his articles, we're all prisoners of the piastre, every one of us.' He gestured in the general direction of the square. 'Prisoners of the seventeen-franc piastre. And in some ways that makes everything quite straightforward; but it also complicates matters. Consider your own case, for instance. Almost anyone could be running the operation at Perec Frères because there are so many people around here doing the same thing, despite their superficial differences. And it's this simplicity, this common ground, that ultimately makes it all so confusing.'

'So you don't believe that I'll ever be able to solve the case . . . '

'You've done very well to date, Monsieur Guéry. Far better than I would have predicted. You've found out what your brother was doing here, and you now have a clearer understanding of the circumstances surrounding his murder.' He paused. 'But I do think it's time for you to go home, back to Antibes, before it's too late. You should be satisfied with what you've achieved and grateful that you're still alive.'

Guéry assembled his damaged features into something resembling a smile. 'I appreciate your concern,' he said. 'I really do. But I can't leave Saigon until I've found out precisely what happened to Olivier. I'm afraid it's just one of those things.'

Once again, Guéry was being given good advice here; but once again, he chose to ignore it. I still don't quite understand why he should have done so, and I imagine Bergerac found it rather mystifying too. Despite the fact that Guéry had never been especially fond of his brother, he was prepared to risk his own life in order to bring his brother's killer to justice. I have often wondered since why this should have been the case, particularly given the unheroic qualities that Guéry typically demonstrated in every other area of his life. And I suppose the best answer I can provide relates to the fact that he was a reader: a man who loved reading and a man with a very high regard for the conventions of his preferred genre. As we know, he tended to see things from a rather literary perspective, and now here he was, in Saigon, of all places, living out his very own Série Noire—surrounded by spies and informers and *femmes fatales* and mysterious strangers and 'clues' and everything else one associates with that kind of literature. And if he were to give up and go home at this point, having made some partial discoveries and gained a slightly better understanding of what had happened to his brother, it would be like abandoning a novel a hundred pages or so before the end. If he were to return to Antibes, that is to say, without having solved the case, the novel he was living would come to an abrupt and unsatisfying conclusion; and this was something that Guéry, as an avid reader of Simenon and his colleagues, simply couldn't tolerate. So he had to go on, motivated of course by certain psychological and emotional imperatives, but also motivated, at a deeper level, by the desire to finish the 'novel' he had started—to bring everything to a satisfying conclusion, to discover precisely who had pulled the trigger, and why.

* * *

After another couple of cognacs, Guéry left Bergerac and walked back to his hotel. His nose was beginning to ache, and he was feeling unbelievably tired. Not just physically tired either, but tired of everything—tired of the peculiarities of the case, tired of his own ignorance, and increasingly tired of all the unsolicited advice he kept getting. Everyone he had met so far seemed to agree on one thing: that he, Guéry, was completely out of place in Saigon, and that he should go back to Antibes as soon as possible. After a while, this refrain had become a little insulting, quite frankly, and rather dispiriting too. Was he really such a picture of incompetence and stupidity? Was it entirely inconceivable that he might achieve something here, and live to tell the tale?

Apparently so.

When he got back to the Majestic, he took off his shoes and stretched out on the bed. The bridge of his nose was still sore, so he decided to call down to reception for some ice. He reached for the telephone on the bedside table, and that was when he noticed that something was awry. Of course, Guéry himself was not a particularly tidy person. Some might even say that he lived in a state of abject squalor. But like many such people, he had a clear sense of where everything should be and could tell at once if an object had been moved or misplaced.

In this specific instance, he had left an apple core on the bedside table, but it was no longer there. He got up and looked around the room for it. It wasn't on the dining table either, or on the sideboard by the door. Only after searching for some time did he find the missing apple core lying under his bed, covered in dust and partially concealed by an old *Caravelle* magazine. And that was just the beginning. Almost immediately, he noticed a number of other things that were out of place. A dirty shirt that had been draped over the back of a chair was now lying on the seat itself, beneath several items of discarded underclothing and a wire coat hanger. He had left a collection of his notes on the desk by the window, and these too were disarranged—a tariff card lay where an advertising flyer should have been, and an empty cigarette packet had replaced a fragment of yesterday's *Journal de Saigon*. It was the same thing in the bathroom. A glass of water that he had been using as an ashtray was standing on a shelf when it should have been on the toilet cistern, and an empty bottle of 4711 that he had left on the floor was now lying on top of a pile of soiled clothes in the corner.

It could all mean only one thing. At some point over the last couple of hours, while he was talking to Vitelli or Bergerac at the Continental, his room had been searched.

Whoever it was hadn't done a very good job, but perhaps they had been lulled into a false sense of security by the disarray in which they had found the place. They probably didn't imagine that someone who lived in such a *bordel* would notice a misplaced shirt or a few rearranged papers.

Guéry walked back into the other room and began looking around to see if anything was missing. His passport and traveller's cheques were still in the desk drawer, along with his grandfather's ivory cigarette holder and some unchanged francs. He looked through the disorderly piles of notes he had been reading earlier that day, but nothing had been taken from there either—not even the precious title page that had been found on his brother's body. Then it suddenly occurred to him that the book itself might have gone. He walked over to the bedside table and opened the drawer. Although it had obviously been inspected in his absence, *Tu Parles d'une Ingénue* was still where he had left it, surrounded by aspirin capsules, earplugs, and half-smoked cigarettes.

He lit one of the cigarettes and lay down on the bed.

It was rather unsettling to think that someone had been there, in his room, searching through his belongings. And the fact that he had no idea who was responsible for this outrage made it particularly disturbing. It couldn't have been thieves, he realized, otherwise they would have taken his passport and his traveller's cheques. So it must have been someone else— but who and why? Perhaps it was the same three men who had assaulted him in the alleyway. But how had they managed to get into his room, if that was the case? There was no sign of forced entry, and the lock on the door was a solid one. Did they have accomplices within the hotel itself?

He reached over to the bedside table and tapped his cigarette against the edge of an ashtray that also belonged elsewhere.

Or perhaps it was the police, trying to find out what he had discovered during the course of his investigation. They would certainly have had the authority to retrieve his key from the hotel manager. But then, of course, if they had wanted to search the room, they could have done so quite openly, without resorting to this kind of subterfuge. No, it must have been someone with something to hide—most probably the same people who were running things at Perec Frères, and therefore most probably the same people who had killed Olivier.

The thought made him feel slightly nauseous.

If that was true, if it really had been his brother's killers who had searched the room, then what would have happened if he had come back half an hour earlier, say, and discovered them there? Would he have been shot dead too, just as Olivier had been? He couldn't help imagining the scene: the door opening to reveal two (or should that be three?) evil-looking men with thin, ratty faces, one of whom would have pulled out his nine-millimetre Luger and forced Guéry to sit down at the table.

'Monsieur Guéry,' he would have said, 'we warned you, but you refused to listen. In fact, you refused to listen to everybody, even Leclerc. And now you're going to pay for your stupidity. Prepare to die.'

Or perhaps they would have tried to get some information out of him first, before killing him.

'Tell us what you know about Perec Frères,' they might have said. Or, 'What are you doing here, and who are you working for? Who sent you?'

Something along those lines.

But of course Guéry would have refused to say anything, maintaining a dignified, even heroic, silence—no matter how brutally he was treated.

And then finally, having understood that they were dealing with a man of rare fortitude, they would have put the Luger to his head, just behind his left ear, and prepared to fire. At the last minute, however, Guéry would have wrestled the gun off his adversary—with 'the rapidity of lightning,' to quote the author of *Tu Parles d'une Ingénue*—and killed them both where they stood. Or perhaps, better still, he would have handed the contemptible wretches over to the police, who would have arrived a short time later to 'take it from there' and thank Guéry for having solved the case as they had been completely unable to do so.

This, at least, was how it all unfolded in his imagination. In reality, he just lay there smoking cigarettes and staring at the ceiling until eventually he became tired of this occupation and decided to go downstairs for dinner.

According to the surveillance report I have before me, he ordered a croque-monsieur, some fries, a plate of sautéed vegetables, and a disgusting confection that goes by the name of *café liégeois*. This was followed by a coffee and some more cigarettes—three, to be precise.

He retired for the evening, so the report says, a little after eleven-thirty.

* * *

Before proceeding, I should probably make it clear to the reader just how delusional these fantasies of Guéry's were—and explain why it was so difficult to take him seriously as a 'detective.' Despite his theoretical knowledge of police procedures, he was easily led astray when it came to deciphering the real world. It was around this time, for instance, that he became obsessed by the lilting, sing-song cries of Saigon's ubiquitous street vendors. In Chapter 2, if you remember, I reproduced a musical notation that I had found among Guéry's papers—the one he jotted down during his interview with Arnaud at the Sûreté. It was a song that a nearby street vendor had been singing, he later told me, and I imagine that's when his obsession with these (rather irritating) refrains must have started. He had always been interested in codes and ciphers; and he found musical cryptography particularly fascinating. So I suppose it was only a matter of time before he began to ascribe a hidden meaning to the mercantile cries that are such a notable feature of Saigon's street life. The vendors themselves are everywhere, of course, and they typically carry their wares on long poles slung over their shoulders or in baskets (*cai ro*) that they balance on their heads. But even if you are not able to see these vendors, you are always aware of their presence—and of the specific merchandise they happen to be selling—as their songs can penetrate the deepest recesses of any building, drifting along corridors, up staircases, and through keyholes. *Ai hoa ra mua? Ai hoa ra mua? Ai banh tay ra mua? Ai banh tay ra mua?* Etc., etc. Most people learn to ignore these songs, but for some reason Guéry found them intriguing, and this growing obsession can be traced quite clearly in the notes that he was making at the time.

There was a young sugar cane vendor, for example, to whom he paid particularly close attention. According to his notes, she was in her early twenties, 'slender and pretty,' and she carried her sticks of sugar cane on a flat *cai ro* balanced on her head. Every day at around ten-thirty, she would make her way along rue Catinat, singing the same repetitive refrain: *Ai an mia khong? Ai an mia khong? Ai an mia khong?* Guéry was never able to discover the precise meaning of this simple sentence ('Who wants to eat sugar cane [or not]?'), and perhaps that's why he found it so fascinating. 'Could she be conveying a message of some kind?' he speculated in his notes. 'Does it have something to do with the Viet Minh and the "murder committees" that are operating in the city? And if so, where is this deeper, secondary meaning to be found? Is it conveyed by the actual utterance—*Ai an mia khong?*—or encoded within the tonal inflections of the song itself, which does seem to differ slightly from day to day?' In an effort to reveal the song's underlying meaning, he had even gone to the trouble of carefully transcribing its basic melody:

Ai   an   mia   khong?

But I'm afraid this didn't get him very far—the deeper meaning of the sugar cane vendor's song (if any) remained elusive. And he was equally mystified by the young boys whose occupation it was to sell roasted peanuts and watermelon seeds, and whose cry was especially piercing:

Dau phong ran hot dua hot   dua dau phong ran?

I won't waste your time with any more examples along these lines, but rest assured there were others too—other vendors and other songs. There was a blind man who sold grass jelly and dried figs in the centre of the city. There was an old woman who made brushes with bamboo handles for a living, and whose cry, we are told, was 'soft and plaintive' (*Ban chai khong?*). And there was a letter-writer, a public scribe, who carried around a bilingual dictionary and an old Adler typewriter in its original case. But no matter how hard Guéry tried, he was simply incapable of decoding these songs. In fact, even their literal meaning could sometimes be elusive, and he would need to see the merchandise itself (what a linguist would call the 'referent') before he was able to make sense of the 'signifier.'

So why, you may wonder, am I telling you all of this? It obviously provides a little bit of local colour, which has been neglected in the narrative thus far; and it is important, at this stage, that the reader should be reminded of the 'strangeness' of the place, particularly from the perspective of someone like Guéry, who had never before travelled so far from the Côte d'Azur. But what I'm really trying to emphasize by mentioning this curious obsession of Guéry's is the fact that he was profoundly ill-suited, in almost every way, for the task that he had set himself. It wasn't entirely beyond the realm of possibility that the Viet Minh were transmitting encoded messages in this manner, but it was highly unlikely. And in any case, even if they were employing the street vendors to convey such messages, this clearly had nothing to do with the investigation that Guéry himself was conducting. So why would he bother pursuing a lead like this in the first place, and in such minute detail too? It's hard for me to say—it was just the way he saw the world, I suppose. He always found it difficult to distinguish between things that mattered and things that were of no significance whatsoever: background noise, filler, fripperies of one kind or another. And yet the irony, of course, is that he did eventually solve the case—he did eventually find out what happened to his brother, Olivier Guéry—despite his dilatory or 'digressive' tendencies, despite the fact that he was constantly distracted by matters of little or no relevance to the investigation itself. Somehow, despite all of this, he still managed to succeed where we, the police, had failed; and as you can see from the notes I have summarized here, it was really quite remarkable that he should have done so.

Chapter 10

Le Roi Jean

Three days later, as a consequence of a clerical error by one of the secretaries at the Information Service, Guéry was invited to attend a cocktail party at the residence of the high commissioner, General Jean de Lattre de Tassigny. The reception was being held to celebrate General de Lattre's recent victory in the Battle of Mao Khe, and it was going to be a very exclusive affair—the kind of event that the *Journal* would describe as a 'glittering occasion.' Only the most important civil and military figures in Saigon had been invited, so whoever was responsible for including a personage of Jean-Luc Guéry's stature on the guest list had obviously made a grievous mistake. For some reason, though, Guéry took his invitation at face value, and at the appointed hour, suitably attired, covered in eau de cologne and with his hair plastered to his head, he presented himself at the general's residence on boulevard Norodom.

Guéry was careful to arrive at 6.45 precisely, as specified by the invitation, and after identifying himself to the guard at the gate, he was led along a gravel pathway to the residence itself. The Hôtel du Général, as it is known, is a rather imposing two-storey structure built in the classic colonial style (stucco balustrades, louvred shutters, geometric tiling, etc.). Once inside, Guéry was ushered into a large, rectangular room with high ceilings and arched windows. A decorative screen covered in Chinese dynastic imagery stood in one corner, and on the other side of the room, a small band was playing unobtrusively. The room was already quite crowded, and when a waiter arrived with champagne, Campari, and various liqueurs, Guéry had to repeat his order three times before it was understood. The general had yet to make an appearance, so Guéry wandered aimlessly for a while, drifting here and there as if he actually belonged at such a rarefied gathering. Whenever a waiter appeared, he would take another glass of champagne or one of the liqueurs, and before long he was beginning to feel a strange enthusiasm for the proceedings. Yes, by God, he did belong here, among all these dignitaries and socialites; he wouldn't have been invited otherwise, would he? And it was this growing sense of conviviality that led Guéry to strike up a conversation with a man who was standing by the folding screen in the corner, scrutinizing one of its lacquered panels.

'It's beautiful, isn't it?'

The man turned to face Guéry. He was extremely thin, almost malnourished, and he was wearing a suit made of blue serge, which hung loosely on his emaciated frame.

'Indeed,' he said. 'I was just admiring this scene.' He gestured toward an imperial palace that had been depicted from above, slightly flattened and at an oblique angle. 'They seem to be celebrating something. The guests are walking across this footbridge, and the emperor himself is sitting in this central pavilion, being entertained by musicians and dancers.

The courtiers are all gathered around him, as if they are too scared to do anything else, and these dignitaries here are waiting patiently for their chance to pay homage.' He smiled. 'How charming it all is, and how appropriate too.'

After disposing of the usual formalities, Guéry learned that his interlocutor was a correspondent for *Life* magazine, and that he had just returned from Hanoi, where he had dined with General de Lattre on more than one occasion.

Guéry explained that he was representing a newspaper by the name of *Le Journal d'Antibes*; and when he did so, the man asked him if he knew Lucien Bodard and Jean Lartéguy.

'Only as respected colleagues,' he replied. 'As *frères d'armes*, one might say.'

'That's wonderful,' the man exclaimed, 'because they're right over there.'

Looking furtively over his shoulder, Guéry discovered, to his horror, that the celebrated war correspondents were standing only a few metres away.

'Shall I call them over?'

'No, no, no,' Guéry said as breezily as he could. 'The night is young. I'll catch up with them later.'

Before his new acquaintance could say anything, they were joined by a third man, who introduced himself as Monsieur Maurice Loubière.

Once again, they exchanged idle pleasantries, and Guéry learned that Monsieur Loubière was the general manager of a local aviation company, Comptoirs Saigonnais de Ravitaillements (COSARA). He had come to Indochina in 1929 to do his national service and, after mastering Vietnamese, had decided to stay for good. During the war, he had established a company that sold food and supplies to the armed forces, and that was when he had realized just how difficult it was to transport freight in a country with such limited infrastructure. So in 1947, along with a Vietnamese business partner, he had established COSARA, a company whose fleet now included five Bretagnes, four DC-3s, and a couple of Junkers.

The mention of the DC-3s reminded Guéry of the young journalist who had died the year before in mysterious circumstances.

'Have you heard of Hugo Lefèvre by any chance?' he asked.

Monsieur Loubière considered this question for some time before responding. 'No,' he said finally, 'I don't believe so.'

'He was a journalist who came out here last year to investigate the trafficking of piastres. He was returning to Paris on a DC-4 when it crashed into the Persian Gulf, near Bahrain. There were no survivors and his body was never found. Someone suggested the other day that Pierre Vitelli, the proprietor of the Hotel Continental, may have had something to do with this disaster.'

'Really? Why?'

'Lefèvre had accused him of being involved in the piastre trade—and I suppose, by implication, the drug trade too. In the weeks before he left Saigon, Lefèvre sent a number of telegrams to his editor in Paris saying that he feared for his life.'

'Did he provide any specific names?'

'No. I believe he only referred to the *clan des insulaires*— the Unione Corse. But it obviously had something to do with Vitelli.'

'I would be very careful about drawing such conclusions, Monsieur Guéry. Particularly in a place like this, where you can be so easily overheard.'

'Indeed.' This was the correspondent for *Life* magazine, who had been listening silently thus far. 'And I certainly wouldn't put a question like that to Colonel Savani.'

'Colonel Savani?'

'The local director of the Deuxième Bureau. He's another Corsican, like Vitelli, and he's standing over there by the flag.'

Guéry felt his conviviality suddenly depreciate by a couple of degrees.

On the other side of the room, he could see a man with a long, angular face and slightly tinted glasses. This was Colonel Antoine Savani.

'He first came out to Indochina in the late thirties,' Monsieur Loubière said, 'and then again after the war. No one really knows what he did during the war itself, but he's been the director of the Bureau since 1948.'

'And he knows Vitelli?'

'Undoubtedly, Monsieur. As our friend says, they're both Corsican, and they both have strong ties to Marseille. Like Vitelli, Savani is also married to a Vietnamese woman, and he speaks the language fluently. Perhaps that's why his negotiations with the Binh Xuyen were such a great success.'

It was clear that Loubière was speaking euphemistically.

'What was the nature of these negotiations?' Guéry asked.

'Savani managed to convince the Binh Xuyen to shift their allegiance from the DRV to the emperor—in exchange for certain privileges, of course—and they've been surprisingly reliable allies ever since. He works very closely with another French officer, a man by the name of Roger Trinquier. They both graduated from Saint-Cyr in the same year, and they're both actively involved in the counterinsurgency programme.'

'I see.'

Perhaps unwisely, Guéry was about to ask Monsieur Loubière to elaborate, when another two guests joined their circle. These new arrivals introduced themselves as Mademoiselle Yvette Giraud, a visiting singer, and Monsieur René Branellec, the editor in chief of Radio France-Asie. Mademoiselle Giraud had come all the way from Paris, they were told, to appear on a radio programme that was recorded live every Sunday evening in the theatre of the Hotel Majestic. The programme itself was called *Recreation*, and it was designed to entertain the soldiers of the Expeditionary Corps.

'A worthy enterprise,' Monsieur Loubière said, 'if ever there was one.'

The correspondent for *Life* magazine agreed (as did Guéry); and for some time, they exchanged more pleasantries along these lines.

As far as Guéry could tell, this largely involved discussing the private lives of the other guests at the party. There was a Monsieur Guy Fourès, for instance, who had made a fortune trading rice in Cholon and then squandered it all on the horses. There was a Madame Jacqueline Armand, whose lover was a lieutenant in the army, and when he was transferred to Saigon, she had enlisted in the PFAT, a female auxiliary unit, just to make sure that he didn't get into any trouble. And there was even a story about General de Lattre himself. Apparently, his son had been having an affair with a Vietnamese woman who was a former mistress of the emperor; and that was why his father had arranged for him to be transferred, just recently, to the 1st Bataillon de Marche du Régiment des Chasseurs. But of course this was little more than hearsay, and one couldn't possibly hope to verify such stories.

There was one story in particular, though, that Guéry found quite troubling—and entirely plausible. It concerned a man by the name of Paul Gannay, who had served as the inspector general of the Banque de l'Indochine for many years. (If you look at any piastre note, from one to five hundred, you'll find his signature right there, on the left-hand side, guaranteeing its status as legal tender.) According to Monsieur Branellec, Gannay had recently undergone a rather traumatic experience.

'In his capacity as inspector general,' the editor said, 'he had taken it upon himself to investigate the illegal trade in piastres; and he was especially interested in the foreign exchange office on rue Guynemer, which is where many of the irregularities seemed to be occurring. Not long after he began making these enquiries, however, his valet, a handsome young Vietnamese boy, was kidnapped, along with one of his most prized possessions: a late nineteenth-century reproduction of the Apollo Belvedere. As you may have surmised, Monsieur Gannay is one of those people who are given to practising the Grecian vice. And this has been common knowledge around here for many years. So he was particularly devastated to lose the young man in question— along with his statue of Apollo. We were never told precisely what the kidnappers' demands were, but after a protracted series of negotiations, Gannay managed to recover his young employee and his precious *objet d'art*. Everything returned to the way it had been before, with only one crucial difference. From that day on, Monsieur Gannay lost all interest in the illegal piastre trade, preferring to occupy himself with amateur archaeology and cocktail parties such as this one.'

Everyone else found this story highly amusing, but for Guéry it was quite the opposite. Not only did it remind him of Olivier's fate, but it also made him contemplate, very seriously, the danger that he himself was facing. After all, if the inspector general of the Banque de l'Indochine was not safe from gangsters of one kind or another, then what chance did he have of making it out of Saigon alive? Even the residence of the high commissioner was full of potential enemies, of people like Antoine Savani, who would think nothing of putting a bullet in his head and dumping him in the Arroyo Chinois. The very thought made him give an involuntary shudder, as if he had just ingested some disgusting foreign delicacy. And so he did what he always did under such difficult circumstances: he made sure that things got even worse.

When I talked to him about it a couple of weeks later, Guéry's memory of the rest of the evening was somewhat hazy. He could remember drinking a series of sugary liqueurs and countless glasses of champagne. He could remember discussing Napoleon's victory at Austerlitz with Monsieur Nguyen Huu Tri, the minister of defence. He could remember tearing his cigarettes in half in order to make them last longer. He could remember trying to find the correspondent for *Life* magazine and being told, by Yvette Giraud, that he had already left the party. He could remember accidentally spilling a glass of Chartreuse on General René Cogny, the chief of staff for the high commissioner. He could remember telling a member of the band that his piano was incorrectly tuned. He could remember offering his professional services to Messieurs Jules Haag and Pierre-Jean Laspeyres, the publishers of *Le Journal d'Extrême-Orient*. He could remember laughing so uproariously that he almost fell over. He could remember requesting that the band play 'Monk's Mood' and being told that it was not in their repertoire. He could remember admiring a pair of spectator shoes worn by Monsieur Hoang Cao Tang, the director of Vietnamese programming at Radio France-Asie. He could remember hearing a female voice say, '*Il a l'air d'un déterré*,' and he could remember feeling certain that it was he, Jean-Luc Guéry, who looked as if he had just been dug up from a grave. He could remember dropping his cigarette and burning a large hole in the upholstery of a Second Empire chaise longue. He could remember running into his nemesis, Monsieur Auteuil, the junior officer from the Information Service on rue Lagrandière, who graciously explained that his *carte de presse* was still not ready. He could remember proposing a toast to Admiral Paul Ortoli and being told that the recipient of his toast was in fact a man by the name of Jean Aurillac. He could remember feeling a sudden longing for Antibes and the Plage des Ondes. He could remember running out of cigarettes and being obliged to cadge one from Monsieur Jean Letourneau, the minister of overseas territories. He could remember gazing for some time at the picture of the imperial palace on the folding screen in the corner. He could remember discussing the notion of eternal recurrence with Professor Vien Phuoc, an emeritus professor of moral sciences at the Sun Yat-Sen University. He could remember asking a young lady to dance and being told that it was not that kind of party. But all of this was nothing compared to the indignity and humiliation of what was still to come. And life being what it is, he would remember the following scene with a kind of preternatural clarity for the rest of his days.

Guéry was wandering around trying to find a waiter when the band began to play the first few notes of the 'Marseillaise.' This was the sign that the general himself had finally arrived; and as ever, he made a dramatic entrance. Everyone stopped what they were doing and turned to applaud the hero of Mao Khe, his wife, and their entourage. The applause was loud and enthusiastic. It was the beginning of what would come to be known as *l'année de Lattre*, and the general was the most popular man in the country. In December 1950, de Lattre had been appointed high commissioner for Indochina and commander in chief of the French forces in the Far East, thus combining for the first time these two different roles. Over the following year, he won a series of major victories in the north of the country and managed to prevent the fall of Hanoi; but he also lost his only son, Bernard, who was killed at the age of twenty-three in the Battle of the Day River. And then, in January 1952, having fallen ill and returned to Paris for surgery, the general himself would die of bone cancer. On the day of the reception, though, all of this misfortune still lay in the future, and de Lattre was simply enjoying the adulation of the various dignitaries who had come to celebrate his latest victory.

Needless to say, Guéry had no intention of introducing himself to the general. Even in his advanced state of conviviality, he realized that such a course of action would be extremely ill-advised. So once the excitement generated by de Lattre's arrival had subsided, he resumed his search for a waiter—having one thing, and one thing only, on his mind. It took a couple of minutes, but eventually he found what he was looking for. In order to reach this elusive figure, however, Guéry was obliged to make his way through a dense crowd of chattering people. And when he finally arrived at his goal, he was so relieved that he immediately lunged for the waiter's silver tray without pausing to take in his surroundings.

'Monsieur,' a voice behind him said, 'I believe it is customary, in such circumstances, to give the ladies precedence.'

Guéry turned to apologize and found himself staring directly into a pair of piercing blue eyes. These eyes were framed by a proud, Gallic face that was instantly recognizable. To his utter dismay, Guéry realized that he was being addressed by the high commissioner himself, General Jean de Lattre de Tassigny.

Graduate of Saint-Cyr, veteran of the Armée d'Afrique, hero of two world wars, General de Lattre was a formidable figure, someone to be taken very seriously indeed. He was famous for his eloquence, his ability to inspire, and his courage on the battlefield. Even while he was out here in the tropics, he was always immaculately dressed and expected the same degree of perfection from his subordinates. On one occasion, so the rumour goes, he fired a stenographer because he disapproved of her clothing and thought her hair was dirty. And when he first arrived in Saigon, he publicly reprimanded the guard of

honour for their slovenly appearance. So one can only imagine
what he made of our old friend Jean-Luc Guéry, who even at
the best of times looked like a recently disinterred vagabond—
and this certainly wasn't the best of times.

'I'm . . . I'm very sorry, General,' Guéry stammered. 'I . . .
I didn't see you there.' He paused for a second. 'Nor you, Madame
de Lattre. Please . . . please accept my deepest apologies.'

'Of course,' Madame de Lattre replied. 'It's very crowded in
here, and it's difficult to see what you're doing.'

At this point, Guéry should really have taken his leave, but he
found it impossible to do so. It was the first time in his life that
he had encountered an historical figure of this stature; and he
was transfixed by the sight of those immortal, aquiline features.
He felt like Bernadette Soubirous on her knees, in ecstasy, before
the apparition of Our Lady of Lourdes. And so, thus immobilized,
he made the fatal mistake of introducing himself.

General de Lattre seemed slightly surprised by this
impertinence. 'Do you live in Saigon, Monsieur Guéry?' he asked.

'No,' Guéry replied, 'I'm only visiting.'

'I see . . . And how long will you be staying here?'

'I'm not sure.'

This was followed by a long silence.

'Are you here on business?' Madame de Lattre
asked eventually.

'Not really—well, yes, I suppose. I'm on assignment here,
representing Le Journal d'Antibes.'

'How interesting.'

There was another long silence, and after a while Guéry
said, 'I should congratulate you, General, on your recent victory.'

De Lattre made a vague gesture with his hand. 'I'm afraid
we still have a long way to go, Monsieur Guéry. But we'll get
there in the end.'

Guéry nodded enthusiastically and then lapsed into silence once more. Out of the corner of his eye, he could see the members of de Lattre's entourage exchanging glances, and the general himself seemed to be studying something just beyond Guéry's left shoulder. But he was still paralysed by the splendour of this messianic figure; and the silence grew longer and longer, like a piece of elastic, until finally he blurted out the first thing that came into his head.

'I wasn't always a journalist, you know. For some time, as a younger man, I wanted to be a writer . . . I even wrote a novel inspired by Gide's *Counterfeiters*, but none of the reputable publishers were interested.'

General de Lattre responded to this confession with a look of profound indifference. 'Really?' he said.

'Yes,' Guéry continued, having already committed himself to this inconceivable folly. 'As a matter of fact, I'm planning on writing another novel when I get back to Antibes. And I've decided that this one is going to be lipogrammatic.'

The word hung in the air like a terrible curse, and suddenly all eyes were on Guéry.

'I don't suppose you're familiar with the term—it's fairly arcane, after all . . . It comes from the Greek adjective *lipogrammatos*, which means "missing a letter." And it's used to describe a piece of writing that deliberately excludes one or more letters.'

This information was received in silence by the general, his wife, and their entourage.

'The Germans say *Leipogram*; the Spanish say *lipogramacia* or *lipograma*; and we say *lipogramme*.'

'If we choose to say it at all, Monsieur Guéry.'

'Quite so, General, quite so. But the practice itself has been around for a very long time, and it can be found in many different cultures. In the second or third century, for instance, Nestor of

Laranda wrote a lipogrammatic *Iliad*, and Tryphiodorus of Sicily did the same thing a hundred years later with the *Odyssey*.'

General de Lattre nodded his head very slowly.

'We find other examples in Spanish literature,' Guéry continued in an increasingly deranged tone. 'Castillo Solórzano's *La Quinta de Laura* includes a story that was written without using the letter Y. In 1640, Francisco de Navarrete y Ribera published a courtly novel, *Los Tres Hermanos*, which doesn't contain the letter A. And around the same time, Lope de Vega wrote five stories— one with no A, and the others missing E, I, O, and U, respectively.'

'Fascinating,' de Lattre said. 'Quite fascinating.'

'For some reason, the Italians seem to have a strong aversion to the letter R. In 1633, Orazio Fidele wrote a poem of two thousand lines without once using this particular letter. Antoine-François Riccoboni did the same thing in one of his later stories. And in 1802, an Italian cleric by the name of Luigi Casolini published a collection of sermons that also avoided using the letter R. Apparently, he had a speech impediment that made it difficult for him to pronounce the R sound, and so he decided that it would be better to eliminate this letter altogether.'

General de Lattre, his wife, and their entourage said nothing.

'As for our own literature, this too provides us with numerous examples. In the early seventeenth century, Salomon Certon published a collection of lipogrammatic verses, each of which suppressed a different letter. Two hundred years later, Joseph Raoul Ronden composed an entire play without using the letter A. And in 1853, having accepted a challenge at a dinner party, Jacques Arago did the same thing with his *Voyage Autour du Monde*—although he later confessed that he accidentally included the word *serait* on page 27.'

Guéry had obviously been researching this subject for some time, and he would have provided many more examples of such writing had General de Lattre not finally run out of patience.

'This is all very edifying, Monsieur Guéry, but I don't really see the point of such an exercise. In fact, I suspect that these works might have been greatly improved if their authors had decided to leave out *all* the letters . . . But that's neither here nor there, and I'm afraid I don't have the time to discuss the matter any further.'

'Yes,' Guéry said, 'yes, of course. I should let you go. I'm sorry that I've detained you for so long. Sometimes, you know, when I'm nervous . . . well, I find myself . . . yes, yes . . . I should really let you go. Sorry.'

General de Lattre and his wife bid Guéry a rather frigid farewell, as if they didn't know quite what to make of this strange bird, this anomalous creature from the Cote d'Azur; then they turned and walked away, surrounded on both sides by their entourage. And this was the last thing that Guéry would remember of the night in question, this image of the general and his wife disappearing into a crowd of laughing, animated people. It is impossible to overstate the catastrophic nature of the encounter I have just described, particularly given the time and place at which it occurred. To be in the presence of General Jean de Lattre de Tassigny, in April of 1951, as he celebrates the successful defence of Haiphong, and find yourself talking about the history of lipogrammatic literature—well, it's difficult to think of a more mortifying experience. But of course Guéry would not understand this until the following morning, when he woke to find himself lying partially naked on the floor of his hotel room. At the time, as the general and his wife receded into the distance, he had other things on his mind, colourful things, syrupy things, things from Armagnac and Calvados and Saint-Barthélemy-d'Anjou—and he was determined to find them as soon as he possibly could.

Chapter 11

The Marbled Ledger

On the day after the disastrous cocktail party at General de Lattre's residence, Guéry did nothing at all. Nothing worth mentioning, at any rate. And the following day was the same. I would later discover that he was, at this time, undergoing what you might call a crisis of confidence. What could he, a mediocre journalist working for an obscure provincial newspaper, hope to achieve here in Saigon? How could he possibly expect to solve the mystery of his brother's murder when even the police had failed to do so? He could fantasize all he liked, but the reality of the situation was that he was wasting his time here, and risking his life too, for no good reason. Everyone he had spoken to was right: this was no place for a man of his dubious qualities, no place for an alcoholic, a gambler, and a failed writer. He should really just go home, back to Antibes, back to his little apartment above the photographic studio on rue des Palmiers, and stop making a fool of himself by acting out these ridiculous fantasies.

As a boy, Guéry had developed an all-consuming enthusiasm for the sport of cycling. Every summer, he would follow the progress of the Tour de France as reported in the yellow pages of *L'Auto*, the daily newspaper whose editor, Henri Desgrange, had founded the race in 1903. Those were the heroic days of cycling, when the riders would almost kill themselves crossing the Pyrenees and would complete every last stage despite suffering the most horrific injuries along the way (fractured collarbones, flayed ribcages, etc.). Guéry was of course fascinated by such heroism; yet even as a child he had found failure and dereliction still more compelling. Every so often, a rider would push himself too hard, particularly in the alpine stages, and he would suffer a complete collapse—both physical and mental—that would oblige him to abandon the race. In the language of cycling, such a crisis was referred to as a *défaillance*, and those who suffered this fate would be formally ejected from the Tour, their failure proclaimed in the following day's *L'Auto* so that the entire country would come to learn of their disgrace. (Such riders, we were told, 'did not have the courage and the energy required to overcome passing *défaillances* and the fatigue inherent to the great road races.') In many ways, as you may have deduced, Guéry's crisis of confidence halfway through his investigation reminded me of the *défaillances* suffered by some of his boyhood heroes. It wasn't just a question of physical debilitation either; it had more to do with a failure of nerve, a loss of morale, and a sudden, overpowering recognition of the futility, the ultimate folly, of all human endeavour—whether it be competing in a cycling race or trying to solve the mystery of your brother's murder.

Altogether, Guéry's *défaillance*, his sudden failure of nerve, lasted for three or four days, during which time he did nothing even remotely productive. He sat by the swimming pool at the Sporting Club for hours, drinking Cinzano and contemplating the shimmering reflection of the water on the underside of the diving board. He wandered aimlessly through the streets of the city. He went to see a performance by Lucienne Boyer at the Municipal Theatre. He bought some overpriced souvenirs at Les Halles Centrales. And I'm told he even looked into the possibility of going to Cap Saint-Jacques for the weekend, despite his long-standing aversion to seafood.

When I read the surveillance reports that were submitted during this period, I actually believed, in my innocence, that Guéry had listened to the advice he had been given and was enjoying a little holiday here in Saigon before taking the plane back to France. But unfortunately this wasn't the case. Just as I was about to reassign the officers who had been keeping him under surveillance, he suddenly decided that it was time to pull himself together and finish what he had started. Aside from everything else, he was beginning to run out of money, having lost so much at the casino, and it was clear that he couldn't sit by the pool forever. If he was going to solve this mystery, he would have to get moving. So yes, after three or four days, to our surprise, Guéry somehow managed to shake off his despondency, and the strange interlude that I've been describing came to an abrupt conclusion.

One morning, he emerged from the Majestic at an uncharacteristically early hour, and instead of making his way, as he usually did, toward the Sporting Club or the Capriccio, he followed the quai Le Myre de Villers along the river until he arrived at rue Pasteur. He then turned left and walked for two or three hundred metres in a northwesterly direction. When he reached the intersection with rue d'Espagne, at the corner of the old Artillery Directorate, he turned right and continued walking until he came to a rather dingy concrete building with steel roller shutters on every window. In some places, these shutters had been opened outward at a forty-five-degree angle, creating little triangles of shade; and on the roofline of the building, where the concrete was particularly dirty, there was a billboard advertising Nationales cigarettes (*Toujours premières!*). It was, as you may have guessed, the location of the Perec Frères offices. After climbing the stairs to the fifth floor and ringing the bell, our 'subject' was ushered inside by a middle-aged Vietnamese woman with pencil lines for eyebrows.

Guéry would later tell me that he hadn't particularly wanted to return to Perec Frères; but at this stage of the investigation, he simply couldn't think of anything else to do—or anywhere else to go. He needed to find out if his brother's company really was involved in the trafficking of piastres and, if so, whose money was being remitted in this way. He also needed to find out, if he could, why Reyes had lied to him and what had really happened to the elusive Jacques Fourier. And the only place he could hope to do any of these things was at the Perec Frères offices on rue d'Espagne.

When he had come to see Reyes the first time, having just arrived in Saigon, he was only made to wait for a couple of minutes. On this occasion, however, almost half an hour elapsed before he was finally shown in to the office that had once belonged to his brother.

'Monsieur Guéry,' Reyes said, rising momentarily from his chair. 'How unexpected. I was under the impression that you had left Saigon some time ago.'

'As you can see, I decided to stay on a little longer. I haven't yet finished what I came to do.'

'I wonder if that was a wise decision, Monsieur.' He gestured toward Guéry's face. 'You've obviously encountered some . . . difficulties.'

'Indeed I have.'

Reyes regarded him impassively through his bifocal glasses. It was clear that he was not going to be as obliging as he had been during their last encounter. Something had changed. He was still polite, but there was an edge to his voice and his grey eyes had lost their affability.

'So what can I do for you, Monsieur Guéry?'

'I'd like to ask you a few more questions about my brother, if you don't mind.'

'Very well. But I should warn you that I have another appointment at ten-thirty.'

'That's fine,' Guéry said. 'This shouldn't take long.' He sat down on the same uncomfortable chair he had used the last time he was there. 'As you know, I've been investigating Olivier's murder, and I've discovered a few things—some peculiarities, some inconsistences—that I'm hoping you can clarify.'

'I'm afraid that's rather unlikely, Monsieur. I've already told you everything I know.'

'Yes, well, I thought I should ask anyway—just on the off-chance.'

Reyes indicated that he should continue.

'When I was last here, you told me that my brother had been gambling rather heavily and that he may have borrowed money from someone to cover his losses.'

'That's what I had heard, yes.'

'You also told me that he had been seeing one of the dance hostesses at the Palais de Jade.'

Reyes nodded.

'And you suggested that either one of these activities may have led, directly or indirectly, to his murder.'

'It was only conjecture. But yes, I may have said such a thing.'

Guéry produced a piece of paper covered in his own distinctive handwriting. 'You said, and I quote: "Once you start frequenting such places, once you start gambling in their casinos and consorting with their dance hostesses, you expose yourself to another way of life. And you can easily run into trouble.'"

'I'm aware of what I said, Monsieur Guéry, and I still believe it to be true. During this period of time, your brother was living rather dangerously.'

Guéry paused for a moment to light a cigarette. He also offered one to Reyes, who declined with a gesture of barely concealed impatience.

'When you told me that Olivier had taken to gambling, I found it difficult to believe. But I accepted it as a possibility. After all, I hadn't seen him for five years, and there was always a chance that he may have abandoned some of his earlier prejudices.'

'Yes, quite.'

'But I managed to find this dance hostess, the one you mentioned, and she told me that she had never once seen Olivier gamble. In fact, she said that he hated gambling. He considered it a waste of money and believed that it was something only stupid people would do.'

'Is that a direct quote, Monsieur, or are you paraphrasing?'

Guéry elected to ignore this. 'I also spoke to a regular at the Grand Monde, and he told me that he had never met anyone by the name of Olivier Guéry.'

'That doesn't mean anything. Your brother may have been using another name.'

'Yes, I considered that possibility. So I showed him a photo of Olivier, and he said that he had never seen him before in his life.'

Reyes shrugged. 'This is just one man, Monsieur Guéry. It's his word against mine.'

'But I talked to other people there too, and they all said the same thing. Olivier had never been to the Grand Monde—or if he had, it was clear that he had never made an appearance at the roulette tables.'

'I stand corrected,' the managing director said with a beleaguered smile.

'And I don't believe his death had anything to do with the hostess at the Palais de Jade either.'

'No? And why not?'

'She didn't even know that Olivier was dead. When he disappeared, she simply assumed that he had grown tired of her or that he had gone back to France. And she was genuinely dismayed when I told her that he had been murdered.'

'So what does that prove?'

'If Olivier had been killed as a consequence of his relationship with the girl, then I imagine she would have known about it. But there was obviously no altercation with anyone at the Palais, and thus no motive for his killing. In short, there was no danger there at all—despite what you told me.'

Reyes shrugged again. 'It was merely conjecture on my part, Monsieur. Nothing more.'

'Perhaps. But then you did say that he had taken to gambling too, and that he had borrowed money to cover his losses.'

'And?'

'And this was also . . . misleading.'

Reyes looked at him for some time before replying. 'Monsieur Guéry,' he said at last, 'are you suggesting that I deliberately lied to you?'

'I'm suggesting that you misled me.'

'And why, pray tell, would I have wanted to do that?'

'Because you wanted to divert my attention from what's really going on here at Perec Frères.'

Reyes laughed. 'I'm afraid that's ridiculous, Monsieur. We've got nothing to hide here. Our business is perfectly legitimate.'

'If that's the case,' Guéry replied, 'then why is your warehouse full of empty crates? Where's the merchandise? Where's all the agricultural machinery?'

Reyes took a cigarette of his own from a silver case and lit it. Then, in a distinctly cold tone of voice, he said, 'Monsieur Guéry, how could you possibly know what we have stored in our warehouse?'

'When I visited the place a few days ago, I happened to notice that the crates were empty.'

'But the crates are all sealed. How could you "notice" that they were empty?'

'I suppose I was curious,' Guéry admitted, 'so I opened a couple. They weren't sealed very tightly.'

'I see. You were *curious*.' Reyes emphasized this last word derisively. 'And so you decided to open a couple of crates.'

Guéry nodded.

'Just like that.'

Guéry nodded again and, despite everything, felt a sudden twinge of shame. It was an emotion that came easily to him, even in circumstances such as these. Even with his brother long dead. Even ten thousand kilometres away from the Côte d'Azur and all his old ignominies.

'So would you mind telling me,' he said, once this feeling had dissipated, 'why there's nothing but empty crates in your warehouse?'

'It's very simple, Monsieur. There's been a delay at the port in Marseille. We've been expecting a shipment for some time now, but it hasn't arrived.'

As he spoke, Reyes was playing with the same cigarette lighter that Guéry had noticed the last time he was there—the IMCO one with the circular lid. It was identical to the lighter that had been found on his brother's body, and the sound it made, as the lid opened and closed, was just as irritating as it had been before.

'Why has the shipment been delayed?' Guéry asked.

'The Confédération Générale du Travail has imposed a boycott on all freighters carrying military supplies to Indochina.'

'But you're not importing military supplies.'

'No,' Reyes said. 'Obviously not. But for some reason the union believes that we are, and we still haven't managed to negotiate the release of our containers.'

'Why haven't you ordered more merchandise, then, and had it shipped from somewhere else?'

'We simply can't afford to. And even if we could, there's really no other viable route. The containers would still have to go through Marseille.'

Guéry thought for a moment. 'But surely you would have stockpiled merchandise to cover contingencies of this kind. Isn't that precisely the point of having a warehouse?'

'The strike has been going on for a long time, I'm afraid. Since October of last year. And our stock has dwindled.'

'Dwindled to nothing?'

'That's right.'

'But the warehouse isn't even empty, Monsieur Reyes. It's the crates themselves that are empty, and that's what I find particularly strange. Why would you maintain a warehouse full of empty crates? It's almost as if you were trying to create the impression that you're still an active company, when that's clearly not the case.'

The managing director tilted his bald head to one side and frowned slightly. 'So what exactly are you suggesting, Monsieur Guéry?'

'When I went to the Sûreté to report the assault I suffered the other night, I spoke to an officer there by the name of

Leclerc. I told him everything that had happened, and I also mentioned the empty crates that I had found in your warehouse. He said that over the last four or five years a number of companies in Saigon have become involved in the trafficking of piastres. Some of these companies bribe the officials at the foreign exchange office in order to secure currency transfers. Others import useless or obsolete merchandise from France, paying for it with BIC piastres. And some companies don't even bother importing anything at all. They simply create false bills of lading that enable them to double their money once the non-existent merchandise is "paid for" in Paris.'

Reyes scrutinized Guéry for a long time without saying a word; and when he finally did reply, his voice was so quiet as to be almost inaudible. 'Monsieur Guéry,' he said, 'are you accusing us of trafficking in piastres?'

At this point, somewhat belatedly, Guéry understood the gravity of what he was doing, because of course the answer was yes—yes, he was accusing them of trafficking in piastres. But if he was right, and Olivier had been killed by someone at Perec Frères, then he was exposing himself to considerable danger by doing so. If they had killed Olivier, their erstwhile colleague, for threatening to reveal what was going on, then they certainly wouldn't hesitate to kill Olivier's degenerate younger brother. Even Guéry could see that he was playing with fire here, but it was too late now to dissemble.

'Yes,' he said rather hesitantly, 'I suppose I am suggesting something along those lines.'

'And you're making this accusation simply because we have some empty crates in our warehouse . . . '

This irritated Guéry, and for a moment he forgot about the danger he was facing. 'No,' he said, 'I'm making this accusation because of all the strange things that have been happening around here, and because this explanation is the only one that makes any sense. It explains why you're taking the trouble to maintain a warehouse full of empty crates. It explains why my brother was shot in the head and dumped in that river over there.' He pointed in the direction of the Arroyo Chinois. 'It explains why my brother's colleague, the one who identified his body, has gone missing. It explains, most probably, why the SDECE are looking for him too. And it also explains why you found it necessary to give me misleading information about Olivier's activities here in Saigon.'

Once Guéry had finished speaking, there was a brief pause. Then suddenly, and quite unexpectedly, Reyes leaned back in his chair and laughed. He seemed genuinely amused by what he had heard.

'Monsieur Guéry,' he said, 'you obviously missed your calling. You should have been a writer of thrillers. Your imagination is so vivid and your sense of intrigue so highly developed—I really do envy you. But unfortunately, in the real world, things are much more prosaic and boring. We're not trafficking in piastres here; we're simply selling agricultural machinery. And as I've already told you, there's a perfectly rational explanation for the fact that our warehouse is empty—one that doesn't involve criminal intrigue or sinister conspiracies.'

'Very well, Monsieur.' Guéry smiled. 'If there's a perfectly rational explanation for everything that's going on here, I'd be interested to know why you have a calendar from 1949 hanging on your wall.'

Reyes swivelled in his chair and looked up at the calendar in question.

'I should congratulate you on your eye for detail,' he said, turning to face his interlocutor once more. 'I believe this is another skill that every writer of thrillers should possess.

But I'm afraid there's nothing sinister about this particular "clue" either. We simply haven't received a calendar from Vendeuvre for two years, and no one has thought to get rid of the old one.'

'But why is it open to July, then, and not December—if what you say is true?'

'Unfortunately, that's a question only your brother could answer, Monsieur. If you remember, this was in fact his office. I was stationed somewhere else until quite recently.'

Guéry nodded and looked around the office. It was just as cluttered and untidy as it had been the last time he was there, and he had to admit that it did look like a functioning workplace—full of catalogues and invoices and overflowing correspondence trays.

'So tell me,' Reyes said, 'what is your theory regarding your brother's murder? Why do you think he was killed?'

Anyone else would have hesitated before answering this question, but not our dissolute friend from Antibes.

'At some point over the last couple of years,' Guéry replied, 'Olivier must have become involved in the trafficking of piastres. I imagine he did so quite willingly, but then for some reason things turned sour. He must have had an altercation with one of his colleagues or with the people who were financing the operation.'

Reyes smiled. 'And you believe that these people, whoever they might be, eventually decided to have him killed.'

'Yes.'

'I'm curious, Monsieur Guéry. Why do you think they would have done so?'

'Most probably because he was threatening to reveal what was going on here.'

This time Reyes laughed. 'But, Monsieur, this is pure fantasy. First of all, as I say, we're most certainly *not* trafficking in piastres. But even if we were, do you really think it would be necessary to maintain that level of secrecy? What you accuse us of doing is actually a fairly common practice in Saigon these days, and I doubt very much that anyone would be killed for threatening to reveal such a thing . . . Not too many people would care, I suspect, one way or the other.'

Guéry studied the end of his cigarette in silence.

'I'm sorry to disappoint you,' Reyes continued, 'but there's really nothing sinister going on here. We have an empty warehouse, it's true, but I've explained why that should be the case. And if you don't believe me, you can always contact the representatives of the CGT in Marseille. They'll verify everything I've told you.'

'And what about this Jacques Fourier? Why has he disappeared?'

Reyes shrugged. 'I've got no idea. He simply didn't turn up for work one day, and we haven't heard from him since.'

'But don't you find it strange that he should have gone missing immediately after Olivier was murdered, and that the SDECE should also have taken an interest in him? Doesn't that strike you as more than just a coincidence?'

Reyes shook his head. 'No, quite frankly, it doesn't.' He paused. 'I fear you are seeing correspondences where there are none, Monsieur Guéry, and that is also typical of someone who cannot properly distinguish between reality and the world of the literary thriller. In reality, things are not always connected, and they don't always carry a deeper significance.'

'No? So why did Fourier disappear immediately after identifying Olivier's body, then? Surely there's a connection there.'

'Not necessarily. He could have disappeared for any number of reasons.'

'And the SDECE?'

'Again, Monsieur, one shouldn't assume that everything is connected. Their interest in Fourier most probably has nothing whatsoever to do with Olivier's case. As you can imagine, the SDECE are very active these days, and they take an interest in many different things.'

At this point, Guéry later told me, he experienced another fleeting crisis of confidence. Everything Reyes had said thus far was entirely plausible. And the story about the containers stranded in Marseille was particularly persuasive. Was it possible that he had got everything wrong? Was he finding clues and uncovering crimes where there were none? Perhaps Reyes was right; perhaps he *was* confusing reality with a thriller or a detective novel. Perhaps he did read too many of those damn things. And perhaps that was why he was turning everything into a Série Noire, complete with mysterious strangers, beautiful dance hostesses, and elaborate conspiracies of one kind or another.

From time to time, over the years, Guéry had experienced the unpleasant sensation of seeing himself as others saw him—from the outside looking in, as it were, quite objectively—and this was one of those times. Without moving from his chair, he found himself exchanging places with Reyes; and when he looked back across the desk at this so-called Jean-Luc Guéry, what he saw was not particularly gratifying. He saw a man rapidly approaching middle age, with too much brilliantine in his hair, half-closed eyes, heavy eyebrows, and a disproportionately large nose. He saw a man wearing a ridiculous cervical collar like some kind of injured dog, with a soiled bandage between his eyes and an angry-looking welt on his left temple. And he also saw a man who was utterly lost in his own fantasies, a man who had been so dissatisfied with his own life, who had failed so many times in so many different ways, that he had finally turned away from reality altogether and instead entered the pages of a thriller, a thriller of his own devising, where every detail carried a deeper significance, where all the gangsters were trying to hide something, where all the women had languid eyes and vertiginous curves (etc., etc.), and where nothing random, nothing absurd or inexplicable, ever occurred, a place where the dead were always avenged, where murderers were always brought to justice, and where investigators such as Maigret or the hero of *Tu Parles d'une Ingénue* were always on hand to provide all the logic and clarity and meaning one could possibly hope for in this world.

What a fool, he thought, what a stupid, misguided, alcoholic fool.

'Monsieur Guéry,' Reyes said, 'I'm afraid I have another appointment in a couple of minutes, so I'm going to have to bring our meeting to a close. I hope you understand.'

'Yes,' Guéry replied, getting to his feet, 'yes, of course.'

Reyes led Guéry through the adjoining office, where his secretary was busy typing a letter, and then along the corridor to the landing. His manner had quite clearly changed over the course of their conversation, and when he bid Guéry farewell, he did so with a smile that could almost be described as amiable.

'Enjoy the rest of your stay,' he said, 'and I hope you have a safe journey back to Antibes. I always did like that part of the country, and Antibes is a beautiful city. Did you know that it was founded by the Greeks, who named it Antipolis, or "opposite city," because of its location on the opposite side of the Var estuary from Nice?'

'Yes, actually, I did . . . '

'Antipolis,' Reyes continued, without acknowledging Guéry's response. 'It's such a strange name for a city. But of course, from our perspective, it couldn't be more appropriate. And it seems to me, Monsieur Guéry, that Antibes is precisely where you belong . . . Not here, where everything is so dirty and dangerous, but back in Antibes, where everything is clean and safe, and you can live the rest of your life in peace.'

It was obvious that Reyes, like almost everybody else in Saigon, had decided that Guéry was not someone to be taken altogether seriously. He was someone to be humoured, someone to tolerate, someone to send to Cap Saint-Jacques for the cool sea breezes and the grilled oysters. And as I've said before, perhaps that was why Guéry was able to get away with some of the things that he did while he was out here—because he was seen by so many people as an absurd figure, as a source of comic relief, like a character that Hergé might have created had he chosen to tell a story along these lines.

After offering Reyes the usual assurances, Guéry turned and made his way slowly down the stairs. It was still only ten-thirty in the morning.

* * *

I imagine that this encounter must have been fairly demoralizing for Guéry, and I would have understood if he had suffered another failure of nerve, another *défaillance*, like the one I described earlier. But as it turned out, he didn't allow Reyes' patronizing attitude to affect his morale; in fact, quite the opposite. It made him even more determined to solve the mystery of his brother's murder, and it also gave him the motivation to do something, a couple of days later, that was rather ill-advised. I would only learn about this misadventure the following morning, when Guéry came to see me in my office at the Sûreté. And when he told me what he had done the night before, I was, quite frankly, horrified. It was an act that required a certain degree of courage, to be sure, but also a great deal of stupidity, as it could easily have cost Guéry his life. But he didn't seem to care—not anymore. He was just happy that he had discovered a good old-fashioned 'clue' and, in so doing, had brought us slightly closer to solving the case.

It was around eleven-thirty on Sunday evening when Guéry left the Hotel Majestic. The officer who had been assigned to keep him under surveillance that night was sound asleep in the hotel foyer (and he would be severely reprimanded the following day for this dereliction of duty). Once Guéry left the Majestic, he walked through the empty streets of the city for about twenty minutes or so. At one point, he was approached by a couple of soldiers who asked to see his identification; and once this had been verified, he was allowed to continue on his way. Eventually, he came to a large concrete building on rue d'Espagne with metal shutters and a billboard on the roof advertising Nationales cigarettes—you know the one.

Guéry was pleased to find that the main entrance to the building was unlocked and that there was no concierge on duty at this late hour. The foyer seemed even more spacious at night, and the wrought-iron elevator cage cast strange elongated shadows on the tessellated floor. After looking around nervously, Guéry made his way up the stairs and along the corridor until he reached the familiar bronze plaque that said *Perec Frères*. Then he kneeled down in front of the door and, using two straightened paper clips and a pair of pliers, began to manipulate the keyhole. This was a technique that he had been taught by one of his more disreputable colleagues on *Le Journal d'Antibes*, but it was the first time that he had been compelled to put it into practice, and it wasn't as easy as one might have expected. In the end, it took Guéry about twenty-five minutes before he heard a faint click and the door to the office slowly swung open. He slipped inside and closed the door behind him. As he was afraid that an electric light might be seen from the outside, filtering through the interstices of the doorway, he took out his cigarette lighter and held it aloft, like an explorer in an ancient temple.

The outer office was exactly as Guéry remembered it to be—sparsely furnished and permeated with a strong leafy smell that he couldn't quite place. He walked over to the desk in the corner and began to examine the various items that had been left there: an Olivetti typewriter, a few inconsequential carbon copies, a magazine called *Modes de Paris*, a small transistor radio, a drawer full of stationery, some hairclips, a hand mirror, and one or two other things of no great significance.

But of course Guéry was more interested in the contents of the inner office, and to his relief, he discovered that Reyes had left it unlocked. Once the door was safely closed, he turned on the overhead light and looked around. Just as it had been a couple of days before, the place was in a state of complete disarray. There were files and invoices and trade catalogues covering every available surface. There was even a fishing rod in one corner, along with an alloy reel and a wooden tray containing several dozen artificial flies. Guéry realized that it wasn't going to be easy to find anything of significance here either; and perhaps that was the reason for the chaos in the first place—perhaps it was some kind of protective measure, a way of concealing what really mattered from prying eyes.

He began by searching through the disorganized piles of paper that had been left on Reyes' desk. As far as he could tell, they all seemed to relate, quite legitimately, to the business of importing and selling agricultural machinery. Then he examined the contents of the two correspondence trays. Everything in there seemed legitimate too, and he was about to turn away, when it suddenly occurred to him to check the date on each of the letters. The first letter, from a company called Société Anonyme des Rizeries Indochinoises, was dated 31 October 1948; the second, from a coffee grower in Dalat by the name of Claude Morère, was dated 6 July 1948; the third, from a rubber company called Plantations des Terres Rouges, was dated 24 February 1949; and so it continued. They were all at least two years old, and every one of them was addressed to Olivier Guéry. He checked the piles of paper on the desk again and discovered the same thing. The casual clutter of the office was obviously deceptive. Everything had been arranged intentionally; and like the calendar on the wall, it all dated back to the late forties.

Guéry felt vindicated by this discovery, but it still wasn't the kind of incriminating evidence he was looking for. It wasn't enough simply to present the police with a few old letters as proof of piastre trafficking. And although it may have confirmed his suspicion that Perec Frères was no longer a legitimate company, he still didn't know who was really running the place.

He walked over to the large grey filing cabinet that stood in the corner of the office, and opened the top drawer. Inside, he found some more old letters, a few obsolete inventories from the warehouse on the quai de Belgique, and a half-empty bottle of Armagnac.

'*Vincit qui se vincit*,' Guéry muttered grimly as he closed the drawer. He conquers who conquers himself.

The middle drawer turned out to contain some of Reyes' personal belongings. There was a degree certificate from the Catholic University of Lyon (Accounting). There was a postcard from one of his female relatives in the Alpes-Maritimes, another from a friend in Tangier, and a third from someone visiting the island of Singapore. There was a Portuguese dictionary with an inscription congratulating him on attaining his baccalaureate. And there were also several photos of Reyes looking younger and happier in various different places. But none of it had anything to do with the trafficking of piastres or with Olivier's murder. He put these things back where he had found them and opened the bottom drawer.

Inside this last drawer, under a pile of old invoices, he found a marbled ledger containing page after page of figures and dates. The most recent entry had been made only three days before. Guéry smiled to himself. He was finally getting somewhere. But of course he still didn't really understand the significance of this discovery. He assumed that each figure represented a sum of money (970,000 piastres, 2,300,000 piastres, 1,600,000 piastres, etc.), but it was impossible to tell whether this money was incoming or outgoing and what its ultimate source, or destination, might have been. Beneath the ledger there was a cardboard portfolio fastened with string. He opened this too and looked inside. It contained several typewritten letters addressed to Reyes, and another twenty or so addressed to Olivier, one of which listed an account number at the Banque de l'Indochine. In addition to these letters, there were also a large number of transfer notes issued by the Office Indochinois des Changes. Guéry selected one at random and checked it against the entry that had been made on the same day in the ledger; they corresponded exactly. So the money was obviously outgoing—it was clearly being remitted to France to pay for non-existent merchandise. But this still didn't tell him where the money was coming from and who was ultimately profiting from these transactions.

He looked again at the letters. In almost every case, they were only two or three lines long, and on the face of it they seemed to be legitimate orders for agricultural machinery. They specified what kind of machinery was required, the date on which the order had been made, and the amount of money the buyer would be depositing into the Banque de l'Indochine. Once this had been done, the money would presumably be transferred to France through the exchange office on rue Guynemer—and in the process, a piastre worth eight and a half francs in Saigon would instantly double in value, giving the company a one hundred per cent return on its 'investment.' It was a profitable enterprise, and certainly far more lucrative than importing and selling agricultural machinery. But who was behind it all? The letters had only been signed with the initials R.T., and there was no other way of discovering the sender's identity. There weren't even any postmarked envelopes that could be traced to a specific location. For a moment, Guéry considered taking everything he had found and presenting it to the authorities; but then he realized that the ledger and the portfolio would soon be missed and this would give Reyes all the time he needed to destroy more incriminating evidence or simply to flee. So instead he made a note of the bank account number on a piece of paper, and also jotted down the five most recent entries in the ledger, along with the serial numbers of the corresponding transfer notes. Hopefully that would suffice.

Just as he was finishing the last of these notes, Guéry heard a sound in the corridor beyond the adjoining office. He quickly replaced the ledger and the portfolio and got to his feet. As he did so, he heard another noise, and this time it was much closer. Someone was opening the door marked *Perec Frères*. Guéry immediately understood that he was trapped; the balustraded windows overlooking rue d'Espagne couldn't be opened, and there was no other way out of the office. With his heart racing, he crouched down beneath the desk and waited.

A short time later, he heard someone open the door and make their way over to the filing cabinet in the corner. Guéry leaned forward slightly and looked up from where he was hiding. A man he had never seen before was standing in front of the filing cabinet, examining the marbled ledger. He couldn't see the man's face from this angle, but it obviously wasn't Reyes. It must have been one of his employees. After a moment or two, he put the ledger back where it belonged and closed the drawer. Then he opened the top drawer of the filing cabinet and poured himself a large glass of Armagnac. Having done this, he turned and walked over to the desk, and for the first time Guéry was able to see his face. It was none other than His Serene Highness, Rainier III, the Sovereign Prince of Monaco. Or at least it was someone who resembled the prince in almost every particular—including the high, aristocratic forehead and the neatly bifurcated moustache.

Guéry retreated as far as possible beneath Reyes' desk and watched as the lower half of Rainier's legs came to a halt directly in front of him. A moment later, His Serene Highness picked up the telephone and dialled a number.

'Yes, hello,' he said. 'It's me. I've just checked, and I can confirm that the transfer was made three days ago.'

There was a pause.

'No, there were no difficulties whatsoever. It would have been received in Paris on Friday.'

Another pause, longer this time.

'That's right. You can tell Trinquier that the merchandise has been ordered and paid for in full.'

More silence.

'Okay . . . okay, goodbye.'

After replacing the receiver, Rainier sat down in Reyes' chair to finish his Armagnac. And it soon became clear that he was in no hurry to do so. He lit a cigarette and leaned back to contemplate the ceiling.

Guéry had found himself in many undignified situations over the years, but none of them quite compared to the one he was obliged to endure for the next twenty minutes.

He spent this time staring at Prince Rainier III's immaculately maintained brogues and wondering if they might belong to the man who had killed his brother. Every so often, Rainier would shift in his chair, and Guéry would be convinced that he was about to be discovered. His Serene Highness had only to stretch his legs out in one particular direction and he would immediately come into contact with something soft and pliable and greasy. Then, having discovered the intruder, he would no doubt pull Guéry from his hiding place and subject him to a long and brutal interrogation. What was he doing there? What, if anything, had he seen or heard? Who was he working for? Etc., etc. Once it became apparent that Guéry knew exactly what was going on at Perec Frères, his fate would be sealed. Rainier would take him down into the basement (if there was one) and force him to his knees on the dirty concrete floor. Then he would produce his Luger, the very gun that had dispatched Olivier into eternity. He would put it to Guéry's head—in the same place, just above the left eye— and after uttering something suitably disparaging, something about amateurs or dilettantes, he would pull the trigger, and that would be the end of the story. No more *femmes fatales*, no more mysterious strangers, and no more sinister conspiracies. It struck Guéry as a particularly absurd and disagreeable way to die, being shot in the head by a scion of the House of Grimaldi, but in his case perhaps it was only appropriate—a fitting conclusion to a life that had been filled with so much else that was equally absurd and disagreeable.

To Guéry's surprise, however, none of the above actually happened.

After twenty minutes or so, Rainier simply rose from his chair, put the empty glass back on top of the filing cabinet where he had found it, and left the office.

Guéry slowly exhaled and got to his feet. After waiting for another ten minutes, he too left the office, making his way cautiously out onto the landing and down the stairs.

According to the surveillance report I have just finished reading, Guéry arrived back at the Majestic at 2.36 in the morning. The reason we know this is because he was in such an agitated state that he managed to get himself tangled up in the hotel's revolving doors and had to be released by one of the night porters. This commotion in turn woke my colleague, who made a note of the time and described Guéry as looking 'visibly perturbed.'

I can imagine his furrowed brow, dishevelled hair, and deranged eyes without too much difficulty because this is precisely how he looked when he came to see me the following morning.

Chapter 12

Some Answers

It was a little after nine, and I had only just arrived at the office myself, when Guéry made his appearance. He was still 'visibly perturbed,' and it was clear that he hadn't slept much the night before. Once he had managed to settle into a chair and light a cigarette, he proceeded to tell me everything that had happened over the last couple of days—concluding with an account of his strange adventure at Perec Frères.

My first reaction was one of unadulterated horror. 'Monsieur Guéry,' I said, 'you do realize that breaking and entering is a crime.'

'Of course,' he replied. 'But I didn't really have a choice. I had to do it.'

'Is that so, Monsieur? And did you find anything there to justify your actions?'

'Yes, as a matter of fact, I did.' He took a dog-eared piece of paper from his pocket and gave it to me. 'I found a ledger in Reyes' office containing a record of all the currency transfers they have made over the last few years. Those are the figures and dates right there.' He pointed to the piece of paper. 'I wrote down the last five. I also found some letters from an unknown source arranging for the transfers to be made.'

'And what did these letters say, exactly?'

'They were orders for various pieces of agricultural machinery. Apparently, the buyer would deposit a sum of money into an account at the Banque de l'Indochine; and then Perec Frères would transfer this money to France, where the equipment would, in principle, be purchased.'

'I see.'

'Needless to say, this strikes me as a rather odd way of doing business.'

I shrugged. 'It may be strange, Monsieur, but that doesn't make it illegal . . . Were these letters not signed?'

'Only with the initials R.T.,' Guéry said, 'and there was no letterhead either.'

I nodded my head slowly.

'As you can see, the most recent entry in the ledger was made several days ago. They transferred nine hundred and seventy thousand piastres to Paris. You can find the serial number of the transfer note there too.'

Again he gestured toward the piece of paper I was holding.

'How interesting,' I said, doing my best to decipher the hieroglyphics I had before me.

'All of which proves that they're still conducting business here in Saigon.'

'Apparently so.'

'And yet their warehouse is empty. When I asked Reyes about this, he said that they had been expecting a shipment for some time, but it had been delayed by a CGT boycott in Marseille.' He paused dramatically. 'So tell me, Inspector, how can they continue to do business here when there's no merchandise to be sold?'

I conceded that this was a difficult question to answer.

'And when I checked the other documents in Reyes' office, they turned out to be at least two years old. They had been deliberately left out on display in order to make the company look legitimate, when in fact it only has one customer—whoever wrote those letters—and a warehouse full of empty crates.'

Despite everything, I had to admit that Guéry was making a compelling case.

'And you say that you overheard a telephone conversation while you were there?'

'That's right. I was in Reyes' office when someone came in to use the phone. It was a man who looked a lot like Prince Rainier.'

At first, I thought I had misheard him. 'I beg your pardon, Monsieur? Who did you say he looked like?'

'Like Rainier III.'

'The Prince of Monaco?'

Guéry nodded.

'The only son of Count Pierre de Polignac?'

'The very same.'

'But it wasn't him . . . '

'No, it was just someone who looked a lot like him. Same forehead, same moustache, same hair.'

'So,' I said after a rather long pause, 'this person, the one who resembled Prince Rainier, did he mention anything of interest while he was on the phone?'

'To be honest, I'm not really sure. He was confirming that the currency transfer had taken place three days before—the transfer to Paris. He said that the person he was speaking to should tell Trinquier that the merchandise had been ordered and paid for in full.'

This startled me. 'I'm sorry, did you say Trinquier?'

'Yes, that was the name. I heard it quite clearly.'

I flatter myself that I am a good judge of character. I tell myself that this is an important part of my job—the ability to take a person's measure quickly and accurately. And as you know, I had long since dismissed Guéry as something of a comedic figure. But at that moment, for the first time, I was forced to revise my opinion of the man. Of course, he was still an absurd character in many ways. He was still a failed writer, a compulsive gambler, a chronic alcoholic, and an avid collector of colourful phobias and neuroses. But as soon as he mentioned the name Trinquier, it suddenly became clear to me that he wasn't *only* those things. There was, I realized, a lot more to Jean-Luc Guéry than met the eye—which was probably just as well, given his rather unprepossessing appearance.

'Is this the bank account number here?'

I touched the piece of paper with my finger.

'Yes,' Guéry replied, 'that's it.'

'And you're sure that you heard the name Trinquier?'

'Yes,' he said, 'quite sure.'

'Very well. Please excuse me for a moment, Monsieur.'

I picked up the phone and dialled a number that I had long since memorized. After ringing two or three times, it was answered by a man with a refined, slightly feminine voice.

'Monsieur Édouard,' I said, 'it's Inspector Leclerc here. I need you to do something for me, please.'

'Yes, Inspector?'

'I need you to find out who this bank account belongs to.'

I gave him the number.

'Just a minute.'

While I was waiting, I looked over at the poor dishevelled figure sitting across the desk from me.

'Monsieur Guéry,' I said, 'would you care for a glass of water?'

He raised his bloodshot eyes. 'No, thank you. I'm fine.'

This obviously wasn't the case, but I smiled anyway and turned my attention to the page of figures and dates that he had given me. It was, I thought, the diplomatic thing to do.

'Inspector Leclerc, are you there?'

It was Édouard.

'Yes, go ahead.'

'I've got what you need. The account is registered to a company by the name of Perec Frères.'

'Yes, I imagined it would be. And do you have a list of recent transactions there?'

'I do.'

'Could you tell me if the company happened to make a withdrawal four days ago?'

'Yes,' Édouard confirmed, 'they did.'

'Of nine hundred and seventy thousand piastres?'

'Exactly.'

'And when was this money deposited?'

There was a pause.

'The day before. On the third of May.'

'I see . . . Could you tell me who deposited the money?'

Another pause.

'It was deposited by a company called Rizerie Franco-Indochinoise. Apparently, they're based in Haiphong, on rue de Nantes.'

'Are you familiar with this company, Monsieur Édouard?'

'No,' he replied, 'it's a name I haven't heard before.'

'Could you please check the last five deposits. Were they all made by the same company?'

This time there was a longer pause, and I could hear the sound of papers being shuffled.

'Yes,' Édouard said finally, 'the only deposits that I can see here were all made by the Rizerie Franco-Indochinoise. And in every case, the money was withdrawn by the beneficiary the following morning.'

I thanked Édouard and replaced the receiver.

'Well, Monsieur Guéry,' I said, 'this is all very intriguing. The account is officially registered under the name of Perec Frères, and all of the deposits were made by a company called Rizerie Franco-Indochinoise.'

'I've never heard of it.'

'Nor have I, and nor has my contact at the Banque de l'Indochine.'

'And what about Trinquier?' Guéry asked. 'Do you know anyone by that name, Inspector?'

'Yes, as it happens, I do. And if I'm right about this, it would certainly explain a few things.'

'So who is he?'

I lit a cigarette of my own—the first one of the day—before answering. 'Do you remember you asked me about the SDECE the last time you were here?'

Guéry nodded.

'And I told you about the volunteers they're recruiting from the hill tribes, mostly T'ai and Meo, to fight on our side.'

'Yes,' he said, 'I remember.'

'Well, Major Roger Trinquier is the commanding officer in charge of that operation. He's responsible for recruiting these volunteers and overseeing their training at Cap Saint-Jacques.'

This time it was Guéry who looked startled. 'Are you suggesting that the SDECE are the ones who are ultimately running Perec Frères?'

'Not the SDECE as a whole, but perhaps a small part of that organization.'

'The section commanded by Trinquier . . . '

'Precisely. The SDECE is actually composed of four different services: intelligence, decoding, counterespionage, and paramilitary. Trinquier's unit belongs to the last of these, and reports directly to the high command of the Expeditionary Corps. It's called the Groupement de Commandos Mixtes Aéroportés—the GCMA.'

'And they're responsible for recruiting and training these supplementary forces?'

'That's right.'

He thought for a moment. 'But why would a government agency need this kind of money? It doesn't make sense.'

I smiled. 'I'm afraid it does, Monsieur Guéry. It makes perfect sense. The success of Trinquier's operation depends on his ability to recruit volunteers from the hill tribes. But of course one must pay a price for such loyalty. These people don't fight for nothing.'

'So they're essentially mercenaries.'

'Essentially, yes.'

'But wouldn't the government pay for their services and their training?'

'Not anymore, Monsieur. It's proving to be an expensive war, and once the government has paid for everything else, there's very little left over for programmes of this kind. Nowadays, I believe Trinquier has to get his money from other sources.'

'So he's trafficking in piastres . . . '

'I can't be sure, but it's beginning to look as if that might be the case.'

Guéry leaned back in his chair and stared up at the ceiling for a long time. Then he suddenly lowered his gaze and said, 'So that would explain who assaulted me in the alleyway. The SDECE wanted me to stop investigating the case—to leave Saigon before I found out what was going on at Perec Frères—so they delivered that "warning." And then, once it became clear that I wasn't planning to leave, they decided to search my room at the Majestic to see if I had discovered anything incriminating.'

I nodded. 'Most probably.'

'And that would also explain why the SDECE were looking for Fourier—because they were ultimately his employers . . . They were simply looking for an employee who had gone missing.'

'Yes, Monsieur.'

'So if all of this is true,' Guéry concluded, raising his voice to emphasize the point, 'then it must surely have been the SDECE who killed Olivier. It couldn't have been anyone else.'

This was going too far, and I felt obliged to say so. I told Guéry that even if the SDECE were behind the operation at Perec Frères, it didn't necessarily mean that they had murdered his brother.

'But it does give them a strong motive,' he insisted.

'Does it really? And what might that motive be?'

'Perhaps he was threatening to reveal their involvement in the piastre trade, so they decided that he had to be silenced.'

'Perhaps,' I replied. 'But as you know, the trafficking of piastres is a fairly common practice these days, and I'm not sure that they would find it necessary to kill someone for this reason alone.'

'They did say that they were going to kill me if I didn't go back to France.'

'They may well have *said* this, Monsieur. But the deadline they gave you expired some time ago, and you're obviously still alive.'

Guéry agreed, rather reluctantly, that this was true.

'So we shouldn't automatically assume that Trinquier was responsible for your brother's murder. It could easily have been someone else.'

'Maybe so. But there are still some things I don't understand.'

I waited.

'If piastre trafficking is really such a common practice around here, then why are they going to so much trouble to maintain the secrecy of the operation? Why was I assaulted in the alleyway and told to leave? Why was my room searched?'

'I suppose the SDECE is still a government agency, and piastre trafficking is, strictly speaking, illegal. So it's not too surprising that they're being as secretive as possible.'

Guéry seemed unconvinced by this answer. 'You also say that operations of this kind are not being funded by the government . . . '

I nodded.

'If that's the case, then where is Trinquier getting the money to transfer to Paris in the first place?' He looked over at the piece of paper I had before me. 'One and a half million piastres. Two million piastres. Nine hundred and seventy thousand piastres. Where's it all coming from?'

I shrugged my shoulders. 'Your guess is as good as mine, Monsieur. Trinquier is a very resourceful man. I'm sure he has a hand in a great many . . . enterprises.'

'Also illegal?'

'Perhaps. I don't know. It's impossible to say.'

A circling fly landed on one of my files, and Guéry studied it for a moment or two in silence.

'I hope, Monsieur, that all of this satisfies you.'

His eyes suddenly refocused. 'I'm sorry,' he said. 'I don't understand.'

'I hope that you are satisfied with what you have achieved here.'

'To be honest, Inspector, I don't feel that I've achieved anything at all.'

'Nonsense. You have discovered who's really running Perec Frères. You have discovered what they're doing there. And as you say, you have most probably discovered who killed your brother, and why they did so. This is all very impressive—particularly for a novice such as yourself.'

Guéry inclined his head modestly.

'But at this point,' I went on, 'there's really nothing more you can do. So please leave the rest to us. We'll take care of everything.'

'And what do you plan to do about it?' Guéry asked.

'We'll investigate further and, if necessary, try to build a case against Trinquier.'

He gave me an appraising glance, then said, 'But you're not going to, are you?'

'We're not going to what?'

'You're not going to investigate, and you're not going to build a case against Trinquier.'

In retrospect, I obviously should have lied. I should have told Guéry what he wanted to hear. If I had done so, he most probably would have considered the case closed—at least as far as he was concerned. He would have checked out of the Majestic the following day and gone back to his quiet little life in Antibes, satisfied that he had solved the mystery of his brother's murder and brought the perpetrators to justice. But there was something about his innocence, his relentless integrity, that suddenly angered me. I was tired of dealing with this strange and tormented creature who filled my office with the smell of

4711 and filterless Gauloises, who inspired pity and impatience in equal measure, and who seemed always to be standing, like Cavafy, at a slight angle to the universe.

'You're right,' I said, stubbing out my cigarette. 'We're probably not going to investigate any further, and we certainly won't be bringing a case against Trinquier. We're fighting a war here, Monsieur. Nobody cares about piastre trafficking. Nobody cares about empty crates and old trade catalogues and false bills of lading. I'm sorry, but it's true. The only thing they care about is winning this war—and yes, if possible, making a bit of money on the side.'

Guéry seemed rather taken aback by this tirade, and I immediately regretted losing my temper.

In a more reasonable tone of voice, I said, 'Monsieur Guéry, I promise you I'll do my best to find out if Trinquier is actually running Perec Frères, and if this proves to be the case, I'll discuss the matter with my superiors. I imagine it will then be dealt with internally.'

'And if it turns out that he *was* responsible for Olivier's murder, what then?'

'There are mechanisms in place to deal with such eventualities, Monsieur. One way or the other, I promise you the case will be resolved.'

'And Fourier?'

'Yes, we'll try to find him too.'

Guéry turned in his chair and looked out the window, where there was nothing to see but a blank wall and two or three branches of a dying tamarind tree. He was clearly unsatisfied by what I had said, and I could understand why he might have felt that way. After all, this was not how a proper Série Noire was supposed to end; it was all wrong—too premature, too unsatisfying, and far too realistic.

'I realize this is disappointing for you, Monsieur Guéry, but one must be pragmatic. And the reality of the situation is that there's nothing more you can do here. Trinquier is one of ours, so let us deal with him in our own way.'

'And what should *I* do, then?' Guéry asked. 'Go home, back to Antibes, secure in the knowledge that my brother's killer will be brought to justice?'

'Yes,' I said with a thin smile, 'precisely.'

'But it's not going to happen, is it?'

I chose to ignore this. 'Monsieur Guéry, you've achieved a great deal since you've been here, but I'm afraid this is the end of the line. I've been telling you all along that you should go home, and this time I really mean it. To investigate any further would be very dangerous indeed. As I say, we're in the middle of a war here. Have you not noticed the wire netting on the cafés? Have you not heard the grenades detonating all over the city? Have you not seen the artillery fire from the roof terrace of your hotel? This is a war, Monsieur, like any other, and Major Trinquier will do whatever it takes to win it. That's what makes him such a good soldier and such a dangerous adversary.'

For some time, the only sound in the room was the whirring of the electric fan as it swivelled to and fro. Guéry was gazing out the window again; and I was beginning to wonder if there was something happening out there, when he finally broke the silence.

'Very well,' he said, turning to face me once more. 'I'll take your advice, Inspector. I'll go home.'

I looked at him disbelievingly. 'You'll go home . . . '

'That's right. I don't think there's anything else I can do here.'

'And you're satisfied with this outcome?'

He smiled. 'I suppose I'll have to be, won't I?'

'That's a very wise decision, Monsieur. Can we hold on to this?'

I gestured toward the piece of paper he had given me.

'Of course. Please do.'

He thanked me for my time and got up to leave, but just as he was opening the door, something occurred to me.

'Monsieur Guéry,' I said, 'please don't tell anyone else what you have told me here today. If you were to do so, I fear that your life would be in great danger.'

He paused in the doorway. 'Don't worry,' he said. 'I won't tell a soul.'

Then he turned and walked out of my office, and I went back to my coffee and my newspaper, quite convinced that I had finally seen the last of Jean-Luc Guéry.

Chapter 13

The Smell of Fir Trees

Guéry went to bed early that night in order to finish reading *Tu Parles d'une Ingénue*. He was still sure that the book contained some kind of encoded message from his brother, but he was finding it difficult to ascertain precisely what that message might be. The novel's hero, the legendary agent OSS 117, had been asked to recover a stolen file that related in some way to international arms trafficking; but there seemed to be no connection between this case and what was going on at Perec Frères. No matter how closely he scrutinized particular passages or even individual sentences, Guéry could find nothing to distinguish the novel from any other thriller—and certainly nothing that had any bearing on the case that he himself was trying to solve.

He was just coming to the end of Chapter 9 (in which OSS 117 seduces, or is seduced by, an adolescent girl with an 'overflowing sensuality' and 'perverse eyes'), when he heard a knock at the door. He looked at the clock on the bedside table. It was two-thirty in the morning.

After getting out of bed and putting on a pair of trousers, he made his way over to the doorway.

'Who's there?'

Silence.

He tried again, but there was still no reply. So he armed himself with a sommelier knife from the sideboard and cautiously opened the door. Once his eyes had adjusted to the dimly lit corridor, he was astounded to find Weiling, the dance hostess from the Palais de Jade, standing there. It was as if a character from the novel he had just been reading had come to life. She was wearing a tight-fitting *cheongsam* that revealed 'the agreeable lines of her young body,' and there was an orchid made of red crinoline in her hair.

'Monsieur Guéry,' she said, 'I'm sorry to disturb you.'

'Not at all.' He hesitated. 'Please . . . please come in.'

She followed him inside, and they both sat down at the small dining table by the window.

'Can I get you a drink?' Guéry asked, suddenly feeling rather dehydrated himself.

'Yes, please.' Weiling smiled. 'I think I need one.'

With the miniature knife safely concealed in his trousers, Guéry got up and walked over to the sideboard, where there were several half-empty bottles standing on a silver tray.

'Cognac?'

'That would be fine.'

He filled two glasses, one of which he gave to his visitor.

Once he was sitting down again, he asked Weiling how she had managed to find him.

'It wasn't too difficult,' she said. 'I tried the Continental first, then the Grand, and then I came here.'

'And how did you get my room number?'

She smiled once more. 'I told the concierge that you had requested my . . . services.'

'Oh,' Guéry said, 'I see.'

'Yes, he was very obliging.'

Guéry offered her a cigarette, and then lit one for himself.

'Monsieur Guéry, you appear to have injured your face . . . '

'Indeed.' He touched his nose tentatively. 'It actually happened after I came to see you at the Palais. On my way back here, I was assaulted by three men I had never seen before in my life.'

Her 'large, soulful eyes' grew even larger. 'But, Monsieur,' she said, 'that's terrible.'

Guéry gave a stoical shrug. 'It's really nothing. I'm feeling much better already.'

This wasn't strictly true, but it seemed like the right thing to say under the circumstances.

They looked at each other for a moment in silence, then Weiling said, 'Again I must apologize, Monsieur, for disturbing you at this hour.' She glanced over at the unmade bed in the corner. 'I wouldn't have done so if I didn't have something very important to tell you.'

'Yes?'

'Tonight, while I was working, I heard someone mention your name. They said that you were still here in Saigon— still making a nuisance of yourself, still causing trouble. And then they said something I didn't quite understand: *Ça sent le sapin.*'

Guéry felt a sudden pressure at the base of his ribcage. 'That was the phrase they used? They said they could smell a fir tree?'

Weiling nodded. 'I don't know what it means, but it didn't sound very good.'

'No,' Guéry said, 'it's not very good at all. On the contrary, it's bad. Very bad. In the old days, they used to make coffins out of fir trees. So if you can smell a fir tree, it means that someone is going to die soon . . . Was there anything around that actually did smell like a fir tree?'

'No.'

'Perhaps some plywood or a crate of some kind?'

She shook her head.

'No model aeroplanes or Christmas trees?'

She shook her head again, more sadly this time.

'And I don't suppose there was an actual coffin nearby, was there?'

This time she didn't even bother shaking her head. She just looked at him with a mournful expression on her face, as if he were already on his way to the guillotine.

'I didn't think so . . . '

'I'm sorry, Monsieur.'

Someone once said that the prospect of being hanged concentrates the mind wonderfully, but Guéry didn't find this to be the case. He could hear a strange pulsing sound, which appeared to be coming from inside his head; his lungs weren't inflating properly; and his tongue felt as if it had doubled in size.

'So who were these men?' he asked. 'Had you seen them before?'

'They were the same men I saw at the Palais the night you were there. Only, tonight one of them was missing'

'But you still recognized them—they were definitely the same men . . . Big and strong, like Graeco-Roman wrestlers, with cold, unforgiving faces.'

'Yes,' Weiling said uncertainly, 'I suppose so.'

'Do you know who they are?'

'I know that they work for the French intelligence service. That's all.'

He raised his eyebrows. 'And how do you know that?'

'One learns a lot, Monsieur, just by dancing and listening.'

Guéry had a very clear memory of dancing with her that night at the Palais de Jade. He remembered the band playing 'Les Feuilles Mortes.' He remembered saying that it was a beautiful song. He remembered the way her body had moved to the music. He remembered the fact that he had only survived by imitating the other men on the dance floor and by trying to imagine what the ambassador of the Dominican Republic would have done in his place. And he also remembered her suddenly freezing, mid-sentence, and telling him to leave, right away, for his safety and for hers too. Forget about your brother, she had said, forget about his murder. Go home to Antibes. This place is far too dangerous for someone like you. Then she had turned and walked away without a backward glance.

'So when you saw these men, the night I was at the Palais, why were you so concerned? Why did you suddenly ask me to leave?'

'I could tell from the way they were looking at you that there was something wrong. I could tell that you were in trouble.'

'I see. Did you know then that they were working for the intelligence service?'

'Yes.'

'So why didn't you tell me?'

She looked at the Cinzano ashtray on the table in front of her. 'I don't know. I was scared. Scared for myself, scared for you. I thought it would be best for you to leave immediately, and I didn't want to waste time explaining why.'

Guéry nodded slowly. 'And then tonight you saw the same men, only there were two of them this time . . . '

'That's right. They were sitting at one of the tables near the dance floor.'

'You were dancing?'

'No. I was at a nearby table.'

'And you heard them mention my name.'

'Yes.' She tasted her cognac for the first time. 'At least I assumed it was yours. They referred to someone by the name of Guéry.'

'Can you remember anything else they said?'

'No. It was very loud, and I could only hear the odd word or phrase. I heard your name, and then I heard them say that you were still here and that you were still causing trouble.'

'And that they could smell a fir tree . . . '

Weiling looked at him sympathetically. 'That's what it sounded like anyway. I thought I should tell you, so I came here as soon as I could.'

At this point, Guéry remembered the warning I had given him earlier that day as he was leaving my office. As it turned out, I was right: his life *was* in danger. And Weiling's unexpected visit had confirmed several other things too. If the men who had assaulted him in the alleyway really were SDECE agents, then it was clear that the SDECE or one of its subordinate agencies must be behind the operation at Perec Frères. It was also clear that they would do anything to maintain the secrecy of this operation, even if it meant killing someone. And if they were prepared to do so in this particular case, then there was every reason to suspect that they had done the same thing before—by shooting Olivier, for instance, and dumping his body in the Arroyo Chinois.

'But why would these men want to kill you, Monsieur? Does it have something to do with your brother?'

'Yes,' Guéry replied, 'I believe it does. After seeing you at the Palais that night, I went back to Perec Frères, and I discovered that the place is actually being run by the SDECE. They're using it as a front for the trafficking of piastres.'

'Really?' Weiling seemed genuinely surprised. 'And what about Olivier? Was he involved in this too?'

'I'm afraid so. As far as I can tell, it all started in 1949, by which time he had been working there for about two years.'

'So why was he killed, then?'

'He must have had a falling out with his employers, with the SDECE. Perhaps he was threatening to reveal what was going on at Perec Frères, so they decided that he had to be eliminated.'

'And now they're planning to do the same thing to you . . . '

'Yes. They've obviously run out of patience.'

After thinking for a moment, Weiling said, 'So does this mean that you're going to leave Saigon, Monsieur Guéry?'

There was something in her voice, a slight tremor or a note of anxiety, that made him look at her before replying. And as he looked at her, it suddenly occurred to him that he had no idea who she was or where her allegiance actually lay. All he knew was that she worked at the Palais de Jade and that she had once conducted an affair with his brother. So had she really come all this way just to warn him that his life was in danger? Or had someone sent her there—perhaps Reyes or Trinquier himself—to deliver another message, a final warning? A week or so earlier, if you recall, I had told Guéry that Saigon is a city of subterfuge and lies, and that no one in this place can be trusted, not even those who claim to be on your side. As he looked at Weiling (with her curves and her eyes and her agreeable lines), he remembered this advice and wondered what she was really doing in his hotel room at two-thirty in the morning. He was also reminded, at that moment, of everything he had learned over the years about *femmes fatales*: their beauty, their allure, and, above all, of course, their fatality. On the face of it, Weiling seemed to be helping him, but was this actually the case? Was she to be trusted, or was she really working for Trinquier? Had she been sent there, in fact, to kill him, having first discovered everything she could about his investigation? I had also asked him, earlier that day, not to tell anyone what he had found out about Perec Frères; and yet that was precisely what he had just done. He had told this strange woman everything he had discovered about the place, thus demonstrating what a liability he was to the SDECE, and now there was only one thing left for her to do . . .

Guéry fingered the sommelier knife in his pocket, but even as he did so, he realized that it would be of no use to him whatsoever. It was designed for opening bottles of wine, not self-defence, so its folding blade was only about three centimetres long; and if she was really going to kill him, she would most probably use a gun anyway, and he would be dead before he could do anything about it.

He withdrew his hand from his pocket and, feigning nonchalance, lit another cigarette.

'May I ask,' he said, 'why you're helping me? After all, by doing so, you're placing yourself in a great deal of danger.'

'It's really very simple, Monsieur. I don't want to see you get murdered.'

'That may be so, but why risk your life for the sake of a complete stranger?'

'I suppose,' she said, 'I feel sorry for you.'

Guéry wasn't particularly surprised by this response. It wasn't the first time he had been the object of someone's pity.

'And why do you feel sorry for me?'

'Because your brother is dead. Because you're trying to achieve the impossible. And because you obviously don't belong here.'

'I don't belong here?'

'No. You're too nice for a place like this. You don't stand a chance against these people.'

Somehow this was both flattering and insulting at the same time.

'But that can't be the only reason you're helping me,' Guéry said. 'Does it have something to do with Olivier too?'

Weiling's eyes focused on the ashtray once more. 'Perhaps.'

'Are you sorry that he's dead?'

There was a long pause, then she said, 'Yes, I am sorry. I enjoyed our time together. He was always so full of life. He made you feel as if anything was possible.'

Guéry wasn't surprised by this response either. He was only too familiar with his brother's moronic *joie de vivre*, which was generally held to be 'infectious.' For his part, Guéry had always found it rather tiresome, but it was one of the things that people liked most about Olivier, and it had always made him particularly popular with the ladies. They seemed to favour cheerful, enthusiastic, and well-adjusted people.

'Yes,' he said, 'Olivier's *joie de vivre* was certainly very infectious.'

She nodded her head vigorously. 'That's the word for it: *infectious*. Whenever I was with him, whenever we went out together, life always seemed so promising. It was as if we could do anything we wanted, as if the world had been created for our pleasure, and I always felt so young and so free.'

Guéry sighed inwardly. 'So how did you feel when he disappeared?'

'I was very sad. As I said at the Palais, I thought he must have grown tired of me or gone back to France. Either way, it was very . . . disappointing.'

'It surprises me that you never tried to find out what had happened to him—why he had disappeared and where he had gone.'

'But I did, Monsieur. I told you the other night, remember? After a week or so, I went to his apartment to see if he was there, but it was completely empty.'

'That's right. You said they were redecorating.'

Weiling nodded.

'So do you still miss him, then?'

She lifted her eyes suddenly. 'I do. I sometimes think about the little things we did together—going to the Sporting Club on Saturday morning, walking along the quay, shopping at Les Halles. And it makes me feel sad because I'll never be able to do those things with him again.'

'You could always do them with someone else.'

'Yes, but it wouldn't be the same. There's nobody else in the world like your brother.'

To be honest, Guéry found this all a little nauseating, but he could see that she was being quite sincere. She had genuinely loved Olivier, and it was obvious that she was risking her life not for Guéry's sake, but for the sake of his poor dead brother—whose infectious *joie de vivre* now lay buried under two metres of red laterite in the old Catholic cemetery (*Priez pour lui*). It was also clear that she wasn't working for Trinquier, or anyone else for that matter. She had come of her own accord, simply to warn Guéry that his life was in danger. And once he realized this, he felt a sense of relief so great that he immediately forgot all about the knife he was concealing in his trousers.

'Did you ever go out to Cap Saint-Jacques?' he asked.

'I'm sorry?'

'Cap Saint-Jacques. Did you ever go there with Olivier?'

'No—no, I didn't. He always said it was too far to go. The ferry takes hours and hours, and if you travel by car it can be dangerous. Why do you ask?'

'I was just wondering. I'm told it's very pleasant out there, what with the sea breezes and the grilled oysters and everything.'

'Yes,' she said, looking at him rather strangely, 'I believe it is very nice.'

'Perhaps I'll go there one of these days. Before I leave.'

'So when *are* you going to leave, Monsieur Guéry?'

He smiled. 'Not just yet. I still have a few more things to do.'

Weiling stared at him incredulously. 'But, Monsieur, this is madness—after everything I've just told you. You must leave Saigon at once. Tomorrow morning, if possible.'

'That's what everybody keeps saying. I was at the Sûreté this morning, and the officer I spoke to there gave me the same advice. He told me to go home, back to Antibes.'

'So why don't you, Monsieur? It's good advice.'

'I'm very close to solving the case. I just need a couple more days.'

'But you've already discovered what your brother was doing here, and you now know the identity of his killers. Surely the case has been solved.'

'Not quite, I'm afraid. There are still some questions that haven't been answered.'

Weiling frowned. 'Such as?'

'If you remember, there were traces of opiates in Olivier's blood. I need to find out why they were there. I also need to find out what happened to Fourier, Olivier's colleague at Perec Frères. Why did he disappear around the time of the murder? What happened to him, and why is he being pursued by the SDECE? . . . And of course I still don't know exactly why Olivier was murdered. Did he threaten to reveal what was going on at Perec Frères, or did they kill him for some other reason?'

'Are you really prepared to risk your life in order to answer these questions?'

Guéry produced another stoical shrug. 'Yes,' he said, 'I suppose so.'

As I've observed before, the real mystery at the heart of this narrative is why Guéry should have consistently demonstrated such courage while he was here in Saigon—despite everything we know about his character and despite the fact that he had never been especially fond of his brother in the first place. It surprised me more than once, and on this particular occasion I'm sure it must have surprised Weiling too. Not many of the men she had encountered in her life would have responded as Guéry did to the warning she had just delivered. Even the toughest Binh Xuyen gangsters would have taken such a threat very seriously indeed. But not Jean-Luc Guéry. Not this strange, dysfunctional creature from the Côte d'Azur. For some reason, he had decided to solve the mystery of his brother's murder, and he wasn't going anywhere until he had done so.

'I must say this is not a particularly wise decision, Monsieur. But I admire you for making it. You're very brave.'

Guéry raised his hand in a deprecatory gesture. 'It's nothing,' he said. 'I'm only doing what anyone else would do in my place. After all, family is family.'

'Yes,' she replied, 'family is family.'

Guéry asked her if she would like another cognac.

After hesitating for a moment, Weiling nodded her head and smiled. 'Yes, please. That would be nice.'

He walked over to the sideboard to refill their glasses, and as he did so, he glanced at the clock on his bedside table. It was already a quarter past three.

He would later tell me that Weiling stayed there, at the Majestic, for another two hours and that between them they very nearly finished the bottle of cognac they were drinking. In the kind of novel that Guéry liked to read, such an intimate nocturnal encounter would have come to a rather predictable conclusion: the hero of the story would inevitably have seduced (or been seduced by) the beautiful *femme fatale* with the 'agreeable lines' and the 'large, soulful eyes.' But of course this was not one of those novels, and Guéry was not one of those heroes. Quite the opposite, in fact. Although Weiling certainly had what the author of *Tu Parles d'une Ingénue* would call a 'promising anatomy,' Guéry simply couldn't find it within himself to realize that promise. It was all too intimidating for a man who had spent his life reporting on petty crimes and traffic fatalities for *Le Journal d'Antibes*. He had naturally seen beautiful women before, in the cafés and casinos of the Côte d'Azur, but I don't imagine he had ever seen anyone quite like Weiling, and it must have been altogether too much for the poor man. So instead of doing what the ambassador of the Dominican Republic, or OSS 117, or even Olivier would have done in his place, he simply sat there, smoking his cigarettes and drinking his cognac. Needless to say, one shouldn't assume that Weiling would necessarily have been receptive to any advances Guéry might have made, and it would be inappropriate for me to indulge in conjecture of that kind. But I can tell you what *did* happen—and that was practically nothing.

They discussed the case some more; they talked about Olivier; they revisited the subject of Cap Saint-Jacques; and then Weiling left and Guéry went to bed.

Disappointing, really, but what can you do? That was just the way he was, and there's nothing to be gained by pretending otherwise.

Chapter 14

An Unexpected Development

There was obviously a lot happening in Guéry's life at this point in time, and yet for some reason he was still preoccupied with the issue of accreditation. By this stage, it didn't really matter one way or the other whether he had a *carte de presse*. After all, he had already managed to achieve a great deal without one. But even so, he was still bothered by his 'unofficial' status here in Saigon, and it had clearly become a matter of professional honour to secure the same credentials enjoyed by luminaries such as Lucien Bodard and Jean Lartéguy.

Thus, on the morning after Weiling's visit to the Majestic, despite the fact that his life was in danger, despite the fact that the SDECE had decided to 'eliminate' him only the night before, the first thing he did was go directly to the Information Service on rue Lagrandière to enquire about his elusive *carte de presse*.

As ever, he was made to wait for some time before being shown into Auteuil's office—only to find that the latter had once again forgotten who he was.

Guéry reminded him and explained that he was there to collect his card.

'Yes,' Auteuil replied, 'yes, of course. Please take a seat, Monsieur, and I'll find out what has happened to your application.'

He turned in his chair and opened the metal filing cabinet that was standing against the wall to his left.

'Guéry, Guéry, Guéry,' he murmured, sifting through the contents of the middle drawer. 'Ah, here it is.'

He pulled out a thin yellow file and turned to face Guéry once more.

'Let me see.' He opened the file and ran his finger quickly down the first page; then he closed it again and looked up at his visitor. 'I'm afraid, Monsieur, that your card is not yet ready. It may take several more days.'

As we know, Guéry was a man with many imperfections and failings. He was slovenly, indecisive, melancholic, easily offended, secretive, morbid, prone to restlessness and occasional bouts of debilitating nostalgia. But he also had his virtues, and one of these virtues was patience. On this occasion, however, he was simply pushed too far, and something inside his head must finally have given way. (The standard literary image of a floodgate being opened comes to mind here—particularly if one was raised, as I was, on a tributary of the Loire.)

'Monsieur Auteuil,' he said angrily, 'I came to see you on my very first morning in Saigon, and I was informed that it would take several days for my application to be processed. When I returned, however, I was told that it would take another couple of days. You said that you would have heard something by then—either way.'

'Indeed.'

'But now you're telling me that you still haven't heard anything, and that I'll need to wait for yet *another* couple of days. I'm afraid this is simply unacceptable.'

Auteuil gave him a placatory smile. 'I'm very sorry, Monsieur, but these procedures can be rather unpredictable. Although accreditation is usually confirmed within a day or two, it can sometimes take a little longer . . . '

'But this is the third time I've visited your office. It's the third time I've been told to wait for another couple of days. And quite frankly, I'm beginning to suspect that it won't be the last time either.'

'Please, Monsieur. I can assure you that your application is being given serious consideration, and you'll be notified of the outcome in due course.'

'But why is it taking so long?'

Auteuil shrugged. 'I don't know. As I've told you before, these applications are approved or rejected at a higher level. I simply make the submission on your behalf.'

'If I was representing *France-Soir* or *Le Figaro*, do you really think I would have been kept waiting like this?'

Auteuil said nothing.

'Well, do you?'

He looked startled. 'Forgive me, Monsieur. I didn't think you were expecting an answer to that question.'

'Well, the honest answer would be no. If I was representing a major newspaper or magazine, I *wouldn't* still be waiting for accreditation. It's only because I'm representing a newspaper no one has ever heard of that I'm being treated in this derisory manner.'

'Monsieur, I assure you that we have the highest regard for *Le Journal* . . . ' He glanced surreptitiously down at the file: '*Le Journal d'Antibes*. But we're in the middle of a war, and for this reason it may be necessary to prioritize certain newspapers over others.' He paused. 'Is *Le Journal d'Antibes* published on a daily basis?'

'No. It's published twice weekly. On Wednesdays and Saturdays.'

'And what would the circulation be, roughly speaking?'

'About two thousand.'

Auteuil smiled once more. 'Yes, well, I believe *Le Figaro* has a circulation of about two hundred thousand—so you can see the difference.'

'But will my accreditation ever be approved? Will I ever get a card?'

Another bureaucratic shrug. 'I simply can't say, Monsieur. It's not my decision to make.'

'I see.'

'But please do come back in a couple of days, and your card may well be ready.'

'It *may well* be ready?'

'Yes.'

'That doesn't sound very promising.'

'I'm afraid it's the best I can do. As a junior officer, I ultimately have no control over these matters. Your accreditation has to be approved by the director himself.'

'Very well,' Guéry said, rising from his chair. 'Thank you for your time, Monsieur Auteuil. I'll come back again on Friday, and hopefully my card will be waiting for me.'

'Splendid. Please do. And in the meantime, perhaps you might like to spend a few days at Cap Saint-Jacques—if you haven't already.'

Guéry stared at him in disbelief. 'I'm sorry, did you say Cap Saint-Jacques?'

'Yes,' Auteuil replied, 'Cap Saint-Jacques. The swimming is very good out there, you know, and the cool sea breezes are wonderfully refreshing. You'll think you're back in Antibes.'

I suggested earlier that patience was one of Guéry's principal virtues, and this is a good example of what I'm talking about. Any other man would have been tipped over the edge by this final act of condescension, but not Guéry. By now his anger had dissipated, and instead of telling Auteuil what he could do with his Cap Saint-Jacques and his cool sea breezes, he simply smiled and said, 'Thank you for the recommendation, Monsieur. I'll be sure to take your advice.'

The junior officer returned his smile. 'Good, good,' he said cheerfully. 'And don't forget to try the grilled oysters while you're there. I hear they're really quite outstanding.'

* * *

After leaving the Information Service that morning, Guéry should have come straight here to report what Weiling had told him the night before. That would have been the sensible thing to do. But when did Jean-Luc Guéry ever do the sensible thing? I suppose it must have happened from time to time (given the laws of probability), but certainly not on this particular occasion.

Instead of making his way to the Sûreté headquarters, then, he decided to return directly to his hotel. He would later tell me that his encounter with Auteuil had left him feeling rather dispirited, and he simply didn't have the energy to do anything else. Yet even so, having seen what the SDECE had done to his brother (bullet in the head, Arroyo Chinois, etc.), he should have known better than to risk his life in this way. He should have sought our protection immediately, as anyone else would have done under similar circumstances; but all he could think about was the bottle of aspirin capsules standing on his bedside table, the jug of cold water in the refrigerator, and the second-rate thriller he still hadn't finished reading.

With this in mind, Guéry decided to take the shortest possible route back to the Majestic, and that meant braving all the clamour and confusion of Les Halles Centrales. He had just done so, and was making his way down boulevard de la Somme (where the city's scribes and fortune-tellers like to congregate), when he heard someone call his name. He turned around to find a man with a pale, powdery face and an oversized belly standing there. It was, of course, his old friend Bergerac.

'Monsieur Guéry,' he said effusively, 'what a pleasant surprise. I had no idea that you were still here.'

'I keep meaning to leave,' Guéry replied. 'But somehow I never get around to it.'

Bergerac laughed. 'I'm afraid that's a common condition in this part of the world. Everyone's convinced that they're just about to go home, but no one ever does.'

'And what about you, Monsieur Bergerac? Are you planning to leave some day?'

'Me? Good Lord, no. I've resigned myself to this place. I don't think I'd survive anywhere else. And certainly not in France—for one thing, it's far too cold there.'

Guéry smiled.

'I know it's early,' Bergerac said, 'but would you care to join me for a drink? There's a nice place we could go to just down the road.' He gestured in the direction of the quai Le Myre de Villers. 'It's very peaceful at this time of day. One can enjoy an apéritif and watch all the ferries coming and going.'

This was not the kind of offer that Guéry was capable of refusing. 'Of course,' he said. 'With pleasure.'

After setting off together, they walked in silence for a minute or two. Then Bergerac said, 'So what have you been doing this morning? Anything interesting?'

'I've just come from the Information Service. I'm still waiting for my *carte de presse*. They keep promising me that it will be ready in a couple of days, but it never arrives.'

'That's French bureaucracy for you—the single greatest contribution we've made to this country.'

'Yes, but I suspect it's something else too. They're just not taking me seriously.'

'No? And why not?'

'Because I work for a newspaper that no one has ever heard of. Because I'm not Lucien Bodard or Jean Lartéguy.'

Rather judiciously, Bergerac decided to change the subject. 'Tell me,' he said, 'how is your investigation proceeding otherwise? Have you discovered anything of significance?'

Guéry hesitated for a second before replying. 'Well, I have discovered a few things since I last saw you . . . '

'Go on, Monsieur.'

'I've discovered that Perec Frères is being run by the SDECE.'

Bergerac turned to him in surprise. 'Really?' he said. 'So they're the ones who have been using the place as a front for the trafficking of piastres?'

'That's right.'

'But why would they be doing such a thing?'

'The officer I spoke to at the Sûreté told me that they need money to pay their supplementary forces—the men they've been recruiting from the hill tribes.'

Bergerac nodded thoughtfully. 'I see.'

'Apparently, the operation is being run by a Major Trinquier, who's in charge of a small paramilitary unit within the SDECE.'

'And that's who you believe killed your brother?'

'Not Trinquier himself, but certainly one of his men.'

'Why would they have found it necessary to do so?'

'I imagine Olivier was threatening to reveal what was going on at Perec Frères, and he had to be silenced.'

'How scandalous,' Bergerac said. 'If that's true, it's an absolute outrage.'

Guéry agreed.

He then gave his companion a highly selective account of the reception he had attended at General de Lattre's residence—focusing on his encounters with the correspondent for *Life* magazine, the visiting singer, and the editor in chief of Radio France-Asie.

'And what about that Fourier character you mentioned the last time I saw you?' Bergerac asked. 'Have you managed to find him yet?'

'No. Unfortunately, he's disappeared without a trace. And for all I know, he may be dead too.'

'Did you ever finish reading the book you found in his apartment? I've forgotten its title . . . '

'*Tu Parles d'une Ingénue.*'

'Yes, that's the one. Have you finished reading it?'

'Not yet, no.'

'So you still don't know why your brother was carrying the title page when he was killed?'

Guéry shook his head. 'It's a complete mystery.'

'Another one,' Bergerac said with a smile.

'Yes, I'm afraid so. Another one.'

They kept on walking until they reached the end of boulevard de la Somme. Then they crossed over to the quayside and followed the river in a northerly direction. Although it was still relatively early, the quay was crowded with people. There were emaciated coolies loading and unloading different types of cargo, small groups of sailors disembarking for the day, passengers waiting to board the local ferries, and street vendors advertising their wares in loud, adenoidal voices. It was difficult for Guéry to see any of this in detail, of course, but occasionally a figure would appear out of nowhere to offer him a packet of contraband cigarettes or a tray of lychees or some kind of red gelatinous substance that had been cut into squares. Whenever this happened, Bergerac would intervene on his behalf, dismissing the vendor with a wave of his hand, before guiding Guéry on through the crowd.

'So where is this bar we're going to?' he asked after a while.

'It's not too far away. We're almost there.'

Somewhat belatedly, Guéry was beginning to wonder if he should have declined Bergerac's offer. The crowd was growing in density, and he was suddenly aware of just how little he could see. Everything was perfectly clear for a couple of metres in each direction, but then it all dissolved into a blur of shifting shapes and colours—any one of which could have been an SDECE operative.

'I do need to be rather careful in places like this,' he said. 'I've been told that my life may be in danger.'

Bergerac gave him a curious sideways glance. 'I can understand why that might be the case, Monsieur, given the nature of your investigation. But who warned you?'

'The dance hostess who knew my brother came to see me last night. She told me that she had overheard two men from the SDECE discussing the case. They said that I was still making a nuisance of myself, still causing trouble. And then one of the men said that he could smell a fir tree—*ça sent le sapin.*'

'In the figurative sense?'

'Yes, in the figurative sense.'

'And she was sure about this? She definitely heard your name, and she was certain that these men were from the SDECE?'

'Apparently so, yes.'

Bergerac said nothing, and for several minutes they walked on in silence. Then he asked Guéry if he could speak candidly.

'Yes, of course.'

'As far as I can see,' he said, 'your work here in Saigon is done. You've found out who killed your brother, and why they did so. This is quite an achievement for a man of your . . . limited experience. But now, quite sincerely, I think it's time for you to go home.'

'That's what everybody keeps telling me.'

'It's very good advice, Monsieur. You should take it.'

'Perhaps,' Guéry said. 'But I'm not ready to leave just yet. There are still a few outstanding matters that I need to resolve.'

'Despite what you were told last night? Despite the fact that the SDECE have decided to kill you?'

'That's right.'

'Are you absolutely sure?'

'Quite.'

'And I can't persuade you to reconsider . . . '

'No.'

There was another pause.

'In that case,' Bergerac said in a tone of voice he had not used before, 'I'm afraid you leave me with no alternative. I'm going to have to ask you to come with me.'

At that moment, Guéry felt something cold and hard dig into his side.

He stopped walking and looked down at the source of the pressure.

Bergerac, harmless old Bergerac, the procurer of Algerian prostitutes, who powdered his face like Louis XIV and wore silver rings on his fingers, Bergerac, the man even Guéry found it difficult to take seriously, with his perpendicular ears and his huge, spherical belly, this same Bergerac, Guéry's only friend in Saigon, the only one he really trusted, was holding a large and dangerous-looking pistol against the side of his ribcage.

And yes, needless to say, it was a nine-millimetre Luger— the very gun that had been used to kill his brother.

Chapter 15

The *Sirocco*

Guéry was so surprised by this sudden development that he smiled involuntarily and almost laughed, as if it were some kind of elaborate practical joke. But of course the gun was very real—very hard, very metallic—and Bergerac was not smiling. Far from it. The wrinkles around his eyes had almost entirely disappeared, and he was looking at Guéry with a disconcerting combination of malevolence and pity.

'I—I—I don't understand,' Guéry finally stammered. 'What's the meaning of this?'

'I'm sorry, Monsieur, but you only have yourself to blame. You were told to leave Saigon more than once, and yet you chose to ignore these warnings. I believe the technical term for this is hubris; and a literary man such as yourself should know that hubris is always punished.'

Bergerac had draped a jacket over his right arm, the one holding the Luger, and he rearranged it now so that the weapon was completely concealed. Although they were standing on a crowded quay, surrounded by people, no one could see what was happening.

'And please don't do anything stupid. If you try to call for help, you'll be dead before you've uttered your first syllable— and I'll be gone. Nothing could be simpler, I assure you.'

'But you're going to kill me anyway, aren't you? Isn't that the plan?'

'Let's not get ahead of ourselves, Monsieur Guéry. What I want you to do now is turn around very slowly and walk toward the boat moored behind you.'

Guéry obeyed, and as he was turning, he felt the pressure of the gun barrel shift from his side to the base of his spine.

'Move,' Bergerac said, 'but slowly. If you try anything, I'll kill you right here.'

Again Guéry did as he was told.

The boat was a large ferry with a covered upper deck that was open on both sides and surrounded by iron railings. The word SIROCCO was written on the hull in capital letters, and there was a tricolour hanging limply from the stern.

'Get on board. I already have the tickets.'

As Guéry was approaching the gangway, he saw a Vietnamese policeman standing to one side; and Bergerac must have seen him too, for the pressure at the base of his spine suddenly increased.

'Keep walking. Don't say anything.'

Just as they were reaching the foot of the gangway, however, the policeman stepped forward.

'Messieurs,' he said, 'if you please . . . '

For a moment, Guéry was convinced that deliverance was at hand, that his life was about to be saved. But then the policeman held out a small, perforated piece of paper and said, with an ingratiating smile, 'Would you like to buy a lottery ticket? It will only cost you five piastres, and you could win a fortune.'

Guéry felt the pressure from the Luger increase by another few degrees.

'No, thank you,' he said. 'Not today.'

Once they were safely on board, Bergerac directed him up a narrow flight of stairs and over to a table on the other side of the ferry. There were at least a dozen such tables, surrounded by slatted wooden chairs, and they were almost all occupied by soldiers on leave—many of whom were drinking from bottles of beer and playing card games. They sat down facing each other, and as soon as they had done so, Bergerac leaned forward slightly in his chair. It took Guéry a moment to realize what was happening. Bergerac wasn't about to share a confidence; he was simply repositioning the gun so that it could be trained on Guéry beneath the table.

Shortly afterward, a whistle blew and the ferry started moving.

'This was all very well-timed, Monsieur Bergerac. I'm impressed.'

'Let's just say we were fortunate.'

'I'm not sure that I would describe myself as fortunate, given the circumstances.'

Bergerac said nothing. He was looking at a group of soldiers sitting at a nearby table.

'May I ask where you're taking me?'

There was no response.

'May I ask where you're taking me?' Guéry repeated.

This time Bergerac registered what he was saying. 'Yes, Monsieur, you may. We're going to Cap Saint-Jacques. We'll be there in a few hours.'

* * *

Before continuing any further, I should probably explain how Guéry could have been abducted like this, in broad daylight, despite the fact that he was being tailed by two of my best officers at the time.

They had followed him from his hotel to the Information Service on rue Lagrandière; and from there, through Les Halles Centrales and down boulevard de la Somme, to the quai Le Myre de Villers. That much had been easy enough. Once they reached the quayside, however, things started to go wrong. Simply put, they lost him in the crowd—but perhaps it would be better if I quoted directly from the report at this stage. And from my perspective, as you can imagine, it makes for a rather sobering read.

'The subject and his companion,' we are told, 'were observed walking in a northerly direction along the quayside. The quay was extremely crowded at this time of day (11.20), and every so often, as could be expected, the two men were obscured from view. At a certain point, they came to a halt and seemed to be discussing something of considerable importance. Rather than stopping too, and thus drawing attention to ourselves, my partner and I joined a queue of people waiting at a nearby ticket office. Once we had done so, however, we turned around to find that the subject and his companion had disappeared. After walking back and forth along the quay for several minutes, my partner finally located the two men. They had boarded the Cap Saint-Jacques ferry and were sitting at one of the tables on the far side. We made our way as quickly as possible to the point of embarkation, but unfortunately it was too late. By the time we reached the river's edge, the gangway had been pulled aboard and the ferry was already departing. There was simply nothing we could do; the subject was gone.'

So there you have it: *the subject was gone*. Just when Guéry needed us most, we were unable to intervene, unable to do anything to help him. He was left to face this danger alone, with a nine-millimetre Luger trained on him beneath the table. And the man who was holding this gun, the one we have been calling Bergerac, was obviously not who he had claimed to be. He had most probably never met an Algerian prostitute in his life, and had certainly never had anything to do with supplying women for the BMCs. But this was something we would only discover much later, once our own inquiry had been conducted. At the time, my men had no choice but to abandon their pursuit and return to headquarters, while 'the subject and his companion' continued on down the Saigon River—past the entrance to the Arroyo Chinois, past the Messageries Maritimes building, through the mangrove-fringed delta, where the Binh Xuyen had once made their living as river pirates, and all the way to Cap Saint-Jacques.

* * *

After travelling in silence for some time, Guéry said, 'I don't suppose your name is even Bergerac, is it?'

The other man smiled. 'No, Monsieur, it's not.'

'Would you mind giving me your real name, then?'

'Not at all. There's no longer any need to maintain this pretense.'

There was a pause.

'So?'

'Can't you guess, Monsieur Guéry? Isn't it obvious by now? I thought you considered yourself to be some kind of detective.'

Guéry didn't much care for the tone of the other man's voice. 'Quite frankly,' he said, 'I've got no idea who you are—so why don't you just tell me?'

'Very well, Monsieur, I shall . . . My name is Fourier. Jacques Fourier.'

Guéry stared at him for a moment in stunned silence. 'I'm sorry,' he said at last, 'I don't understand. Are you trying to tell me that *you're* Fourier?'

'That's right.'

'Jacques Fourier.'

'The very same.'

'So you were lying the whole time—about who you are, about what you do, about everything.'

'Yes, Monsieur, I was lying the whole time.'

'You used to work at Perec Frères?'

'I did.'

'And you used to live in that apartment on place du Joffre—number 24?'

'Indeed.'

'And it was you, then, who identified my brother's body in the morgue?'

Fourier nodded and smiled once more. He was obviously enjoying himself. 'Yes,' he said, 'that was me too.'

'So you knew Olivier . . . '

'Of course. May his soul rest in peace.'

'And Reyes.'

'Yes. He was a colleague of mine. A junior colleague, I might add.'

'And that book, *Tu Parles d'une Ingénue*—that belonged to you too?'

'It did . . . Actually, it still does. Strictly speaking.'

'So can you tell me why Olivier was carrying the title page in his pocket when he died?'

Fourier shook his head. 'Not yet, Monsieur. You'll have to wait.'

'But you do know?'

'I suppose so, yes.'

'And what about the murder itself—do you know who killed Olivier? Were you there when he died? Did you . . . '

Another possibility suddenly occurred to Guéry, and for the first time that day he recognized the true nature of the danger he was facing. Up until this point, he had continued to confuse Fourier with his previous incarnation—the agreeably louche Monsieur Bergerac. Despite everything that had happened, Guéry still saw him as a slightly absurd, slightly grotesque, colonial caricature, with mineral powder smeared on his face and silver rings embellishing his fingers. But he now realized, somewhat belatedly, that this was a very dangerous mistake to have made, for the man sitting across the table from him was in fact a complete stranger, one who bore only a superficial resemblance to his old friend Bergerac. This stranger may have shared the same obese and perspiring body with the old Bergerac. He may have possessed some of the same vanities and vices. But otherwise they were two completely different people, and the man he was looking at now, the one who called himself Fourier, could be capable of anything—even murder.

After all, the facts did seem to speak for themselves. Fourier had been working alongside Olivier at Perec Frères. He had mysteriously disappeared around the time of the murder. A page torn from one of his books had been found on Olivier's body. He had lied about his identity on more than one occasion. He had pretended that he had never heard of Perec Frères. And he had abducted Guéry at gunpoint that very morning, using a nine-millimetre Luger to do so.

All things considered, then, only one conclusion seemed possible.

'Did you kill my brother?' Guéry asked.

Fourier glanced furtively at the nearest table of soldiers. 'Monsieur Guéry, now is not the time to discuss such matters.'

'Tell me, please. I need to know. Did you kill my brother?'

'I'm afraid I can't answer that question. Not yet anyway.'

After a pause, Guéry said, 'Could you at least tell me if you were involved in the piastre trafficking at Perec Frères?'

Fourier nodded. 'I was.'

'And are the SDECE actually running the operation there?'

'Yes, they are.'

'So where are you taking me now, then?'

'To Cap Saint-Jacques.'

'I know,' Guéry said. 'But for what purpose?'

'You'll see.'

'Are you going to kill me?'

'You'll find out when the time comes, Monsieur.' Fourier smiled derisively. 'As a reader of detective novels, you should know that everything will be revealed in due course. So please, if you don't mind, a little patience.'

It was clear that he wasn't going to get any more information out of Fourier; but even so, Guéry had learned enough to understand that he was in grave danger. If Fourier had worked at Perec Frères, then he must have been associated with the SDECE at some point in time. It was true that he had gone missing, and that the SDECE had searched his apartment, but that didn't mean that he wasn't still working for Trinquier. And there was no definite proof, either, that the men who had searched his apartment were actually from the SDECE—or, if they were, that they belonged to the specific unit that was under Trinquier's command. Of course, it was always possible that Fourier had been on Olivier's side and that he had been obliged to flee from the same men who had killed his colleague. But if that was the case, why had he not revealed his true identity to Guéry at the very beginning? Why had he followed the investigation so closely (and yet so covertly)? Why had he found it necessary to do what he did on the quay, and why was he holding that nine-millimetre Luger—the very gun that had been used to kill Olivier? No, the most likely scenario was that Fourier was still working for the SDECE in some capacity, and that he had been charged with carrying out the threat that Weiling had delivered the night before. He was going to take Guéry out to Cap Saint-Jacques, find some deserted place in the jungle or the sand dunes or the surrounding rice paddies, and quietly eliminate him—just as he had eliminated Olivier.

But there was one thing he didn't understand. Why take him all that way just to put a bullet in his head? Surely it would have been easier to do it in Saigon, where they were pulling dead bodies out of the river every other day. It was then that he remembered what I had told him about the SDECE having a military base at Cap Saint-Jacques, and everything began to make sense. Killing him in Saigon would have presented certain difficulties. If the authorities found his body floating in the Arroyo Chinois, killed in the same way that his brother had been, then they would be obliged to investigate both cases more thoroughly. Not only would his own death come under close scrutiny, but they would be compelled to reopen Olivier's case too, and that was obviously the last thing that Trinquier wanted. So instead he must have told Fourier to take his captive out to the SDECE base at Cap Saint-Jacques, where he could be killed more easily and more discreetly. By the time anyone in Saigon realized that he had disappeared, it would be too late to do anything about it. They would have no idea where he had gone, who had taken him, how he had died, or even *if* he had died. He would simply have vanished, just as Fourier himself had—only, in Guéry's case, he would be lying under several metres of white sand with a bullet in his head.

'Everybody told me that I should go to Cap Saint-Jacques,' Guéry murmured.

'I'm sorry?'

'Everybody I spoke to in Saigon told me that I should go to Cap Saint-Jacques for a couple of days.'

Fourier said nothing.

'Auteuil, the junior officer at the Information Service, was the first to do so. He told me that the swimming is particularly good out there, and that the cool sea breezes are very refreshing. He said that I would think I was back in Antibes.'

'Really, Monsieur?' Fourier said with indifference. 'How nice.'

'He said that I should leave first thing Saturday morning and come back in the afternoon on Sunday. And if I was travelling by car, he advised me to allow plenty of time for the return journey as you can't be too careful these days.'

'That's very true.'

'Then Vitelli gave me the same advice. He spoke very highly of the place, and suggested that I try the grilled oysters at the Negresco while I was there. He said they're absolutely splendid. Have you ever tried them, Monsieur Fourier?'

'I beg your pardon?'

'The oysters at the Negresco—have you tried them?'

'No, I can't say I have.'

'Vitelli said that I should make sure they're grilled and not fried—and that I could have them with or without garlic, depending on my preference.'

'I see,' Fourier said, smiling in a rather bemused way. 'And which did he recommend?'

'He told me that he preferred them without garlic.'

Fourier nodded his head solemnly. 'So grilled and without garlic, then.'

'Yes. And he also said that they go particularly well with a bottle of Sancerre.'

'Chilled?'

'He didn't say, but I imagine so.'

Fourier nodded once more.

'But I don't suppose I'll get a chance to sample the oysters, will I, Monsieur Fourier?'

'No, Monsieur, you won't.'

'And I don't imagine I'll be going swimming either.'

'I would consider it rather unlikely.'

Guéry turned in his chair and looked out at the dense concentration of mangroves that surrounded the river on either side. It was a landscape of unrelenting monotony, and it smelled too, like something rotting in the sun.

'That's a shame,' he said. 'That's a real shame.'

'But were you actually going to take their advice, Monsieur Guéry? Were you really planning on going to Cap Saint-Jacques one day?'

Guéry considered this for a moment. 'No,' he said finally, 'I don't suppose I was.'

'I didn't think so. You don't strike me as the kind of man who would go in for such things. Grilled oysters and the like.'

'No, but now I regret not going. It might have been nice.'

'Of course you do. But you really should try to see the positive side of this whole business. I'm giving you the chance to do something that you wouldn't have done otherwise. If I hadn't intervened, you would never have made it out there.'

'That's true, although I don't think this really qualifies as a holiday.'

'No, but at least you're going to get a chance to see Cap Saint-Jacques before . . .'

'Before I die?'

Fourier laughed. 'I didn't say that, Monsieur.'

'You didn't need to.'

'Well, whatever the case, you ought to enjoy yourself while you still can. The circumstances may not be ideal, but it is a nice day, and I can already feel the sea breeze on my face.' He lifted his head slightly. 'That Auteuil was right, you know. It's almost like being on the Côte d'Azur.'

This was not actually true, but Guéry refrained from saying so. He was more concerned, at this stage, with the prospect of his impending demise. He was thirty-eight years old, and it was generally acknowledged that he had achieved very little in his life. He had written a few articles here and there. He had managed to endear himself to one or two people. He had fallen in love twice. He had read every word that Simenon had ever written. He had mastered the yo-yo as a young boy, and had once walked all the way from Cannes to Antibes (for reasons we have already discussed). But otherwise his life thus far had been a rather dispiriting litany of underachievement and failure. None of his early ambitions had come to anything. He had never played on the left wing for FC Antibes (or in any other position, for that matter). He had never found a publisher for the novel it had taken him so many years to write. And he hadn't even managed to complete his undergraduate degree at the University of Nice. True, he had interviewed a few minor celebrities and some of his articles had been fairly well-received, but what did that really amount to in the grand scheme of things? Very little— almost nothing. In fact, it was clear to him now that he had wasted the best years of his life haunting the bars, casinos, and racecourses of the Côte d'Azur. And perhaps that was why he had been so determined to solve the mystery of his brother's murder. Not for Olivier's sake, or even their father's, but for his own selfish reasons—so that he could tell himself that he had finally achieved something in this world, something meaningful, something of enduring value. But of course, as it turned out, he had failed in this regard too. He may have discovered who killed Olivier and why they had done so, but his brother's killers would never be brought to justice. And no one would ever know the precise circumstances in which Guéry had died either. He would simply disappear without a trace, without leaving anything behind—no novel, no wife, no children, no legacy, no nothing.

As you can imagine, it wasn't particularly pleasant for Guéry to contemplate all of this, and for some time he felt genuinely despairing. But then he remembered what Fourier had said about enjoying himself while he still could, and he realized that this was actually quite good advice. There was obviously nothing to be gained now by worrying about such things. He may have passed through life without achieving anything of significance. He may have failed at almost everything he had tried, and squandered the precious gift of existence on useless fripperies and moronic vices. He may have failed to ensure his own immortality by giving his name to another creature on this planet or by publishing an imperishable work of literary genius. But there was really nothing he could do about any of that now—not here, not on the 11.30 ferry to Cap Saint-Jacques, not with an agent of the SDECE pointing a gun at him beneath the table.

Guéry decided that it was time to have a cigarette.

'May I?' he asked, indicating a packet of Gauloises that lay between them on the table.

'Of course,' Fourier replied. 'They're your cigarettes.'

Guéry took one and lit it. Then he sat back in his chair and surveyed the passing landscape. It was exactly the same as it had been for the last hour or so—river, mangroves, sky, river, mangroves, sky. He had never seen anything that looked less like the Côte d'Azur in his life.

Once he had finished the cigarette, he immediately lit another one.

Fourier raised his eyebrows. 'You're smoking a lot, Monsieur Guéry. Are you nervous?'

'No—well, yes. But that's not why I'm smoking.'

'So what is it, then?'

'I feel I ought to smoke as much as possible while I still can—before it's too late.'

Fourier smiled. 'That makes sense,' he said. 'If I were you, I'd probably do the same thing.'

After finishing his second cigarette, Guéry lit a third and then settled back into his chair once more.

It was the first time in many years that he had been able to smoke without worrying about contracting cancer of the tongue—or any of the other maladies associated with the consumption of tobacco. For the first time in his adult life, that is to say, he could simply enjoy the cigarette for what it was, without imagining the terrible things it might be doing to his palate, his lungs, his throat, or his poor long-suffering tongue.

There was nowhere to go and nothing he could do about the nine-millimetre Luger beneath the table. For better or for worse, his fate was sealed. All he could do at this point was sit back and look out over the unchanging landscape, listen to the inane chatter and laughter emanating from the surrounding tables, glance from time to time at his companion's greasy, discoloured face, and smoke—smoke every last one of his cigarettes. Needless to say, this was, for the most part, both boring and depressing, and he was still filled with a sense of terrible dread whenever he thought about what was going to happen to him once they arrived at Cap Saint-Jacques. But in some strange way, it was also surprisingly relaxing. To be able to sit there and smoke without fear, to cast aside his old phobias and neuroses, and to know that whatever happened now was completely beyond his control—all of this was strangely . . . nice. That was the word he had used earlier, and Fourier had used it too. It was a banal word, 'nice,' so drained of feeling as to be practically meaningless, but it was the word that came to mind as Guéry lit yet another cigarette and gazed out over the mangroves.

Yes, he thought to himself, this is nice. This is really quite nice.

* * *

They arrived at Cap Saint-Jacques a little after five. Fourier followed Guéry down the gangway, then guided him into a waiting car. The driver was a young Vietnamese man with scented brilliantine in his hair and wire-rimmed sunglasses. He seemed to know where they were going.

After leaving the pier, they followed the coastal road from one end of the bay to the other. To his left, Guéry could see dusty palm trees and fishing nets spread out on the sand to dry. Fourier sat silently beside him in the back, still holding the Luger beneath his jacket.

'Is that really necessary?' Guéry asked him at one point.

'Yes,' he replied, 'I'm afraid it is.'

They continued driving in silence for another few minutes; then the car left the main road and turned inland.

'Are we going to the military base?' Guéry asked.

This time Fourier smiled. 'Patience, Monsieur Guéry, patience. We're almost there.'

As they turned inland, the road suddenly began to rise, winding its way up the side of a small mountain that stood at the northern end of the bay. Although the foliage on either side of the road was becoming increasingly dense, Guéry was still able to catch the odd glimpse of the harbour below, and this gave him some sense of how far they had climbed.

Eventually, they came to a large iron gate flanked by two stone pillars. The driver got out to open the gate, and then closed it again once they were on the other side. Still climbing, they followed a long driveway through the trees. After a hundred metres or so, the car came to a halt on a gravel courtyard outside a dilapidated two-storey villa. To Guéry's surprise, it was precisely the kind of place one might expect to find on the Côte d'Azur—complete with wrought-iron balconies, elaborate stucco mouldings, and a broad marble stairway leading up to the portico at the entrance. But it had most definitely seen better days. In places, the stucco was scabrous and peeling; the wooden shutters were hanging awry; and there were intermittent patches of vegetation sprouting from the cornice.

They got out of the car, and Fourier ushered him up the stairway and through the front door. Once they were inside, they crossed the entrance hall and made their way up another flight of stairs.

'Through here,' Fourier said, opening the first door they came to on the landing. The room they entered was empty, aside from one or two pieces of furniture, a pile of old magazines, and a bicycle leaning incongruously against the wall.

Fourier opened some French doors and led him out onto a large terrace surrounded by a stone balustrade. Even if you were shortsighted, the view from the terrace was spectacular. Beyond the trees, Guéry could see the entire bay, including the coastal road they had just followed, the distant pier, and the vast expanse of the harbour, shimmering in the early-evening sun.

A figure was sitting by the balustrade with his back to them. He was reading a newspaper and smoking a cigarette. On a small table to his left stood two empty glasses, a bottle of Pernod, and a carafe of iced water. Guéry assumed this must be Trinquier.

'He's here,' Fourier said. 'I'm sorry we're late.'

The man turned around and smiled. It wasn't Trinquier. It was someone else.

Sitting there, on the terrace of this dilapidated villa in Cap Saint-Jacques, reading yesterday's *Journal de Saigon* and smoking a leisurely cigarette, was a man Guéry knew very well indeed.

It was his brother—the one and only, late lamented Olivier Guéry.

Chapter 16

Cap Saint-Jacques

'Hello, Jean-Luc,' he said. 'Would you care to join me?'

He gestured toward an empty chair.

Guéry sat down in a daze, unable to believe what he was seeing, unable to believe that he was actually speaking to his dead brother.

'You're . . . you're alive?' he stammered feebly.

'Indeed,' Olivier replied. 'Alive and well.' He grinned. 'In fact, I've never felt better.'

Guéry stared at him without saying anything. He could think of nothing to say. He found himself searching for a bullet hole above his brother's left eye.

'And what about you, Jean-Luc? How are you these days?' He pointed at Guéry's disfigured face with his cigarette. 'I did hear that you'd had a rather unpleasant encounter with some of Trinquier's men. I'm afraid they can be a little overzealous at times, can't they?'

Guéry nodded his head once or twice, very slowly. 'Yes,' he said, 'yes, they can.'

There was a pause while Olivier filled a glass with Pernod and water, then pushed it across the table.

'Here,' he said. 'You look as if you could use this.'

Guéry accepted it gratefully.

'I must say I've been impressed by your tenacity,' Olivier continued, pouring another one for himself. 'I didn't think you would last longer than a few days, but here you are.' He looked at Guéry for a moment, then added, 'Does it hurt? Your face, I mean.'

'No, not anymore.'

'But you still have to wear that ridiculous collar?'

'For another week or so, yes.'

'It must be very uncomfortable in this climate.'

Guéry nodded. 'It is.'

'Very sweaty.'

'Yes, quite.'

'And it does make you look rather strange. Almost Napoleonic—in a defeated kind of way.'

'So I imagine.'

In the brief silence that followed, Guéry heard the sound of distant gunfire from the military base. It reminded him of something geological, like an earthquake or a volcano, and he wondered for a second or two if he might be dreaming.

'I ought to apologize for the manner in which you were brought here,' Olivier said. 'We had to get you out of Saigon as quickly as possible, and we weren't sure that you would even come unless you were obliged to. In any case, I trust my associate treated you courteously?'

Guéry looked around to find that Fourier had disappeared.

'Yes,' he said, turning back to face his brother. 'He was as courteous as he could be, under the circumstances.'

Olivier laughed. 'Poor old Jean-Luc. You're not really used to this kind of thing, are you?'

A familiar condescending tone had entered his brother's voice. It was clear that he was enjoying himself—enjoying his position of superiority, enjoying the game he was playing, enjoying Guéry's ignorance and confusion.

'No, quite frankly, I'm not.'

'But as I say, you've done very well to have made it this far. You've caused everyone a great deal of trouble. Myself included.'

Guéry lit a cigarette. He was beginning to recover from the shock of seeing Olivier sitting there on the terrace, very much alive; and now, more than anything, he wanted answers.

'So,' he said, suddenly enraged by his own ignorance and by the pleasure it was giving his brother, 'are you going to tell me what's going on?'

'Of course, Jean-Luc. That's why we brought you here. I think it's time you solved this "case" of yours.'

There was another long silence, and then Olivier suddenly laughed. 'To be honest,' he said, 'I don't really know where to begin.'

'Why don't you start by telling me what's been going on at Perec Frères?'

'There's no need. You've already discovered that for yourself.'

'You were involved in the trafficking of piastres.'

'That's right.'

'For Trinquier—for the SDECE.'

'Yes.'

'But why?' Guéry asked. 'Why did you do it?'

'Isn't it obvious, Jean-Luc? We were making a reasonable amount of money importing agricultural machinery. We were comfortable, you might say, but not really doing that well. And then one day I was approached by an SDECE agent, who explained that we could make a great deal more money—a small fortune, in fact—by collaborating with Trinquier.'

'So you agreed to do it?'

'Immediately. Why wouldn't I? These aren't gangsters we're talking about here. These are members of the French intelligence service—men who are doing their best to win a war with very limited resources. It was the patriotic thing to do. I had to agree.'

'And it also just happened to be the profitable thing to do.'

Olivier smiled. 'As it turned out, yes.'

'So how was it done, this trafficking?'

'It was all quite simple, really. The SDECE created a bogus company—the Rizerie Franco-Indochinoise—and every so often they would place an order with us for a shipment of machinery. The money to pay for the order would be deposited into an account at the Banque de l'Indochine. We would then take this money and transfer it to France through the foreign exchange office.'

'Where it would ultimately be received by one of your associates.'

'That's right. Once the payment had been converted into francs at the official rate of exchange, our contact in Paris would deposit it into another bank account belonging to the SDECE.'

'So the money would eventually come full circle, having doubled in value in the meantime.'

Olivier nodded.

'And of course there was no merchandise, was there? The bills of lading you presented at the exchange office were all false.'

'I'm afraid so.'

'Hence the empty warehouse.'

'Yes.' Olivier's eyes were shining at the thought of all the money he had made out of that gloomy warehouse on the quai de Belgique. 'It turned out to be a very valuable building indeed.'

'But there's something about all of this I don't quite understand,' Guéry said. 'I've been told more than once that the trafficking of piastres is a fairly common practice around here. Even political parties from the metropole have become involved in the trade. So why all the secrecy in this particular case? Why are the SDECE going to so much trouble to conceal what they're doing?'

Olivier gave him another one of his condescending smiles. 'You really don't know?' he said incredulously. 'I thought you might have figured that out by now.'

'Well, I'm afraid I haven't. So I would be grateful if you could enlighten me.'

'With pleasure, dear boy.' He paused for a moment to refill their glasses, before settling back into his chair once more. 'Do you have any idea why the SDECE is doing this in the first place?' he asked.

'An officer at the Sûreté told me that they need the money to recruit and train mercenaries from the hill tribes.'

'Precisely. But of course you have to pay a rather high price for such services, and they're not getting the funding they need from Paris. It's the same old story. None of those communist deputies understand what we're up against out here.'

'So . . .'

'So they need to get their funding from elsewhere—and that's why they've been obliged to enter the narcotics trade.'

This startled Guéry. 'Narcotics? You mean to say they're trading in opium?'

'That's right. They buy large quantities of the stuff from the Montagnard hill tribes, then they fly it in GCMA planes to the military base here at Cap Saint-Jacques. From here, it's transported by road to Saigon, where they finally turn it over to the Binh Xuyen.'

'They sell drugs to those gangsters?'

'Not quite. The Binh Xuyen are really just acting as intermediaries. They're responsible for processing the opium and then selling it on Trinquier's behalf—to the Chinese or the Corsicans or some local syndicate. They get a healthy commission, of course, and the emperor receives a percentage too, but most of the money goes to the SDECE.'

'Who then arrange for its remittance through Perec Frères.'

'Exactly.'

'Thus doubling their money and laundering it too.'

Olivier nodded.

'And that's where you enter the story.'

He smiled. 'Yes, that's where I enter the story.'

Guéry studied his brother with some distaste. 'Did it ever occur to you that this might be the wrong thing to do, Olivier? Were you ever bothered by the fact that you were collaborating with someone like Trinquier?'

'Honestly, old boy, I'd have to say no. Money is money. That's true everywhere, but particularly out here in the colonies. And the war isn't going to last forever, you know. Sooner or later it will come to an end; and when it does, we're inevitably going to find ourselves on the losing side. So there's really no time to waste. One has to make as much money as possible before it's too late—before everything we've built in this godforsaken place is reduced to ashes.'

At that moment, another barrage of gunfire came from the military base. The sound was so loud that the leaves of a nearby palm tree shivered and a startled bird rose into the air. It was a small bird with vivid, multicoloured feathers, and they both turned to watch as it flew away.

'So tell me,' Guéry said once the bird had disappeared from view, 'how did you end up floating in the Arroyo Chinois with a bullet in your head?'

Olivier laughed. 'That's a long story, but I suppose you would like to hear it.'

'Yes,' Guéry said, 'yes, I would—if it's all the same to you.'

'Very well.'

Although his brother was feigning reluctance, it was clear that this was what he had been waiting for all along: the chance to demonstrate his own ingenuity, his own brilliance.

'My job was actually quite a simple one,' he began. 'Every time the SDECE deposited a sum of money in the Banque de l'Indochine account, I was responsible for withdrawing that money and taking it to the foreign exchange office on rue Guynemer, where I would apply for the necessary transfer note. This I did dutifully enough for almost two years, until one day, as I was walking along the quai de Belgique, it occurred to me that I was carrying a fortune in my briefcase. More money than I could hope to make in a lifetime at Perec Frères. And if I were to disappear with it, this money, somewhere between the bank and the exchange office, no one would ever be able to find me. They could hardly go to the police, could they? It would be the perfect crime. It was a thought that came to me quite spontaneously, but I resisted the urge to act on it then and there. I knew it was something that would require a great deal of careful planning. So on that particular day, I went ahead and made the transfer; I sent the money to France, as instructed. And then, for a long time afterward, I did my best to forget about this momentary impulse. I realized that I was onto a good thing, collaborating with Trinquier, collecting this generous commission for doing practically nothing, and that I should be satisfied with the arrangement as it stood. I also knew that the SDECE, and Trinquier's men in particular, were a dangerous lot, and they wouldn't take kindly to being betrayed. But even so, the thought of that money—that fortune and everything it could buy—nagged at me like a half-remembered song. I couldn't forget the weight of my briefcase. I couldn't stop thinking about the yacht I would buy, the villa in Saint-Tropez, the *pied-à-terre* in Monaco, the parties, the cars, the holidays in Biarritz and Capri. And then one day I finally surrendered to these images. I decided that I would wait until the SDECE made a particularly large payment, and then I would steal it—I would steal it all. I would disappear, somewhere between the quai de Belgique and rue Guynemer, and they would never see me again.'

'So that's precisely what you did.'

'Yes, but of course there were various difficulties that needed to be resolved before I could do anything. For a start, it was obvious that the SDECE would come looking for me if I disappeared with the money—that I would be killed for what I had done. And what's the point of having a fortune if you can't enjoy it, if you're obliged to look over your shoulder a hundred times a day? I considered this problem for quite a while before it finally occurred to me that I would only ever be free if I was dead . . . or at least if they thought I was dead. But even then, if the money went missing on the very day I "died," they would naturally be suspicious. So I decided to make it look as if the money had been stolen from *me*—as if I had been abducted while I was on my way to the exchange office, and then murdered, killed in the line of duty, like a good employee. If they thought I was dead, and that the money had been stolen by someone else, then I could rest easy. I could enjoy my yacht and my villa on the Côte d'Azur without living in fear for the rest of my days.'

'And it was at this point that you recruited Fourier?'

'That's right. If I was going to fake my own death, then I would need to produce a corpse, and that's not the kind of thing I could have done without some assistance. Fourier and I had never been particularly close. We were colleagues and on familiar terms, but that was about it. I could see, however, that he was the type of person who might be tempted by such a proposition. And so it proved to be. I told him what I was thinking of doing, and he immediately agreed to help—for a share of the money, of course.'

'Fifty per cent?'

Olivier smiled. 'Not quite. Actually closer to thirty. It was my idea, after all. I deserved the larger share.'

'Naturally.'

'So anyway, once Fourier had been recruited, we worked together to formulate a plan. On the day itself, I would leave the bank as I always did, following my usual route along the quai de Belgique. After entering rue Guynemer, however, I would suddenly veer off course. Instead of continuing on to the exchange office, I would turn into an adjoining alleyway that led to rue Chaigneau. Fourier would be waiting for me in a car at the other end of the alley. He would then take me straight to his apartment on place du Joffre, where I would spend the rest of the day.'

'And Fourier?'

'He would go back to the office as if nothing had happened. And when my disappearance was reported, he would be as mystified—and suspicious—as everyone else.'

'Until your body turned up the following day.'

'Yes, exactly.'

'So whose body did you use?' Guéry asked. 'And how did you get it? I don't imagine such things are easy to come by.'

Olivier smiled once more. 'You would be surprised, old boy. We're in the middle of a war, remember, and there's no shortage of dead bodies.'

'So tell me, then, how did you manage to get hold of this one?'

'An old associate of mine was serving as the chief medical officer on the *Pasteur* at the time. I explained to him what I was looking for, and he agreed to notify me if he should ever happen to acquire such a thing.'

'And he did?'

'Yes. Not long afterward, one of the legionnaires on the *Pasteur* died en route to Saigon. He had bought a bag of heroin in Port Said, and it ended up killing him and three of his comrades. I imagine the stuff was laced with too much quinine or something along those lines. Anyway, my associate managed to get the body off the ship once it reached Cap Saint-Jacques, and we arranged to collect it several days later.'

Things were gradually beginning to make sense to Guéry. 'So that was *his* corpse in the river—the legionnaire's. And that's why the pathologist told me that they had found opiates in your blood.'

'Did he really?' Olivier seemed surprised by this. 'Well, yes, that would be why. The poor bastard was full of heroin—you could see it in his eyes.'

'So when did you actually get the body?'

'On the night of my disappearance . . . We collected it from a warehouse out by the Gare des Marchandises around ten that evening, and then we drove it to a deserted part of the Arroyo Chinois.'

'Where you shot it twice in the head and dumped it in the river.'

'Indeed. It wasn't pleasant, I can tell you, but it had to be done. And anyway, the poor guy was already dead. He didn't care.'

Guéry thought for a moment. 'So the bullet they found came from Fourier's gun, from his Luger?'

'That's right.'

'Wasn't it dangerous to be firing a gun in the middle of the city? Surely someone could have heard you.'

'Not at that time of night, not out there. And even if someone had heard, they wouldn't have bothered to investigate. One hears such noises all the time these days. Artillery fire, grenades, landmines.'

'So what else did you do to the body?'

'I dressed it in my clothes, the ones I had been wearing when I disappeared, and I left some of my belongings in the pockets—a wallet, a cigarette lighter, a pair of sunglasses. I also made sure that it was carrying my identity card.'

'Were you not worried about the photo on the card?' Guéry asked. 'Wasn't there a chance that someone might notice the discrepancy?'

'Yes, that was a concern, but fortunately the photo wasn't a very good one. The corpse was also rather badly disfigured by then, what with all the bullet holes and everything. And we knew that it would putrefy quickly once it was in the water.'

'I see. And what about the title page, the one from *Tu Parles d'une Ingénue*? Why did you leave that on the body?'

Olivier laughed, clearly proud of this particular detail. 'That was my idea,' he said. 'I had a feeling that you might do something stupid like come out here and try to solve the case, so I thought I should leave you a message. I wanted to tell you to go home. I wanted to let you know that I was perfectly fine.'

'Did the message have something to do with the novel itself?'

'No. It was right there on the title page.'

Guéry tried to visualize the page as distinctly as he could. He could remember the title, the name of the author, and the publisher's logo; but none of this seemed to carry any deeper meaning.

'You didn't get it? I thought that might be the case. And I did tell Fourier that it was probably a little too oblique for you.'

Guéry chose to disregard this jibe. 'So where was the message, then?'

'In the library seal, you fool. Did you not notice that the book came from the Centre Saint-Lazare in Rome? I was trying to suggest that I would be rising from the dead, or that I wasn't dead at all, just like our old friend Lazarus. "And Jesus said unto her, 'Thy brother shall rise again,' and then they took away the stone from the place where the body was laid, and he that was dead came forth, bound hand and foot in graveclothes . . . " I forget precisely how it goes, that absurd story, but you get the picture.'

'Yes,' Guéry said, 'yes, I do. And you're right; it *was* too oblique. How was I supposed to understand something like that?'

'I'm sorry, Jean-Luc, but I couldn't make it too obvious either. I knew that the police would be scrutinizing everything they found on the body.'

Guéry helped himself to another Pernod. 'So what did you do then, once you were finished at the Arroyo Chinois?'

'We went back to Fourier's apartment and waited.'

'For what?'

'It was important that Fourier should be there to identify the body—just to make sure.'

'And he did, I believe, a couple of days later.'

'Yes, that's right. He confirmed that the body was mine, and then, once the funeral was over, we left for Cap Saint-Jacques.'

'So that was the point at which Fourier disappeared too?'

Olivier nodded.

'But I don't understand why you decided to come out here. Isn't it dangerous for you to be so close to the SDECE base?'

'Quite the opposite, actually. It's too soon for us to try to leave the country—if we do, we're bound to be arrested. So we have to lie low for a while, and Cap Saint-Jacques is the perfect place to do it. They would never think to look for us here, just two or three kilometres from the base.'

'But why would they be looking for you? Don't they think you're dead?'

Olivier shrugged. 'Probably, but you never know. They're certainly looking for Fourier, and they may still be wondering about me too. It's always possible. They're clever people, you know, Trinquier's gang; they're not easily fooled.'

'I'm sure.'

'And of course that's why I didn't want you to become involved in the case. I knew it would be dangerous for both of us.'

'Is that why you had Fourier befriend me as soon as I arrived in Saigon?'

'Yes. I had to follow your investigation as closely as I could, and that was the best way to do it.'

'I see.'

'As I say, though, I was rather surprised by the way things turned out. I had no idea that you would actually discover what was going on at Perec Frères. I thought you would spend most of your time . . . doing other things.'

'Like gambling, for instance.'

'I suppose so, yes.'

There was a long silence, then Guéry said, 'When I spoke to Reyes, he told me that you had taken to gambling yourself. Is that true?'

Olivier laughed. 'No, not at all. I think he was just saying that to get rid of you—to give you some motive for my murder. As you know, I've never gambled in my life.'

'Yes, that's what Weiling said too.'

For the first time in the conversation, Olivier looked a little discomforted. 'That's right. Fourier did tell me that you had been to see her at the Palais. How is she?'

'She's well, I suppose. But I don't think she was very happy when you disappeared. She was obviously quite fond of you.'

'Yes, that was all rather unfortunate, but I'm afraid I didn't really have a choice. I couldn't tell her what was happening, for her own safety as well as mine.'

'Couldn't you have taken her with you?'

'I don't think so. It just wouldn't have been feasible.'

'That's a shame,' Guéry said. 'She was very good to me. Very kind.'

'Yes, I know, Jean-Luc. And I feel bad about it; I really do. But it just wasn't *feasible*.'

He emphasized this last word as if it explained everything— and in Olivier's world, of course, it did.

'You're far too sentimental, old boy,' he went on. 'I liked her well enough. We had some good times together. But I couldn't allow her to complicate things. I had to let her go.'

For a moment, the sound of the band playing 'Les Feuilles Mortes' came back to Guéry, and he remembered how it had felt to be out on the dance floor with Weiling, imitating all the other men and trying to imagine what the ambassador of the Dominican Republic would have done in his place. The lyrics of the song came back to him too, and he was suddenly filled with an immense feeling of pity— pity for everyone: for the girl Olivier had abandoned, for the legionnaire whose body now lay in the old Catholic cemetery

(*Priez pour lui*), for the young Vietnamese driver with the wire-rimmed sunglasses, for Fourier, who had obviously half-believed all the lies he told (or at least wished they were true), and even for his brother, Olivier, the man sitting before him on the terrace, who would sacrifice anything and anyone for a briefcase full of piastres.

'And I suppose that was why you finally decided to have me brought here—because I was beginning to complicate things.'

'That's partly true, yes. You were starting to cause too much trouble, and we were particularly concerned about the fact that you were talking to the police. First Arnaud, and then Leclerc. But that wasn't the only reason we brought you out here. Believe it or not, we also did it for your own good.'

'For my own good?' Guéry repeated sceptically.

'Yes. We had heard that the SDECE were going to have you killed, and so we had to get you out of Saigon as quickly as possible.'

'Hence the Luger.'

Olivier smiled. 'Yes, old boy. Hence the Luger.'

Guéry studied the tiled floor of the terrace for a moment without saying anything. 'So what do you suggest I do now?' he asked finally.

'Isn't it obvious?' Olivier replied, laughing. 'It's time for you to go home. Case closed. You've done everything you came here to do. You wanted to solve the case, and that's precisely what you've done. You had the chance to live another life for a while—a more exciting, more interesting life. But now it's time to go back to Antibes, back to that newspaper of yours. What was it called again?'

'*Le Journal d'Antibes.*'

'That's right. It's time to return to your own life, Jean-Luc. It's time to stop playing detective.'

'You want me to walk away from all of this—the narcotics, the piastre trafficking—without doing anything about it?'

'What is there to do? If you went to the police, they would simply hand me over to Trinquier; and what would that achieve? I would be killed, and the trade would continue as before. Nothing would change.'

Guéry looked down at the ground once more, and as he did so, he noticed the desiccated body of a dead lizard lying in one corner of the terrace.

'I've spoken to Fourier about this,' Olivier said, 'and we've decided to make you an offer. A very generous offer. If you go home now, if you forget about everything we've discussed here today, we'll give you fifty thousand piastres for your trouble.'

Guéry lifted his eyes. 'And if I don't accept this offer, what then?'

'If you don't accept it, I fear your "story"—this Série Noire you've been living, this fantasy—may end rather badly.'

As Olivier said this, all of the bonhomie suddenly disappeared from his voice, and Guéry had the impression that he was being offered a rare glimpse behind the scenes.

'Are you threatening me, Olivier?'

'No, I'm merely warning you. Of course I would never do anything to harm you, Jean-Luc. After all, you're my brother, you're family. But this is a dangerous business, and I can't guarantee that I'll always be there to protect you.'

Guéry said, 'I see.' And he did, quite clearly. It was obvious that Olivier was only interested in one thing, and that was safeguarding the fortune he had just recently acquired. Nothing else mattered to him—not the girl he had abandoned, not the dead legionnaire whose body he had stolen, and certainly not his brother, his degenerate, underachieving brother, who had caused him nothing but trouble for as long as he could remember. All that mattered to him now was the Riva yacht he would buy once he returned to France, the villa in Saint-Tropez he would fill with expensive things, and the holidays he would take in all those places where rich people like to go.

Guéry lit another cigarette; then he rose from his chair and walked over to the balustrade. After a moment, Olivier joined him, and for a long time they stood there together in silence, looking out over the bay.

By now the sun had almost entirely disappeared beyond the horizon, and the lights along the waterfront were flickering on one by one. From this distance, it could easily have been the gentle curve of the Promenade des Anglais, or the waterfront at Cannes. But of course it was neither of these places. They were seventy kilometres from Saigon, and a long, long way from the Côte d'Azur.

Guéry turned to his brother.

'Did you happen to follow the Tour last year?' he asked.

'No,' Olivier said, giving him a surprised glance, 'I haven't followed it for years. I've had other things on my mind.'

There was a pause.

'Do you remember the year Honoré Barthélémy lost an eye?'

'I'm afraid not.'

'He crashed during Stage Nine, on the way to Nice, and a piece of flint from the road pierced his left eye. Once the dust had settled, he pulled the shard out, remounted, and finished the stage.'

'Is that so?' Olivier said in a distracted tone of voice.

'Then a couple of days later, he crashed again, breaking his wrist and dislocating his shoulder. But he still managed to finish the race . . . When he reached the Parc des Princes, he was given a hero's welcome. The crowd hoisted him onto their shoulders and carried him around the velodrome.'

'What year would that have been?'

'Nineteen-twenty.'

After thinking for a moment, Olivier shook his head. 'No, I'm sorry. It's all gone.'

Guéry threw his cigarette away and leaned on the balustrade.

'I don't suppose you can remember the year that Pélissier won either.'

'Not really.'

'Desgrange had said that he would never win the Tour because he didn't know how to suffer. But he went ahead and won it anyway.'

'And who's Desgrange?'

'The editor of *L'Auto*. Henri Desgrange . . . You don't remember following the race in *L'Auto* every year? You don't remember the yellow paper they used to print it on? Or the pictures we would cut out and paste on the wall?'

Again Olivier shook his head. 'You've got a good memory for such things, Jean-Luc. Small things, arcane things—things that don't really matter to anyone else.'

Guéry ignored this. 'Surely you remember the time we went to Nice to see the peloton arrive. That was the year Nicolas Frantz won—although your favourite, Leducq, did manage to take three stages.'

'Would this have been some time in the early thirties?' Olivier asked.

'I'm pretty sure it was 1927. We went to Nice for the day, just the two of us, and we didn't tell anyone that we were going. We caught the train first thing in the morning, which meant that we arrived far too early. All the shops were still shuttered and the cafés were closed. So we walked down to the beach and waited there for a couple of hours, smoking cigarettes and throwing stones at the Jetée-Promenade.'

'I'm sorry, old boy.' His brother smiled broadly. 'This is all ancient history for me. I can't remember any of it.'

'I'm talking about your life, Olivier. The things you did when you were young.'

'I know you are. But the world intervenes, doesn't it? One moves on to other things, other places. One *changes*.'

For Olivier, this was another word that explained everything, and Guéry could see that there was no point in arguing otherwise.

'Yes,' he said blandly, 'I suppose one does.'

But Olivier was already thinking about something else. He turned and walked back to the table. 'Do you feel like some dinner?' he asked over his shoulder. 'I imagine you're quite hungry after that long journey.'

Guéry didn't reply. He was still leaning on the balustrade and looking out over the bay. There was something about the scene that was vaguely familiar; and it occurred to him, once again, that he might be dreaming. But then he remembered what it was. During his visit to Perec Frères, he had noticed a watercolour hanging on the wall of his brother's old office. It was obviously a landscape, but it was so generic that it could have been painted anywhere in the world. At first, it had reminded him of the *calanques* between Marseille and Cassis, and then it had looked more like Rio de Janeiro. But he now knew that it depicted neither of these places; and he knew this because it had been painted exactly where he was standing. It had been painted right there in Cap Saint-Jacques, on that very terrace and at roughly the same time of day, when everything that was solid seemed to be dissolving at the edges.

'Are you coming, old boy?' his brother asked.

'Yes,' Guéry said, 'I'm coming.'

He turned to go inside. And as he did so, there was another barrage of gunfire from the military base—but it was quieter this time, and nothing moved, not even the leaves on the trees.

Chapter 17

A Final Encounter

Several days later, I was in my office when the telephone rang. It was Guéry. Without explaining why, he asked me to meet him at the Sporting Club in an hour's time. I was there within fifteen minutes.

When I arrived, he was sitting out on the covered terrace by the swimming pool. There was a newspaper on the table in front of him, along with a packet of Gauloises, a lighter, and two or three empty beer bottles. He had obviously been out there for some time. He was still wearing that ill-fitting leather brace of his, the one that made him look like an Easter Island statue, but the plaster on the bridge of his nose had been removed, and the raised welt on his left temple was beginning to subside.

He immediately told me everything that had happened over the last couple of days, beginning with his enforced journey out to Cap Saint-Jacques.

Once he had finished his story, I asked him if he had decided to take the fifty thousand piastres.

'No,' he said. 'I told them they could keep their money. But I did promise that I wouldn't go to the police.'

'And yet here you are . . . '

Guéry smiled. 'No, Inspector. Here *you* are. I'm simply enjoying a nice quiet beer at the Sporting Club.'

'So would you mind telling me, more precisely, where your brother and Fourier can be found?'

He shook his head. 'I'm afraid that's impossible. I gave them my word. I promised I wouldn't tell anyone where they are.'

'And may I ask why you did so?'

'It may seem strange, Inspector, but family is family. And despite everything he's done, Olivier is still my brother.'

At this point, I was momentarily distracted by the sound of someone diving into the pool; and when I turned around to face Guéry once more, I found him studying me thoughtfully.

'You don't seem particularly surprised by what I've told you,' he said.

'No, Monsieur. Quite frankly, I'm not surprised at all. If the SDECE were behind the piastre trafficking operation at Perec Frères, it was obvious that they had to be getting their money from somewhere. And this was one of the more likely possibilities.'

'That they were involved in drug trafficking too . . . '

I nodded.

'Olivier told me that they sell the opium to local syndicates, but also to the Unione Corse and the Chinese.'

'That would be right.'

'So what happens to it then, once it's been sold?'

'A lot of the opium would be consumed right here in Saigon, but some of it would eventually find its way to France, where I imagine it would be used to supply half the heroin laboratories in Marseille.'

'I see.'

'Yes,' I said. 'It's not a very pleasant business.'

Guéry watched as a young woman mounted the lower diving board, which was only a few metres above the surface of the pool. She had clearly performed this kind of dive before, and her body entered the water at an angle that allowed her to swim a considerable distance without surfacing.

Only when she finally came up for air did he turn to me and say, 'So what do you propose to do about all of this?'

'I'm afraid there's nothing I can do, Monsieur Guéry. The operation is simply too big. There's no way I can take on Trinquier and the SDECE and hope to achieve anything.'

'But will you at least be closing my brother's case—and disinterring the legionnaire buried under his name in the Catholic cemetery?'

'Honestly, Monsieur, I think it would be best for all concerned if we left things as they are. Closing the case would create far too many . . . difficulties. And as for the legionnaire— well, I think you would agree that there are worse places to spend eternity.'

Guéry was silent for a moment or two, as if he were trying to imagine a worse place than Saigon to spend eternity (and finding it difficult to do so).

Of course, I couldn't really blame him for feeling this way. Since arriving in Saigon a couple of weeks earlier, he had been beaten, abducted, patronized, insulted, and ridiculed. He had lost most of his money at the Grand Monde and the Cloche d'Or. He had humiliated himself in front of General Jean de Lattre de Tassigny. He had been completely deceived by almost everybody he had encountered; and he had discovered that the murder he was trying to solve wasn't really a murder at all— but simply another one of his brother's egregious money-making schemes. It wasn't exactly the Série Noire that he had been anticipating. And it was clear, now, that none of the guilty parties would be brought to justice either. Even the poor dead legionnaire would be left where he was, buried under two metres of red laterite and another man's name.

'I realize that it's disappointing for you, Monsieur Guéry, but one must be pragmatic. And this is really the best possible outcome . . . Indeed, more than anything, you should be grateful that you're still alive.'

At first, Guéry didn't seem convinced that this was necessarily a good thing; but he eventually reconciled himself to the realities of the case. And then he told me something that I had been waiting to hear for a very long time.

'I'm leaving Saigon tomorrow morning,' he said. 'I've done all that I can do here.'

I nodded my head sagely. 'I agree, Monsieur. It's time to bring things to a close.'

'But the flight is a long one, as you know, and I need some supplies. So I had better be going . . . '

'Yes, of course,' I said, with a feeling of immense relief and profound gratitude. 'One must be prepared for all eventualities.'

It turned out that we were both walking in the same direction, so I offered to accompany him as far as the Pharmacie Normale, where he wanted to buy a bottle of aspirin capsules and some chloral hydrate for his journey.

We took the usual route through Les Halles, then turned left onto boulevard Bonard. When we reached the Continental, however, I happened to see someone I knew sitting on the terrace; and so, in the end, that was where Guéry and I went our separate ways. I can't remember now exactly what we said in parting, but I do remember asking him, as an afterthought, if he had managed to secure his *carte de presse* from the Information Service.

He gave me a wry smile. 'No,' he said. 'The card never did arrive. I don't know why. I followed their instructions to the letter . . . I even went to Cap Saint-Jacques for the weekend.'

I laughed at this. 'Never mind, Monsieur. I'm sure you'll get it eventually.'

'Yes,' Guéry said, shaking my hand. 'It's just a matter of waiting—waiting and hoping. That's all we can ever do.'

Then he turned and walked away.

I watched as he crossed the road, narrowly avoiding two VNA lorries and a car with diplomatic plates. Only once he had safely reached the other side did I turn away myself. And that was the last time I saw Jean-Luc Guéry. He was walking in the direction of the river, if I remember correctly, fending off a couple of shoeshine boys and trying to light a cigarette.

Not long after he returned to France, I was surprised to hear that he had published a series of articles in *Le Journal d'Antibes* accusing the SDECE of being involved in the international narcotics trade. At the time, these articles caused quite a stir, and his accusations were reprinted in a number of major newspapers (including *Le Monde*, *Le Figaro*, and *France-Soir*). It was clear that he was no Lucien Bodard or Jean Lartéguy; but the articles themselves were written with a certain flair, an indisputable accuracy, and an eye for detail that could only be described as novelistic. If you don't believe me, you're welcome to see for yourself. There were three articles in all, published on consecutive Saturdays in July of 1951, and I'm sure that they can be found without too much difficulty in the newspaper's archives.

As far as I know, Guéry's novel, the one inspired by Gide's *Counterfeiters*, still hasn't been published; and there's been no sign of his lipogrammatic folly either. But if you ever find yourself in that part of the world, on a Wednesday or a Saturday, you might like to read some of his other articles—on local politics, petty crime, or the fluctuating fortunes of his beloved FC Antibes. In places, when he's sufficiently enthused, I'm told that they can be quite good too.

Acknowledgements

While writing this novel, I have referred to a wide range of sources, but I have found the following particularly useful: Émile Bergès, 'Chants et cris de la rue à Saigon,' *Indochine* 162 (1943); Lucien Bodard, *The Quicksand War: Prelude to Vietnam*; Alfred W. McCoy, *The Politics of Heroin: CIA Complicity in the Global Drug Trade*; and, of course, Jean Bruce, *Tu Parles d'une Ingénue* (OSS 117, No. 1). I am grateful to Philippe Peycam for kindly allowing me to reproduce his map of colonial Saigon; and I would also like to thank Nora Nazerene Abu Bakar, Charles Ardai, and Barrie Sherwood for their generous assistance and invaluable advice.